AMALGAM HOUND
Criminal Investigation Bureau:
Special Investigation Unit

`CONFIDENTIAL`

CONTENTS

Chapter	Title	Page
Chapter 1	Looking Up at the Stars from a Cage	001
Chapter 2	Hound for the Girl	039
Chapter 3	The Style of the Inhuman	091
Chapter 4	Loveless Monster	137
Chapter 5	Faithful Weapon, the Hound	183

Midori Komai
Illustration by: Domino Ozaki

CHARACTERS

"As an investigator, I'm merely doing the right thing."

Theo Starling

Former army corporal and rising star in the Criminal Investigation Bureau's Detective Operations division. While he maintains a tight focus on his investigations, he is sometimes so fervent about arresting the perpetrators of the crimes that he doesn't see what's right in front of his nose. He's unsociable, straitlaced, and a workaholic. Traumatized by his time on the battlefield, Theo is plagued with nightmares. He hates Amalgams because of his experience losing his entire family, and he is cold toward Eleven as well.

Age: 28
Height: 172 cm
Special skill: Marksmanship
Interests: Drinking, crossword puzzles

CONFIDENTIAL

"I will execute any duties I am ordered to."

Eleven

Automagiton Amalgam human model Hound No. 11. She looks like an innocent girl, but she is a weapon of war made to crush all enemies and is capable of changing her appearance at will. Given that she does not have emotions, the expression on her face never changes, but she seems perplexed when people treat her like a human being. She looks up to Theo as her master and tries to be useful to him.

Age: Mid-teens (appearance)
Height: 151 cm (default)
Special skill: Mimicry
Habit: Facial-expression analysis

"The girl's a weapon. But I want to welcome her as a colleague. She's quite marvelous."

Emma Canary

A sorcerer who uses magic via firearms. She started at the bureau at the same time as Theo but works on the magic side of operations. A cheerful person, she sets the mood for the team. She's well versed in Amalgam technology, and although she is quick to grasp Eleven's nature, she still tends to dote on her as a junior investigator.

Age: 28
Height: 168 cm
Special skill: Crystallization of magic
Interests: Walking while eating, watching movies

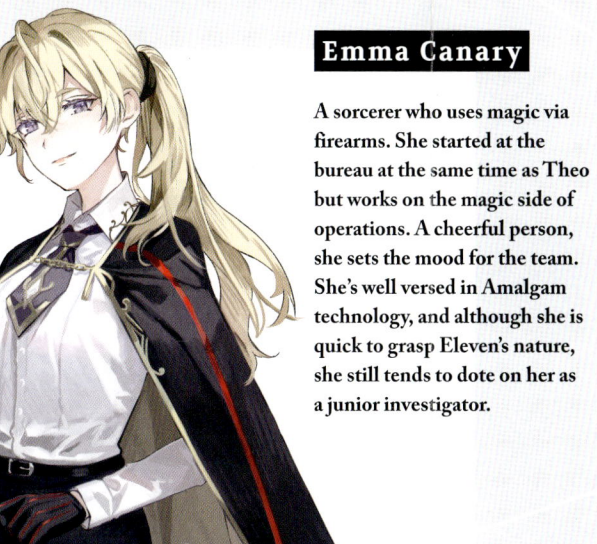

"I'm just worried here. About the both of you."

Tobias Hillmyna

An old hand at the bureau, he's been watching out for Theo and his cohort since they were students at the academy. He's kind but the type to use a smile to apply pressure. Tobias is mindful of the state of the team and a little *too* helpful with Eleven as his new junior investigator. He lost his left arm in an air raid and uses a high-performance prosthetic known as a synthetic.

Age: 36
Height: 184 cm
Special skill: Portraiture
Interests: Driving, darts

AMALGAM HOUND

Criminal Investigation Bureau: Special Investigation Unit

Midori Komai

Illustration by:
Domino Ozaki

Vol. 1

YEN ON
New York

AMALGAM HOUND

Criminal Investigation Bureau: Special Investigation Unit

Midori Komai

Illustration by: **Domino Ozaki**

Vol. **1**

Translation by Jocelyne Allen
Cover art by Domino Ozaki

This book is a work of fiction. Names, characters, places, and incidents are the product of the author's imagination or are used fictitiously. Any resemblance to actual events, locales, or persons, living or dead, is coincidental.

AMALGAM HOUND SOSAKYOKU KEIJIBU TOKUSOHAN Vol. 1
©Midori Komai 2022
Edited by Dengeki Bunko
First published in Japan in 2022 by KADOKAWA CORPORATION, Tokyo.
English translation rights arranged with KADOKAWA CORPORATION, Tokyo through TUTTLE-MORI AGENCY, INC., Tokyo.

English translation © 2024 by Yen Press, LLC

Yen Press, LLC supports the right to free expression and the value of copyright. The purpose of copyright is to encourage writers and artists to produce the creative works that enrich our culture.

The scanning, uploading, and distribution of this book without permission is a theft of the author's intellectual property. If you would like permission to use material from the book (other than for review purposes), please contact the publisher. Thank you for your support of the author's rights.

Yen On
150 West 30th Street, 19th Floor
New York, NY 10001

Visit us at yenpress.com • facebook.com/yenpress • twitter.com/yenpress • yenpress.tumblr.com • instagram.com/yenpress

First Yen On Edition: March 2024
Edited by Yen On Editorial: Rachel Mimms
Designed by Yen Press Design: Andy Swist

Yen On is an imprint of Yen Press, LLC.
The Yen On name and logo are trademarks of Yen Press, LLC.

The publisher is not responsible for websites (or their content) that are not owned by the publisher.

Library of Congress Cataloging-in-Publication Data
Names: Komai, Midori, author. | Ozaki, Domino, illustrator. | Allen, Jocelyne, 1974– translator.
Title: Amalgam hound / Midori Komai ; illustration by Domino Ozaki ; translation by Jocelyne Allen.
Other titles: Amarugamu haundo. English
Description: First Yen On edition. | New York : Yen On, 2024– |
Identifiers: LCCN 2023055526 | ISBN 9781975374143 (v. 1 ; trade paperback) |
    ISBN 9781975374167 (v. 2 ; trade paperback)
Subjects: LCGFT: Light novels.
Classification: LCC PZ7.1.K67568 Am 2024 | DDC [Fic]—dc23
LC record available at https://lccn.loc.gov/2023055526

ISBNs: 978-1-9753-7414-3 (paperback)
       978-1-9753-7415-0 (ebook)

10 9 8 7 6 5 4 3 2 1

LSC-C

Printed in the United States of America

CONFIDENTIAL

Chapter 1
Looking Up at the Stars from a Cage

AMALGAM HOUND
Criminal Investigation Bureau:
Special Investigation Unit

There was a light she could never forget. Blue eyes, blue gaze—a light brimming with good faith and conscientiousness that she never expected to be turned toward her.

As the girl looked up at the night sky through the smashed roof, she extended a hand toward the light from a past countless light-years away. Blue stars glittered in the dark distance. The hand reaching out was pale almost to the point of transparency. The movement was like a finger held out to a small bird and carried with it a purity that was out of place in the stuffy room. Childish fingertips were bathed in moonlight.

There was no expression on her face. Her hair was the color of clouds in the winter sky, with pointed, bestial ears peeking through the strands. A fluffy tail poked out from beneath the hem of her tank top and whapped against the concrete floor. The silver fur had a metallic luster, different from her hair. The animal ears and tail were incongruous with the rest of the girl's slender frame, but this odd appearance was nothing out of the ordinary in this place.

Human shadows writhed inside the room with her, showered in the cold light of the moon. All had silver parts eating into their human forms; all were chained to the walls. They swung their heads and limbs from side to side, ranting and raving, ignorant of the saliva that hung from their mouths, threatening anyone who met their eyes.

Almost as if to proclaim to all and sundry that even now while their bestial nature took hold of them, they were still human beings.

The girl, however, simply took in the stars with her gray eyes, as though the chaos in the room around her didn't even register in her mind. Somehow none of it mattered to her. The howls, the moans—they did not merit her attention.

These writhing shadows would die the following evening anyway. The curtain would rise on the show—a fight to the death—the losers would die, and the winners would remain captive here. That was all. The girl quietly awaited her moment.

As she closed her eyes, her eyelids held fast to that beautiful blue—and for her—unforgettable light.

∎

The shrill ringing of his alarm clock jolted Theo Starling awake. He stared up at the ceiling and slowly let out the breath he'd been holding. He wiped his forehead damp with sweat and inhaled deeply. Even now, two years after he'd left the front lines of the continental war, his days started with a nightmare.

Magic and science had developed together in lockstep in Adastrah, and the country was blessed with abundant natural resources compared with the rest of the continent. Those resources had also long been ravaged by the war between the many nations on that same continent. And while Adastrah had concluded cease-fires with hostile neighbors over the last year—and there was even movement toward a permanent treaty—the land still suffered ongoing upheavals.

Theo had been a military man for only a relatively short period of time. But he would never forget the Alkabel campaign, which ended up being the largest battle in history. It was also his final tour.

The main theater for this battle was the city of Alkabel. After the large bell tower that was the symbol of the city was razed, the intense fighting continued day and night for a full month, taking many friends from Theo and torturing him even now in his nightmares.

* * *

...Remembering all that isn't going to do anyone any good now, though.

He forced his stiff body to rise. As he shuffled into the bathroom, he could still see the billowing black smoke, the dirt and debris floating through the air, and his friends being knocked flying by explosions while the booming roar of destruction echoed in his ears.

He washed his face, peered into the mirror, and scowled. His blue eyes were cloudy with the nightmare, and they were framed by faint but dark bags. When he pushed back his wet bangs, he couldn't help but remember the way he'd washed away dried blood, dark like his own red hair. He saw an ashen arm falling to the earth and whirled around to find a dirty shirt poking out of the laundry basket.

Whether he was asleep or awake, the nightmare had no intention of letting go of him.

Unable to hold back a sigh, he sluggishly got on with his morning ablutions. And then he furrowed his brow at a sudden memory and tightened his necktie.

Flitting through the back of his mind against the backdrop of the battlefield was the figure of a young soldier. Immediately after his unit, No. 133, had completed its diversionary mission during the Alkabel campaign, it was annihilated in an air raid. Theo had been the only survivor. And he'd been buried in a pile of rubble on the brink of death himself until a soldier came racing over to him. Because of the equipment they were wearing and their neutral voice, he couldn't see the soldier's face or tell what gender they were. This soldier heroically pulled him out from the debris, slung his arm around their shoulders, and started walking while Theo's feet dragged beneath him. The soldier was small and slender but clearly accustomed to carrying people, no doubt one of the nursing school students mobilized for the war.

But when another bomb fell, the soldier shielded Theo from the explosion, and their young body was blown to pieces. Theo had also been badly injured, but a sense of duty and deep guilt made him carry what was left of the soldier—nothing more than a head and torso—back to the base. The soldier had no dog tags, and Theo couldn't abandon the person who had saved him to this anonymous fate—not after he'd already lost his entire squad.

He didn't know what had happened after that. By the time he regained consciousness in a hospital bed, all the necessary procedures had already been carried out. Not only did he not know who the soldier was, but he didn't even know where they had been laid to rest.

His memory was hazy. But his nightmares brought him back to that hell in painfully vivid detail every single night. The friends caught in the explosion, flying helplessly through the air. Himself buried in brick and glass. And then the soldier who saved him would always appear, protect him from the bomb, and be blown apart. But, curiously, each time he picked up the body, the soldier would repeat the same words: "Please retreat." "Please run." "Don't concern yourself with me." And then the nightmare would replace the soldier with something else. The cracked anti-dust helmet would become a charred head, the scorched military uniform a dress that was in style at the time. The head bore no trace of the long red hair it used to hold, and sweet fingers would crumble to ash, even as they clung to him.

"Why, Theo? How can you be alive, my dear brother, when you left me to die?"

The teary reproach would be swallowed up by the flames, even as it lingered in his ears and made him dizzy.

Before he knew it, Theo was standing at the front door. Naturally, there was no one else in the silent apartment. It was all a bad dream, all in the past. But that silence constantly reproached and berated him, and he fled the house.

Heather, the little sister he'd left with their parents back in his hometown. A young girl with blue eyes and hair a slightly brighter red than his own. A sad girl still in her teens when she was caught up in an attack so sudden, she hadn't even had the chance to flee.

Theo leaped into the car as if to try and shake free from these memories. Even now, five years after the fact, the tragedy remained firmly etched onto the backs of his eyelids, merging with his memories of the war and leaving his mind a tortured mess.

The streets of the city flowed past outside the vehicle windows. A child walked hand in hand with their parents. Young couples smiled at each other happily as they browsed the shops. And despite the fact that he knew it was a fool's errand, Theo couldn't help but search for his sister among the crowds of people. With no place to atone and no one to hate, all he could do was wallow in foolish fantasies.

But whether he liked it or not, time passed, and crime happened. Theo had to get to work.

He took a deep breath to switch mental gears and stepped into the Delverro Municipal Library. The building was essentially unchanged from before the war, having escaped the air raids, and it quietly welcomed the people, inviting them to wander its fields of knowledge. There were sections for new releases and picture books in the front hall, decorated in warm colors, and families stood around, selecting books. He also spotted a younger person in heated discussion with someone older, both with specialized tomes in one hand, and others dotted the area, basking in some quiet time alone.

This was the peaceful every day that Theo was sworn to protect. He looked around with a smile before continuing toward the turnstiles farther in. He lined up in a separate queue from the library patrons and showed his investigator's badge to the employee on duty there.

With a smile, they silently lowered the transit lever. Theo set the palm of his hand on it to complete the biometric authentication, and when he took a step forward, his surroundings changed completely. A guard now stood where the employee had been and saluted Theo in welcome.

"Good morning, Investigator Starling!" he said.

"Mm, morning." Theo nodded in return. "Here's to another fruitful day."

Unlike the warmth of the library, the lobby he made his way through was a sterile office environment with gray as the keynote color. As usual, groups of investigators were already hard at work in the Delverro branch of the Criminal Investigation Bureau, which was kept hidden using the magical camouflage Mimesis for security reasons. Other investigators were also popping into existence the way he himself just had.

Theo moved forward unerringly and entered the Detective Operations Department. He exchanged hellos with investigators on their way out of the office, discussing the rash of recent "goat mask robberies," and took a look at the city of Delverro through a gap in the blinds. The usual number of people were passing by on foot with the usual amount of traffic on the road, and he could see progress in the reconstruction of buildings in the area. He'd heard rumors that the shops dive-bombed by fighter planes would reopen next month completely renovated. Regular life was gradually returning to Delverro.

Given the fact that it housed communication bases and other military facilities, the city had been a prime target for attack during the war, but the abundance of evacuation routes and shelters meant that there had been relatively few deaths compared to the massive scale of the property damage. Even so, residents were left with wounds that wouldn't heal, and public order grew steadily worse. Violent crimes were a constant, and the city was also plagued with robberies. Just yesterday, a group of boys had been caught in flagrante delicto.

Whatever else, Theo was not the only one living his days counting the things he'd lost. Even knowing this, however, the face reflected in the glass of the window was too dark, and he scowled as he closed the blinds.

"...Time for work," he said out loud to get his brain moving on a different track as he turned to his desk.

"Good morning!" A young man opened the door and bustled into the office. "Yes, morning! Hey! Ooh! Nice tie today!"

Many of the investigators returned his greetings with a smile as the man with delicate features made his cheerful way toward Theo, pushing back his youthful brown hair, bright green eyes shining.

"Hey there! Morning, Theo!" he called. "Quite the sour look on your face again today!"

"That's just how my face is," Theo responded with a sigh. "Leave me alone, Tobias."

Tobias Hillmyna shrugged as he poured himself a coffee. "You haven't changed a bit since the academy. Not too many people bother to put on a scowl like yours. Take a cue from the police dogs. The way they wag their tails, it's the best thing in this world."

"How many times do I have to tell you to drop it—?" His voice automatically grew rougher, but he clamped his mouth shut when he noticed someone new arriving in the office.

Golden hair swinging, Emma Canary twirled the cape that was proof of her membership in the Society of Sorcerers and turned her purple eyes on Theo and Tobias.

"Morning, Emma." Tobias welcomed her with a smile. "You were off working in the mountains until yesterday, yeah? How'd it go?"

"Ended up having a wild dance party with a wendigo. And I *loved* the fireworks against the snow." She laughed and patted the katahr in the holster on her hip. Many of the crimes in the country of Adastrah were committed by sorcerers, and so Detective Operations also included Society-licensed sorcerers. A trustworthy colleague, Emma was particularly skilled with firearms.

"Aren't you supposed to get some time off if you've been away on assignment?" Theo asked, abruptly recalling the departmental rules.

"The boss didn't tell you?" Emma raised an eyebrow in surprise. "He said I should come into the office as soon as I got back."

Theo cocked his head to one side and tried recalling if he'd had such a conversation when Detective Operations Captain Reno Paloma poked his head out of his office door and beckoned Theo and his group with one hand. Theo watched with a scowl as the older man retreated into his office, leaving the investigator with no choice but to oblige. Emma grinned, and Tobias made a sweeping gesture toward the door with one hand. The captain no doubt had new orders for them, or a case. Something like that.

Once they were in his office and lined up in front of his desk, Captain Paloma tented his fingers and got a serious look on his face.

"Sorry to just spring this on you," he said. "But we've had a request from the bureau, and we need to put together a special investigation team. So I'm tasking the three of you to focus on responding to Amalgam-involved incidents."

Theo's eyes flew open at the word *Amalgam*.

"Captain!" Emma cried. "Amalgams are automagitons. Shouldn't they be under military jurisdiction or the Society of Sorcerers?"

"I damn well know that!" Paloma snapped. "But there was this report on how easily incidents involving Amalgams can turn brutal. The Army Intelligence Service is moving on this, too, but heinous crimes fall under the jurisdiction of DetOps. You'll have to work with the army and other specialized organizations to handle the Amalgams. This request comes straight from the bureau chief."

The captain reached out and handed the investigation files to Theo.

"...Amalgam use was originally limited to the battlefield, yes?" Tobias said. "Fidelity to orders is supposedly their strong suit. How are they involved in any incidents in the city? They're giants. They can take a hit from a tank and keep going. They carry a battleship's worth of weapons. I find it hard to believe they could be diverted into illegal channels."

He was exactly right. Automagitons were strategic weapons born from the fusion of magic and science. Even among these, however, the Amalgam was revolutionary. With a simple human form resembling a clay doll, they were equipped with battleship-class weaponry, could withstand any offensive, and advance over any terrain without requiring any supplies whatsoever. They were prized on the front lines as giant soldiers.

For over ten years, they had been the army's main military force, replacing human beings and helping to minimize the number of dead combatants in the continental war. But to avoid information leaks to enemy nations, all material relating to the Amalgams was strictly controlled by the army, and the details remained confidential.

Theo also found it rather hard to believe that these things could be contributing to the rise in crime in Delverro. First and foremost, people would be thrown into an immediate panic if a giant soldier was walking around town.

Paloma ran a hand over his shaved head and sighed at length, a grave look on his face. "No one knows how, but Amalgams *are* being diverted. That's a fact."

"What?!" Emma gasped.

"Intelligence services are also working to track them down, but even they can only do so much," Paloma continued. "That's why you three will work together as a special investigation unit and approach the Amalgams from the criminal side. You can handle other cases when there's no new Amalgam work to take care of, but essentially, I'll need you to focus on Amalgam incidents. You're the lead on this one, Investigator Starling."

Theo yanked his face up at the unexpected assignment. He felt the eyes of his two colleagues on him. "Me, sir? Hillmyna has more experience as an investigator…"

"True, you're one of our younger investigators." Paloma nodded. "But your clear rate's impressive, and that military service history of yours shows you've got grit. The bureau chief's also got a high opinion of you. None of us have any previous experience to lean on with a case like this, but I want you to dig up the truth with the help of a veteran investigator like Hillmyna and a sorcerer like Canary."

"…I will do my best, sir," Theo said.

"Depending on how the investigation goes, we can think about assigning you more people. Now get out there and do me proud." They were dismissed.

Theo walked out of the captain's office with his colleagues, his head spinning in surprise. How on earth could the war machine Amalgams be involved in civilian crime? He had the case file in his hands, though, meaning that their work for that day was settled.

Back at their desks, Tobias crossed his arms thoughtfully. "Amalgams, hmm? I don't know anything about them other than what's been reported."

"Most info's top secret," Emma told him. "To keep from arousing interest in them. And I guess that's to be expected."

"Anyway—Tobias, Emma. Are you all right with this? I mean... me as team leader?" Theo asked, a little worried, and both Tobias and Emma looked at him curiously.

"Captain Paloma said it all," Tobias replied. "I trust your judgment, too."

"And Tobias is here in case you do mess up," Emma added. "Plus, I've got the magical side of things. You tend to just go ahead and make decisions anyway, so it's probably easier to have you lead the team."

"...You make it sound so simple," Theo said. "Is that really it?"

"That's it. Now!" Tobias clapped his hands together. "How about we take a look at the file? Our team's first case."

As ready as they would ever be, they began flipping through the files.

The report was about an illegal fight club in the city. This in and of itself was not particularly unusual. With the war, distribution routes broke down, people lost their jobs, and given that the issues with goods, services, and the economy in general were still a long way from being resolved, some regions saw an increase in the number of people living hand to mouth. The more physically gifted among them ended up regulars at underground fight clubs. The fights took place illegally in vacant lots and abandoned buildings, with bets placed on the fighters' outcomes. The payouts could be quite large, so clubs like this were fairly popular.

But at the club in question, the fighters were said to be unusual. Parts of their bodies were silver, which was curious in and of itself. The report noted that these silver areas were transformed into parts from a different creature. It seemed unlikely that this could have been makeup or prosthetics. In the photos taken surreptitiously, a fighter with a boar head was fighting a man with crab pincers for hands.

Apparently, the draw of this particular illegal club was superhuman fights to the death between bizarre, semi-human brawlers. A spectacle of slaughter, freaks on freaks, inflamed the spectators.

The suspicion was that these fighters were Amalgams.

Theo closed the case file and looked at Emma. "…So? As a magic professional, what's the likelihood that they're Amalgams?"

"From just the look of them, I'd say it's possible, but…" She frowned. "Couldn't it simply be clever synthetics?"

"Ahhh, I'd say no to that. Arms and legs are one thing, but this boar's head—there's no way," Tobias interjected, pointing at a photo of the boar combatant losing the fight. "That's not even real fur. And from what I can tell by looking at the head crushed by the crab claws here, there's no mechanical parts or motor of any kind. It would be impossible to make a synthetic like this. I say this definitively as a synthetics user."

"…So then this is strange." Emma looked at the documents and photos with a troubled expression. "The Amalgam is a specialized weapon. Powerful regenerative abilities, no need for resupply. And above all else, they don't die."

Theo saw what she was getting at. "At this fight club, though, they're forced to fight to the death."

"If they're real Amalgams, they can't die," Emma responded. "Or, well, I mean, they *can* die. But they can keep regenerating until their core's destroyed. That's their power source. So they can just walk off getting their head crushed. The way these fighters look is bothering me, too. Setting aside the whole silver thing, why animal parts?"

Theo shrank a little at her intensity as he flipped through the documents. "You mean an Amalgam can transform into a real human being, too?"

"No." She shook her head. "An Amalgam's camouflage ability is at best enough to blend into the environment. To hide while it regenerated from a wounded state, it would mimic the gravel or plants in contact with it. They reproduce even the texture of the surface, so they're better at camouflage than, say, octopuses or chameleons. But they can only take on that simple clay-doll form you see in the newspapers. They'd have a hard time mimicking actual living creatures."

"...So then, the whole silver thing and animal parts are suspicious from the get-go," Theo said.

"Right. Which is why I thought synthetics, but it's not that, either, yeah?" Emma looked completely baffled. "There are just too many contradictions here for an Amalgam. I haven't got a clue how they're doing this."

Theo scowled. "What would be the point of making people like this fight? Where's the advantage? People are going to talk about animal-human hybrids, and it's hard to imagine that an illegal fight club wants that kind of buzz. They are, in fact, under investigation right now by us because of that buzz. I can't see the purpose of it."

"Maybe it's surprisingly simple," Tobias said brightly, but his eyes were serious. "They're really just trying to get the word out, like 'Hey, Amalgams exist, folks'? A trap for people who come sniffing around."

Theo leaned back thoughtfully. "We'll have to coordinate with the municipal police in the area to shut down the club. If it's a trap, all the more reason to put it out of business."

"Well, even if there *is* an Amalgam in the place, we can take control as long as we grab its commanding officer, right?" Tobias said. "I hear they're pretty faithful to orders."

"Right." Emma nodded. "They are autonomous, but their intelligence is set pretty low for how powerful a weapon they are. We're screwed if the owner gets nervous, though. I'll go ahead and apply for permission to use arts rejectors. I'm sure they'll allow it. We *are* a special team to deal with Amalgams, after all."

The words were no sooner out of Emma's mouth than she was racing to the captain's office. Ever since their academy days, she had always been impossibly quick to act.

As Theo considered weapons in the event that it was a trap, Tobias said, "Try to keep your cool even if there really is an Amalgam, Theo."

Reflexively, he lifted his face. Tobias was worriedly looking his way, and he found this would-be parental gaze extremely unpleasant.

He clicked his tongue. "You just make sure to keep your guard up. Otherwise, you might end up losing your right arm, too." He indicated Tobias's arm with his eyes, and Tobias patted his right shoulder with his synthetic left hand.

"When that happens, I'll get them to give me an arm that can fire missiles," he joked. "Anyway, just remember you're not alone out there."

"…I know. Don't underestimate me."

A vision of flames and black smoke flickered in the corner of his eye, but Theo pushed this away and started making plans.

■

The fight club opened at nine in the evening. Given that it was still early spring, the night breeze was chilly. Theo tugged the collar of his coat up, yanked his hat down over his eyes, and kept watch, taking care to prevent his face from being seen. People were moving away from the better-lit part of the city, down a road where the streetlamps grew sparse. Young, old, rich, poor—they all marched toward the abandoned warehouse with a curious enthusiasm. It was an unusual sight, so many people coming together in a deserted area with no shops, away from the main roads.

In cooperation with the municipal police, Theo and his team chose to slip into the fight club as audience members. He left Tobias and Emma to cover the rear entrance where they assumed staff would be while he entered the venue through the front door by himself.

The exterior was definitely that of a broken-down abandoned factory, but once he made it through the door, it was outfitted like a real-deal fight club. He walked past posters of popular combatants and notices of the results from the last few days as he proceeded toward the seating area.

The music playing over the speakers made the air shake with the heavy bass; a mirror ball glittered overheard, and kiosks were scattered around the club. Instead of actual seats, a simple scaffolding in the form of stairs circled the ring. It was very uncomfortable to sit on. As for the so-called ring, it was simply a square space partitioned off with a fence that stretched up to the ceiling. The fence had only one entrance for the fighters, and that was currently locked. There were conspicuous bloodstains on the floor of the ring. It wasn't hard to imagine the kind of rough treatment fighters had faced here, how many deaths the arena had seen.

Theo wrinkled his nose in a scowl. The venue was dusty and stank of mold. And it was obviously poorly ventilated—cigarette smoke hung in the air, creating a white cloud that hovered near the ceiling. When he looked out on the audience area, no one was paying attention to their surroundings the way he was. The spectators were pulling out cigars, food, drink, each killing time how they preferred.

The crowd of people began to take their seats and face forward at last as voices called out from here and there about the start of the match. That night's spectacle of slaughter would be upon them soon, and some of the audience members were already obviously excited, getting unusually worked up before the first bell had even sounded.

"Blood! Blood! Kill! Kill! Get 'em! Smash 'em!" they shouted with familiar ease.

Theo sniffed at the thoroughly disagreeable sight as the music died down and the seating area grew dark. The ring was brightly lit up.

"*Welcome to one and all!*" a voice announced over the loudspeaker. "*Thank you for your patronage tonight! Witness once again no-holds-barred battles! Gushing blood and flying flesh! These death matches end only with someone's life! First up, in the red corner! A human weapon from the great northern sea, a man who rips out the very hearts of his opponents with his tremendous right hook! Yeti the Giiiiiaaaaaant!*"

The spotlight popped on to reveal a large man stepping into the venue through the fighter entrance. His face was gnarled with old wounds, and he tossed aside his white robe to show off a torso equally covered in scars. A throaty cry rose up to welcome him, and he threw his arms into the air, grinning toothlessly. His fists were colored silver and covered in countless needles.

"*In the blue corner! A rising star dominating the ring, shooting for the throne at impossible speed: Panzer Pantherrrrr!*"

A slender fighter appeared from the opposite corridor. The audience also welcomed him with loud cheers, but he likely couldn't hear them, thanks to the fact that his ears were scarred completely over with severe burns. He doffed his black robe, revealing painful burn scars on his back as well. From the knees down, his legs were lustrous and silver, the limbs of a top predator.

Both men seemed to be popular fighters—just the pair facing each other was enough to elicit louds cries from the audience.

"*Now! Place your bets!*" continued the voice over the loudspeaker. "*If you feel fortune favors Yeti the Giant, purchase the red ticket! But if Panzer Panther's the blessed bloke, choose the blue!*"

Hands shoved money at the ticket sellers. The audience was apparently used to fighters in strange shapes and sizes. No one questioned anything they saw.

Theo stared at the fighters. So the transformation *was* only partial. They could still be synthetics. It was too soon to say that he was looking at Amalgams. He gave the signal for his colleagues to be on standby and chose to watch how things played out.

Both combatants had won all their matches thus far, so it was only natural that they moved with a familiarity and immediately went for the jugular, aiming for the kill. They were evenly matched in terms of physique and size—but eventually, Panzer Panther found an opening, poked out Yeti the Giant's eyes, kicked in his windpipe, and knocked him out when he faltered.

But the match wasn't over yet.

Before the audience had stopped shouting, Panzer Panther grabbed his opponent's head and smashed it against the concrete floor to end Yeti the Giant's life. The bell to signal the end of the bout sounded at last.

With cheers rising up inside the venue, Theo watched for his moment to intervene. Considering the audience's extreme excitement, not only would they not shrink back if he fired his gun, but they would likely grow even wilder. Could he even interrupt the fighting to begin with?

While he struggled to decide what to do, the second match began. The time between bouts was extremely short, and nothing more than a perfunctory attempt was made to wipe up the blood on the concrete. The progress of the card was very fast.

...*Why do the different fighters have different transformations?*

Theo frowned and set his mind to work as the third match was about to start.

"And now for our third event of the night!" the enthusiastic announcer cried, his voice echoing throughout the venue. "In the red corner! Our king, beloved champion, and winner of thirty fights in a row! The blood-soaked mask, Mad Bradleyyyyyyyy!"

The giant who stepped into the ring was so enormous, he made the cage look small. The audience erupted into cheers loud enough to shake the building. Mad Bradley's back was colored silver, his skin turned into a carapace. Drops of blood clung to the iron mask covering his face, creating a rusted red pattern.

He was clearly a popular fighter, but perhaps the timing of Theo's intervention depended on his opponent. Theo turned his eyes to the blue corner and froze.

"His opponent, in the blue corner! The lone little woman in our club, she's already snatched up three victories! The beautiful, adorable rookie, Fluffy Houuuuuuuund!"

Lewd laughter, cheers, whistles, and catcalls almost loud enough to pop his eardrums filled the air in the venue. A girl who looked to be no older than fifteen advanced into this chaos with a cool expression on her face. Her feet were bare, and she didn't so much as glance at the bloodstains beneath them.

She was like snow personified. White-blond hair flowed gently past her cheeks; her eyes were similarly pale, and her porcelain skin seemed almost bloodless. All this combined with the neat proportions of her face made her look like a very skillfully produced doll. But in one way, she was no different from the other fighters—she, too, had been partially transformed into a beast. Pointed ears poked out from her hair, and a furry tail swung down from her backside. Both ears and tail were of course silver, tinged with a metallic luster. Other than this, however, her body was undeveloped like that of a young boy, slender as a willow. She was too slim to even be a dancer. Hers definitely did not seem like the body of a death-match brawler who had clinched three consecutive wins in this fight club.

The vendors could barely sell tickets fast enough while the spectators were on the edges of their seats at this unexpected match.

Theo was stunned for a moment, frozen in place, but he soon tapped the wireless transceiver hidden inside his collar. "…Given how small she is, she'll avoid sticking too closely to her opponent. When a gap opens up between the two of them—Tobias, you hit the dog with an arts rejector; Emma, you get the mask."

They both responded with a brief affirmative. Moments later, the bell clanged, and the match began.

The first to move was the massive Mad Bradley. His fist sliced through the air with an audible *whoosh*, and the girl—Fluffy Hound—nimbly dodged the blow. She looked him up and down, all the while maintaining a fixed distance from him. The giant slammed his fist forward again and again, but she evaded it every time without even blinking. Mad Bradley howled in frustration and thrust his clenched hand toward her, all his great weight riding on it.

And then the girl leaped up to the ceiling.

Theo automatically followed her with his eyes. The ceiling was easily more than four meters above their heads, an impossible leap. The rest of the audience began to clamor and yell while Mad Bradley tilted his head back and stared up with visible disbelief.

The girl kicked at the ceiling, blowing away the stagnant cloud of white smoke. She spun around in a somersault, and as she came out of it, she brought her heel down. Mad Bradley quickly threw up his right arm as a shield and readied a counterattack with his left hand.

Krrrrrk! The sound his arm made as it took the kick was unsettling, and his enormous knee broke underneath him. A heel strike from a leg so thin, it threatened to break with the contact. In that single blow, Mad Bradley was brought to his knees.

Not missing the opening when he faltered, Fluffy Hound closed in, taking advantage of the way he leaned forward on his knees. Her fist sank into his defenseless side, and the shuddering *thud* of the impact seemed unfathomable from the look of the blow. Flesh armor rippling, Mad Bradley's massive bulk bounced into the air.

The audience erupted into screams and cheers and wails. Mad Bradley vomited blood. Rather than striking again immediately in a follow-up attack, Fluffy Hound leaped back, and Mad Bradley's wild swing tasted nothing but air. Already, he was cloaked in the desperation of a losing man. The silver carapace wrapped around his back crackled and spread up to his shoulders as he radiated pure murderous rage.

Theo stared in amazement. What on earth was this show he was witnessing?

The girl was so slender he could snap her in two. But she had overwhelmed her opponent with one blow, even though he was many times her size.

Mad Bradley roared so loudly, it was practically deafening. He gave himself over to his rage and charged. With both arms spread out, his enormous body nearly filled the ring, and he closed in on Fluffy Hound like a wall. There was nowhere to run. But the girl's hair only swung slightly to one side as she flipped up into the air, pressing a hand to Mad Bradley's shoulder to leap over him.

Caught off guard, the giant looked back over. But before he could actually turn around, Fluffy Hound hit him squarely in the back with a roundhouse kick. Her leg, supple like a whip, snapped down against his carapace with force that threatened to smash it right open. Mad Bradley fell forward into the cage.

The fence creaked and bulged out toward the audience, sending bits of metal flying. The spectators screamed and tried to get out of the way. Cheers and boos mixed together. The audience was buzzing with excitement, like a hornet's nest with a stick thrust into it.

Kashank! Mad Bradley crushed the metal lattice of the fence in his fists and peeled it back as he got up from the floor. A silver froth gushed out to cover his body, and his flesh swelled even further.

Theo leaped to his feet, turned his gun toward the ceiling, and pulled the trigger. The gunshot cut through the din in the venue.

"That's enough!" he shouted. "Nobody move! Put your hands on your head and get on your knees! Now!"

The municipal police officers raced forward and quickly got the wild crowd under control while Tobias and Emma fired their arts rejectors toward the ring. Bullets of purple electricity shot out, a cry of anguish pierced the air, and a body dropped to the ground. Perhaps because Mad Bradley's abilities had now been restricted by the arts rejector bullet, his physical body stopped transforming, and the silver shell shrank backward.

Fluffy Hound, on the other hand, showed no signs of damage. She merely tucked her creature features away under her hair and clothes and then stopped moving entirely. She did, however, lift her face abruptly. She looked up not at Tobias, who was closer to her, but at Theo.

Her lips pulled apart slightly, and her eyes grew a hint rounder. Theo couldn't help but stare back at her. Instead of speaking, she put her hands on her head and dropped to her knees. Tobias approached her, handcuffs at the ready.

Fluffy Hound immediately whirled around and put a hand on his collar. Emma and Theo turned the barrels of their guns to get her in their sights a second before they heard an androgynous voice over the wireless.

"I need to talk to you. Go around to the back."

It was the girl. She spoke with Tobias and then meekly allowed her hands to be cuffed. She started shuffling out of the venue with the other fighters and the spectators. Theo looked at Tobias questioningly, but Tobias simply shook his head with a hard look on his face. Theo left the police to deal with the aftermath and headed around to the back entrance.

Once Theo and his team were together in the deserted backstage area, the girl stepped away from Tobias, whose eyes grew wide in surprise. The handcuffs he'd snapped around her slender wrists were now sitting in his hands, still locked.

The girl turned around slowly. "Please excuse me. I couldn't speak with you when there were other people around."

"...You're not one of the fighters here?" Theo frowned. "What on earth—?"

Klak! She set a bare foot forward, and black fabric spilled out from her toes. It raced outward, enveloping her legs and moving steadily upward to cover the rest of her body. When it reached her neck, a black skirt billowed around her knees, and the tank top she had been wearing was now a military dress uniform.

"I'm Eleven, a Hound with the Army Intelligence Service. Thank you for your cooperation in this investigation."

For a second, Theo was at a loss for words. Although she looked to be the same age as his dead sister, the way she neatly brought her heels together and saluted indicated many more years of experience than he himself had.

■

Arrested at the fight club were seventeen fighters, nine staff members, the main organizer, and around thirty spectators who had engaged in illegal activities. Two people were hospitalized. The bodies of twenty-nine former fighters were discovered on the premises, including inside of the club itself. There were interrogations, ID checks, transport, phone calls to guardians, and much more, so that even with the

cooperation of the local police, Theo and his team were up all night working frantically. It was past noon when they finally returned to their desks.

Drinking a cup of coffee that was half milk and sugar, Emma muttered lifelessly, "That...that was one hell of a fight club, huh?"

"Seriously," Theo groaned. He looked over the information sorted and posted onto the board.

After a failed attempt at opening a gambling den, this particular gang had started the fight club. They testified that in order to further increase box office revenue, they had been doping the fighters. This doping was the issue at hand.

They'd simply bought whatever the dealer had for sale; they didn't know the details of the drugs they were using. Neither they nor the fighters had the first clue about Amalgams. But the gang did know that taking even just one pill would cause the user to transform in some way.

The more time that passed, the greater the transformation in the affected area. It wasn't clear why the details of the transformation and the body part where it occurred differed from fighter to fighter. But a wide range of changes manifested in the combatants who won their matches and continued to fight over a longer period of time.

As the area of the transformation grew, the fighters became increasingly belligerent, started to have trouble understanding language, and became less likely to die. The murderous matches far surpassed anything any other fight club had to offer—beast-human-hybrid fighters—inciting a wild enthusiasm in the spectators. Encouraged by their early successes, the organizers brought on more fighters, gave them the drug, and produced more monsters.

Theo and Emma sent people to search for the dealer of this drug, to investigate the changes it brought about in the fighters' bodies, and to analyze the drug itself. Tobias was gone, meeting with reporters. Theo looked back at the waiting room.

The girl in the military uniform was sitting very politely and perfectly still on the sofa, knees and hands pressed together. He was at a complete loss as to what to do with her.

"...Is she really an intelligence agent?" he asked.

"You saw the way she transformed, yeah?" Emma replied. "It's a requirement for espionage work. Gotta be able to transform. It was pretty cool how she just went *whsh, whsh, whsh* and *bam*, new clothes. I need to learn that trick."

"Now listen, Emma, I'm being serious here. We can't overlook the fact that she slipped right out of those handcuffs." Theo sighed. Someone from intelligence services was apparently coming to verify her identity, but the question was when, exactly. "Even if she can use magic, it doesn't explain how she could fight like that with that body. She's a monster."

"True." Emma nodded. "Physical enhancement magic can't give you moves like that. But I mean, how else to explain it, other than magic?"

There was a sudden commotion at the entrance to the office, and Theo turned his eyes in that direction. A man with a coat over his arm was being led inside by Tobias. Theo had seen his kind bespectacled face before but only in the newspapers. The head of military intelligence himself, Benedict Guin.

"Whoa, whoa, whoa," Theo whispered. "I didn't hear anything about the number one man coming to meet with us."

Emma was equally bewildered. "Was the fight club that big of a target?"

A warm smile crossed Guin's face as he stepped into the office, his cheeks pushing up his glasses slightly. The Army Intelligence Service was an information-gathering organization that monitored dangerous elements both inside and outside of the country, active day and night. They were even stricter about secrecy than the Society of Sorcerers. Guin's smile seemed impossibly friendly for the head of such a group.

"Excuse me for intruding while you're at work," he said affably. "It seems you've got one of mine here."

"Is she really an intelligence agent, then...?" Theo asked hesitantly.

"Mm." Guin nodded. "We had her infiltrate the club in order to investigate the veracity of the Amalgam claims. And I've heard all about you. You're the Amalgam crime response team, yes? I'd love to chat. I have a few things of my own to talk about."

No one objected, and so they all headed toward the waiting room. The second she spotted Guin, the girl leaped to her feet and saluted him. He smiled and nodded in return before turning back to Theo and his team.

"Allow me to introduce you," he said. "This is Number Eleven. She's a weapon we've currently tasked with tracking and destroying the diverted Amalgams. She's a fine Amalgam herself: extremely stable, perfect for practical operation."

"*She's* an Amalgam?" Theo's eyes grew wide in surprise.

"There's no way!" Emma cried out.

"You're an investigator from the Society of Sorcerers, yes?" Guin responded calmly. "How can you be so certain of that?"

"It's simply not possible to create an Amalgam that's so nearly identical to a human being," Emma said. "The higher capacity the core, the larger the weapon has to be. I heard they settled on that huge size as a compromise to have a core with the necessary capacity. I mean, for a core that could mimic an actual human being, you'd need something way bigger than a regular Amalgam. Putting it all in this little body, there's just no way. Out of the question. The alchemists would lose their minds. If you told me she was a sorcerer, *that* would maybe make sense to me."

As she argued her angle, Emma shifted her gaze from Guin to the girl. The girl met this with her gray eyes, though her small lips stayed pursed, and she said nothing.

"That is an excellent point," Guin replied instead. "This exact mechanism is classified information, and only the relevant personnel are privy to the details. Even within the military, only those ranked general or higher have been informed of its mere existence. It is a special weapon."

"...And yet it has the form of a child?" Theo said.

"Rest assured, that is merely her appearance. These are weapons specially manufactured to take human form and carry out missions too difficult for actual human beings," Guin explained. "To differentiate them from the other Amalgams, they've been given the designation Hound."

"Oh! So that's it!" Tobias said brightly. He turned to the girl with a smile. "So Hound is the model name, and you introduced yourself as the number eleven? You're the eleventh Hound, then?"

"Your head's up in the clouds. *That's* what was tripping you up?" Emma slapped Tobias on the back and turned to Guin. "So what was this specially produced, top secret weapon doing at a fight club? The place had drugs, people turning into monsters—anything else of importance?"

"Your team, of course," Guin replied with a smile. "There are also other cases where we suspect Amalgam involvement. But the issue in the fight club is what that drug actually is and how it's being distributed. When we heard the bureau was putting together an anti-Amalgam unit, we decided this would be an appropriate first case. You may not have the depth of knowledge that Narcotics Control has, but Detective Operations still knows a thing or two about investigating illicit substances. Not to mention we have a number of deaths in this case as well. We assumed shutting down an illegal fight club would be a piece of cake with Criminal Investigation Bureau investigators taking the lead. Which is why we sent Number Eleven in for the undercover operation rather than a human being. This way, she could join up with you fairly smoothly."

"Wait just a second," Theo interjected automatically. The words of Captain Paloma came back to life in the back of his mind. Paloma had said they could think about adding more people to the team. And apparently, one of those people was… "Are you telling us to conduct the investigation with an Amalgam?"

"The record for this particular individual speaks for itself," Guin told him. "She was produced for the specific purpose of operating among human beings. Number Eleven will also respond flexibly to your requests. I'll vouch for her personally."

"You can't be serious. This is an *Amalgam*. A weapon created for slaughter. She'll do anything she's ordered to do." Theo groaned. Without even realizing it, he'd take half a step backward.

In the back of his mind, a flickering light from the past resurrected itself. Licking over the surface of the mountain, the flames burned for seven days and seven nights. The small settlement nestled in the mountains was quickly swallowed up in the blaze. Fiery winds blew and structures melted, houses grew brittle and crumbled, and residents fell amid fire and debris, without even the time to flee. Theo pushed forward through this hellscape, coughing at the hot wind that threatened to set his lungs on fire, too, as he called out for his mother, his father, his sister, until he reached his family home and found that it was nothing more than rubble. Through a gap in the pile of bricks and glass, a charred arm hung down, the bracelet he'd given his little sister for her birthday wrapped around its wrist.

The scene was unforgettable, hellish—and in the center of all the flames and destruction stood an oversized, rampant Amalgam shooting heat rays. The burning hot mass of a monster had mercilessly mowed down the enemy division together with Theo's hometown.

Tobias tried to intervene, but Guin held a hand up to stop him and turned toward Theo. "It seems you understand the Amalgams very well. Yes: So long as she has orders to do so, she will do anything and also become anything."

"Then, in that case, all the more reason—," Theo started.

"Which is why *you* should be the one to give those orders," Guin continued. "How about it?"

Theo was slow to grasp the unexpected proposal.

"Sir," Tobias cut in. "Is it really wise to hand off authority over a top secret weapon to an individual? At least give the whole of Detective Operations command."

"There has to be someone on the scene with the authority to command her, or she's useless," Guin replied. "What we're doing here, you see, Investigator Hillmyna, is merely dispatching an anti-Amalgam weapon to Detective Operations. About the only means of resisting an Amalgam a civilian has is an arts rejector, but with a Hound, you'll be able to handle most threats. You don't know what kinds of crimes you'll be up against; better to have every weapon at your disposal. Naturally, you can choose to put her in your weapons storage most of the time and only take her out in emergencies. Use her how you see fit."

"Have you not considered that I might abuse that authority?" Theo asked.

"What are you talking about, Investigator Starling? That's not like you." Guin laughed. The gentle, drooping eyes behind his glasses shone with a cold light. "Would you order it to kill civilians? You? Given how your family died?"

"So you knew. And yet you still try to hand the reins over to me!" Theo started to raise his voice, but then he heard the *ping* of a message arriving on his cell phone.

"Whoops!" Guin glanced at his watch and raised an eyebrow. "I've got another appointment. Apologies. I slipped out of work myself to come here, you see. I do have to get going. Investigator Starling, no need to overthink this. Consider it a trial run. Just a test as to whether or not the human side can handle a joint investigation with a Hound. Number Eleven will cooperate with you in whatever form you prefer. Ideal investigator, firearm, daily necessity—turn her into whatever's easiest to use and put her to work. Now that she's officially collaborating with the investigation, I'll send over her operating manual."

"Are you serious, Commander Guin?" Theo demanded. "You're actually putting an Amalgam on our team?"

"Mm, quite serious." He nodded. "She's an excellent Hound, and you are well aware of the threat an Amalgam poses. When we were making this decision, we also took into consideration a letter of recommendation from Detective Operations, but that is the biggest reason we're turning her over to you. We couldn't trust someone who doesn't know the fear of Amalgams to handle one. That said, however, you are free to use or not use her. Well then, I'll be on my way." The words were no sooner out of Guin's mouth than the man was leaving the office at a brisk pace.

Theo ran his hands through his hair and turned to the girl still standing silently at attention. "And how about you try saying something, then? I mean, being handed over to a total amateur like me!"

"I have no particular statement to make, Investigator." Her response was mechanical with a hint of warmth. "I simply follow orders."

"Sorry." Emma raised a hand. "Let me just check on a couple things. First, what should we call you? Hound is the designation for all of your kind, right? What's your individual name?"

"For identification purposes, I am called Number Eleven."

"Yeah? So then…Eleven," Emma said somewhat awkwardly, and the girl's gray eyes waited for her next words. "Did you transform into your current appearance for the purpose of infiltrating the club?"

"No, Investigator," the girl—Eleven—stated. "My current form is the initial default setting, and my clothing is designated for when I am working with the Intelligence Service. Neither reflects any particular requests."

Theo looked her over from head to toe once again. She was a little smaller than the average teenage girl. Silver hair wasn't uncommon in Adastrah, but this combination of white blond tinged with a complex luster and gray eyes stood out and nicely suited her neatly proportioned face. People simply passing her on the street would no doubt turn their heads for a second look.

"…So that hair and those eyes are the default setting, hmm?" he remarked. "What is the intention behind that?"

"The doctor said that white is easier to dye," she replied smoothly. "I was told that white was set as the keynote color due to the need to be able to change appearance and personality to suit the commanding officers."

Tobias shrugged lightly. "I don't mean to be rude here, but were you ever afraid for yourself at the fight club? You're small; you're a girl. You didn't run into any trouble?"

"The fight club staff welcomed my appearance as a young woman. All the fighters were chained up in the standby area with a fixed distance between them so they could not touch me. Contact with the staff was also kept to a bare minimum."

"Is that so?" Tobias smiled. "Well, that's, uh, great. So you were safe, at any rate."

"Yes," Eleven replied. "Thank you for your concern."

"Heh." Theo chuckled to himself. She'd clearly picked up on Tobias's solicitousness. Emma punched him in the side, and he gasped for breath.

"Eleven," Emma said brightly. "That arts rejector bullet didn't seem to faze you. Do they not have any effect on you?"

"Arts rejectors produce less of an effect on Hounds than on other Amalgams," Eleven explained. "Our abilities are temporarily limited, but we recover them quickly, and the arts rejector does not limit our physical functions at all."

"In other words, we can't truly restrain you by using an arts rejector on you," Emma noted. "Just like when you were fighting in the club, a human would be no match for you. Is that it?"

"That is exactly correct, Investigator."

"Thank you, Eleven. Well, now we know something important, Theo." Emma whirled around to face him.

He frowned. "...What do you mean?"

"You can order Eleven to stay in the armory while the three of us go out and investigate, but we have no way of knowing if she'll really be staying put. If she starts rampaging or going off on her own, no one in the division will be able to fight back, even using arts rejectors. Meaning that however you feel about it, you'll be on edge unless we keep Eleven where you can see her."

"And what do *you* think? As the expert." He was annoyed at how easily she had hit upon his unvoiced concerns and basically forced him to take Eleven along on the investigation. He scowled at her, and Emma put a hand to her forehead in a theatrical gesture.

"Personally, it's a real honor to work with the country's top secret weapon. I'm gonna get her to teach me all kinds of stuff."

"Well, I suppose you would say that, Emma," Tobias said with an exasperated smile as he looked at Theo. Theo had often seen this look at the academy. "So? What're we doing, Theo? You're the lead on this one. We'll go with whatever you decide. And you got a message a minute ago, too, yeah?"

Theo automatically turned his eyes toward Eleven. As before, she was quietly staring at him like a dog awaiting a command. He let out a long sigh and then lifted his face. "…We won't get anywhere like this. We move as a group of four. Rocky's report is ready apparently, so first stop is forensic pathology. But listen, Eleven. I'm in charge. I don't know what kind of work you usually do for intelligence services, but you will obey my orders from here on out. Anything you learn, you report it to me straight away. Are we clear?"

"Understood. I appreciate the permission to accompany you." Eleven's response to his prickly tone was merely a cool look. "Please specify the desired appearance and personality for me to operate as an investigator."

"Desired appearance? How am I supposed to answer that off the top of my head?" He rolled his eyes.

"You don't want to stay in the form you're in now, Eleven?" Emma asked, and Eleven blinked very slowly. This was the first time Theo had seen her eyelids.

"We do not have such emotions, and there is no evaluation standard for preferences. But in all situations, I have been given instructions for appearance, gender, and personality, so I proposed it as a customary practice."

"I think the way you look now's cute, though," Emma told her. "I like it. That military uniform suits you. Makes you look all serious."

"Indeed." Tobias nodded thoughtfully. "I suppose you would've been given orders for the right look for a military operation or an undercover mission, hmm? But this is Detective Operations—we don't have a set uniform. What do you think, Theo? Have her take on a form that's easier to swallow?" He looked back at Theo, clearly enjoying himself.

Theo clicked his tongue and took a step forward. "What about your current appearance or personality would affect the investigation? You're fine so long as you follow my orders. For the rest, do as you please."

"I understand. Then I will maintain my current status."

An obedient response. Theo gritted his teeth at the vortex of emotion that swirled around near his stomach as they set out. An Amalgam was walking along behind him, heels clacking against the floor, in the form of a girl the same age as his little sister. Her docility, the way she awaited orders, her every response—it was all unsettling. He knew exactly what kind of monster lived beneath that pale skin. And yet. And yet.

Tobias was the tallest of them, but Eleven was still a full head shorter than even Theo and Emma, who were tied for second tallest. No doubt because of that, Eleven's stride was smaller, and her footsteps were quicker than theirs.

No matter how Theo picked up the pace, the sound of her small shoes only quickened to match him. Breathing the faintest bit harder, he glanced back, and a half step behind him, Eleven looked up at him. Large eyes like the surface of a lake reflecting the winter sky stared innocently at him.

She looked too youthful, too innocent for him to be able to unleash his hatred without hesitation or mercy. With no outlet, his emotions came out in his movements, and he yanked open the door to the morgue so fiercely, he almost tore it off its hinges.

Isco Rocky leaped up from the chair where he sat, looking annoyed, and ran a hand through his salt-and-pepper hair. "No need to make such a racket, son. Oh! Where'd you pick up this lovely young lady?"

He was wearing a white lab coat over his thin shoulders, his eyes fixed on Eleven. Theo hesitated for a second, but given that they'd be seeing a lot of Rocky over the course of their investigation, there was no point in trying to hide the truth about Eleven from him.

"...A human-shaped Amalgam, apparently," he said. "Dispatched from intelligence services with the commander's seal of approval."

"Those big fellas count a sweet little thing like this among their number? Well, it's a pleasure, miss." Rocky extended his hand, and Eleven blinked several times before gently placing her hand in his.

Theo furrowed his brow, wondering exactly what she was doing, but Emma shook with laughter.

"Eleven, the way you do that, you're like a dog offering a paw," she said gently. "A Hound's allowed to shake a person's hand, you know."

"A Hooound. Sounds about right for an investigator, hmm?" Rocky mused. "Here, miss, this is how you shake hands."

As she shook properly this time, Eleven looked down expressionlessly at their clasped hands. "A 'handshake' is something people do in order to greet each other or show feelings of intimacy. That I would be the subject of one, it's very…"

"If we're going to be working together, then a handshake's only right, isn't it?" Rocky said. "That's one chilly mitt you got there, though. You cold?"

"No, Investigator," she replied plainly. "It's simply that no blood flows beneath my skin."

"That's all right, then. Having a real Amalgam in the room makes things a lot simpler. Come on—over here." Rocky led the conversation at his own pace and headed farther back into the morgue. Eleven stood there with her hand hanging in the air.

Tobias watched Rocky go with a bemused look and patted Eleven's back. "Don't pay him any mind, Eleven. He's not particularly great at talking to living creatures."

"…He was a bit *too* quick to accept her," Theo noted. "Maybe only the dead matter to him."

"Honestly. Don't talk like that." Emma glared at him and then peered at Eleven. "Eleven, what's with the hand?"

"Oh." Eleven slowly lowered her arm. "It's the first time I've shaken hands. I required some time to process it."

"You did, huh?" Emma said. "Well, you'll have plenty more chances to shake hands from here on out, so try to get used to it, okay?"

Theo averted his eyes. The way Eleven looked bothered him. The extremely quiet, docile teenage girl was perplexed by actions that were perfectly natural. This demeanor invited sympathy and made him want to scream *Why?!* How much easier it would have been if she acted abominably!

Unable to completely hold back his irritation, he followed Rocky to where two bodies were laid out on autopsy tables: Yeti the Giant and another corpse discovered on the fight club premises. Rocky picked up his forceps and tapped Yeti's silver fist. *Clang.*

"The look and feel of it are absolutely metal," Rocky said. "But the tissue itself is his own. In terms of genetic array, I suppose the closest analogue would be a hedgehog. Quite the curious structure right there. My conclusion is that it's been significantly weakened compared with its originator. What we're looking at is basically a fake Amalgam."

"How different is it from an authentic Amalgam?" Theo asked.

"Well, first thing, this isn't any kind of mimicry. The transformation's based on the genetic information. And it doesn't have a core."

"No way!" Emma cried. "A core's essential for automagitons. How could it move without one?"

"Mm-hmm." Rocky turned toward the projector. "The Amalgam core, you see, is the rare mineral fortunite. But the material analysis I ran didn't pick up even a smidge of the stuff. Which means these fellows don't have regular cores. Instead, they were powered by the physical bodies of the fighters—their life energy, as it were. At the end of the day, the human being's doing the heavy lifting in this relationship. As proof, have a peek at this."

He looked back at the group with a bit of excitement as he went around to the foot of the other body—someone who had died two weeks earlier. This person's legs had been transformed into those of a horse. Unlike Yeti the Giant, however, the area of transformation was as decomposed as the rest of the body.

"...This means that the transformation isn't mimicry, a simple assumption of the form of a corpse," Theo said. "It actually died?"

"Pretty much." Rocky nodded. "A normal Amalgam would swallow up the human and use the material for itself. But this is a parasite. It's dependent on the host, so the host dies, it dies. As for the question of why the half-baked transformation, well, that'd be because it's a bit different from your average Amalgam, right from its original structure."

He projected onto the white screen a video of what looked like mercury wiggling around, linking up with red bloods cells. Whatever it was, it was multiplying at a steady pace.

"This is the drug collected as evidence. From the ingredients alone, you'd be hard-pressed to say it's an Amalgam. But when it links up with human blood, it generates a structure that is infinitely close to that of an Amalgam."

"Hence the fake Amalgam." Theo nodded. "What's the mechanism?"

"It forms an Amalgam-like structure in the blood," Rocky explained. "When this touches air, it becomes a silver metallic substance and transforms in accordance with the genetic information it's programmed with. The idea is likely that when the fighter is injured and bleeds, it hardens around the opening of the wound to protect it. And then when the host dies, the parasite dies with it, unable to flee. They're one and the same, after all. And...young lady. I want to check something. Hold out your hand. Just the one is good."

Eleven obediently offered her hand to Rocky. He immediately picked up a scalpel and cut into her palm.

"Hey!" Emma shouted and grabbed Eleven's shoulders to yank her away. "What are you doing, Rocky?!"

"I was just checking something." He nodded to himself. "Mm-hmm. No bleeding, no pain. Those'd be the Amalgam traits, then."

Theo watched out of the corner of his eye as Rocky scribbled some notes in a notebook while he took a look at Eleven's hand. The cut on her palm was gaping wide-open, but all that was exposed was the smooth, white cross section. He could see no flesh nor blood, and it soon closed over again.

"...The fighters bled when they were injured," Theo said. "And they appeared to have a normal pain response."

"That they did," Rocky agreed. "At best, the fake Amalgam protects the host's body; it doesn't take it over. The fighters we have in custody are still human beings. But there's another issue, you see."

He turned off the projector, put down the scalpel, and held out a piece of paper with a grim look on his face. It was a list of the elements found in the blood of Yeti the Giant.

Theo looked at the familiar names and abnormally high numbers, and his eyes grew wider in surprise.

"Whoa," Tobias said, shocked. "Amazing. A patient in the mobile stages of drug addiction has better numbers than these."

"What on earth are these numbers?" Theo asked. "I thought the fighters were only taking the one pill."

"The drug components Amalgamize by linking with the blood, but a large amount of substances is secreted in the process. This is what caused the doping effect. But it also destroys the cells at the same time and brings about an incredible sense of exultation. The fake Amalgam body becomes unable to metabolize even a single pill. Once the transformation begins, the host can never go back to being what it was. I just hope this stuff hasn't made it to the streets..."

This was a preposterous mechanism for a drug. Emma turned her eyes in the direction of the holding cells and murmured, "So that's why the fighters were so ferocious? The effect of the drug, huh?"

"Rocky, send the results of the analysis to the hospital as well," Theo urged. "It might help the doctors."

"I doubt there'll be any saving people that far gone, but... Well, I'll send it over." Rocky clearly had doubts about the possibility of helping the fighters, but he nevertheless turned toward the phone.

A *ping* of notification came from Tobias's cell phone, and when he checked the message, a smile spread across his face. "Finally some good news. I guess they found the dealer who was selling the drugs to the fight club. Let's go check it out, shall we?"

"We'll go right now," Theo agreed. "Rocky, keep me posted."

Rocky waved without looking back at them as they left him to his work and headed for the parking lot. The team had an extra set of footfalls now, and she was moving at a faster pace than the rest of them.

Not even really knowing himself what he was annoyed about, Theo suppressed the urge to click his tongue.

CONFIDENTIAL

Chapter 2
Hound for the Girl

AMALGAM HOUND
Criminal Investigation Bureau:
Special Investigation Unit

When they arrived at the address where the dealer had been found, an apartment building in the middle of a low-income residential area, there was already a crowd of onlookers and a gaggle of police cars. The scene was chaotic, and it was only a matter of time before the media came charging in.

As Theo got out of the car, he felt curious eyes focus on him while Emma looked around.

"Pretty far from the fight club, huh?" she said. "Did they drive the stuff over, or did they do the deals near here, or what…?"

"If we knew where the deals took place, we'd have a lot more to go on," Theo replied. "Anyway, let's have a look at the dealer."

They headed up to the third floor, and as he slipped under the police tape stretched across the doorway, he noticed neighboring residents being questioned by the police.

The apartment was a small bachelor suite, clearly intended for single people. It had only the bare minimum of furniture, and the kitchen was littered with the packaging from a variety of instant meals and drinks. Pajamas lay where they had been tossed onto the bed, and the nightstand had very obviously been used to prepare drugs. Perhaps the dealer never opened the windows—the whole place was dusty and stank of mold.

Theo left Tobias to talk with the Forensics team and moved toward the bathroom. Emma was already there. She signaled him with one hand and got down on a knee in the doorway.

The man who had been identified as the dealer was sitting up against the wall, blood spilling from his stomach.

"Estimated time of death is about three hours ago," Emma told him. "No possessions, no identification. Also nothing in the apartment that would lead to an ID. Cause of death appears to be blood loss due to a serious abdominal injury... Take a look at this wound."

Theo crouched down and peered at the corpse's stomach. Traces of blood ran straight from the wall to the man, perhaps because he had hit the wall opposite the sink and slid to the floor. When Theo turned his flashlight on the man's abdomen, he could make out a gaping hole there. Had something gone right through him? Theo squinted to get a better look and immediately rejected that idea. From what he could see of the wound, it looked like an internal rupture.

"...What was the murder weapon?" he asked. "Couldn't have been an explosive. There'd be a lot more than blood stains if it were."

"Judging from the blood on the wall and the sink area, the victim was standing in front of the sink when he began to bleed profusely," Emma said. "Maybe he tripped or something, backed into the wall, and dropped to the floor. It doesn't add up, though. A surprise attack from the sink's just not possible. And if an assailant approached from behind, he'd see them right away in the mirror. I don't get it." She shook her head. "I asked Eleven, and she just said, 'Maybe he was eaten from the inside.'"

Theo grimaced. "Quite the ugly sense of humor... And where is Eleven?"

"In the shower there." Emma jerked her thumb back.

Blood flowed from the body toward the shower booth, probably because the floor had an incline to it. Theo traced it with his eyes and found that Eleven was indeed standing at the end of that trail. Wondering what she was staring at with such focus, he went to stand next to her and scowled when he saw the blue tiled wall.

Drawn in black ink, there was a picture of a girl in a laurel wreath, stepping onto a mountain of skulls and brandishing a sword. The lines were delicate, and the face in profile, hanging downward with eyes closed, was very girlish. She had that air of beautiful purity particular to young girls, but he felt a chill at the skulls crammed together, covering the wall.

"…Talk about poor taste," he said. "Did he draw it?"

"The intention of the design is unclear, but it appears to be concealing some words," Eleven said quietly and pointed to one part of the drawing with a plastic-gloved hand. "In some areas, the line is drawn over and over to make it thicker. At first glance, these look like the shadows of the skulls, but when I stood in the doorway of the shower, they looked like letters, so I thought it was perhaps intentional."

Theo stared at the bizarre picture. And sure enough, when he stepped back a little and focused only on the thick shadows, hidden words did pop into view.

"'Glory to Roremclad'?" He read them out loud and frowned. "I've never heard this at the bureau. How about in Intelligence?"

"Unknown," Eleven replied. "As a statement, it resembles expressions praising God. Perhaps it's a new religion?"

"If there's a saint who celebrates addicts, I'd love to meet them. Hmm?" He looked into the shower booth and noticed that the drainage lid was off. Stretched out across the opening was a net to catch hair and other debris. At that moment, however, damp red fibers dangled from it.

Eleven abruptly crouched down and pulled something out of the drain. Theo felt the urge to vomit and pressed a hand over his mouth. Her gloved fingers held up part of an internal organ.

"…It escaped," she said. "Through here."

"You *can't* be serious." He arched an eyebrow. "That whole 'he was eaten from inside' thing?"

"The way the blood moves from the body to the shower is unnatural. I thought it might have been a trail left by something crawling away."

Theo cleared his throat. "After seeing Amalgams parasitizing humans, I can't dismiss the idea as absurd."

The body was carried out, and Forensics withdrew, leaving Tobias and Emma alone in the main room of the apartment. As Theo stepped out of the bathroom, Tobias raised a hand.

"I talked to the building's residents," he said. "Apparently, they had their eye on this guy right from the day he moved in. Loud noises, weird smells, dropping his garbage in the wrong place, and I guess the police were pretty frequent visitors. They came and combed through the place a number of times, though, and didn't find any stock or merchandise. Best I can figure is this apartment was for him in his downtime."

Tobias closed his notebook, and Emma nodded before picking up where he left off.

"This guy was famous among other dealers for having sticky fingers with the stock. He had a bit of a target on his back. Which is exactly why we were able to find this place. Still, though, there should've been more drugs here. It's pretty obvious that he had to have been keeping it somewhere else, considering how much of the stuff he was skimming for himself and the quantities he was selling to the fight club."

"But he had nothing in his possession," Theo noted. "How was he keeping in touch with his customers?"

"Looks like he used a landline," Emma said. "I'm having the call history checked."

Was this a dead end? Had they overlooked something? Theo frowned and set his brain to work when a sound interrupted his thoughts. He looked up to find Eleven moving the blinds covering the only window in the apartment.

"…What is it now, Eleven?" he asked.

"The blinds are twisted up here," she told him. "It seems like someone was frequently peering outside through the gap."

"Isn't that just normal wear and tear?"

"The only place where there's no dust is this twisted area. We can assume that it was touched frequently."

He scanned the room once more. It looked like the apartment had almost never been cleaned. The dust on the floor alone was remarkable.

Given the state of the place, there was no way only the blinds would have been cleaned.

Looking curious, Tobias went over to Eleven and peered outside through the gap she noted in the blinds. "I can see the building across the street. The back side. The most you're likely to see there is a car pulling up. Maybe that's his storage site across the way, then? Doesn't look like anyone's living there."

"Or it could simply be where the deals happen," Theo mused. "Good spot, no one watching. Worth checking out."

"There's bound to be some clues there," Emma said. "Nice work noticing that, Eleven. Thanks."

Eleven's eyes grew the slightest bit larger. Theo assumed she would deflect the praise with some comment about how it was her job, but instead she shifted her gray eyes to the left and then the right until finally she said in the smallest voice, "Not at all."

Tobias narrowed his eyes in a smile. "No need to be embarrassed, is there, Eleven? You worked for Intelligence. I'm sure you got your fair share of compliments there, given that you're this top secret weapon approved by the commander himself."

"No. 'Praise' is an action reserved for human beings," she declared quietly. "I am a weapon, a thing. I am outside the target for that action."

"That's not necessarily true." Tobias shrugged. "I praise cars that drive well, and I chat up flowers that bloom beautifully."

"Not so sure about that part…" Theo shot Tobias a look and then turned to the girl. "Don't worry about details like that, Eleven. When someone says, 'Thank you,' you can simply reply, 'You're welcome.' It's a necessary exchange to make communication smoother."

"All right. I will remember that," she replied briefly. But her expression remained slightly baffled, like a child at her wits' end after losing her way.

Theo understood her even less than before and let out a short sigh.

The face that awaited instructions was exactly that of a faithful dog, just as the name *Hound* would suggest, and her slender figure looked to be that of a young girl even though she was in fact a weapon of unknown specifications—a monster in the shape of a person. For a supersecret weapon, the existence of which was known only to the upper echelons of the military, she was curiously human. Was it because he hadn't designated a specific appearance and personality? Or was this her battle strategy? If it was the latter, it was definitely working on Emma and Tobias.

Was he the odd one out here? The way he stubbornly refused to accept her? Theo furrowed his brow.

Eleven looked up at him. Penetrating ash-colored eyes. When he thought about the fact that there was an Amalgam on the other side of them, he immediately felt disturbed and quickly averted his gaze.

"I'm going to check out the building across the way," he said. "Emma, you're with me. Tobias, could you take a look at the pipes with Eleven? She says something escaped through the drain in the shower. Go see if you can find it."

"Roger that." Tobias gave him a jovial salute. "Suppose our best bet there is to poke around in the catch basin, then. Shall we get going, Eleven?"

"...Yes. I will accompany you." Eleven's reply was a beat delayed, and Theo wondered if she objected. But the look on her face was unchanged as she left the room with Tobias.

"Let's go," Emma said, and Theo finally started to move.

They avoided the crowd of onlookers as they left the scene, and Emma smiled wryly. "So do you hate her, or are you worried about her? Maybe try making up your mind?"

He glared back. "I'm not particularly worried about her. There's no point in worrying about a monster."

"Yeah?" Emma raised her eyebrows at him. "She does look the way she does, though. And she's obedient and cute. She seems like a good kid."

"...How can you simply accept her like that? For all that you supposedly know as a sorcerer, you're surprisingly..." *Lacking in judgment*, he hesitated to say.

As they crossed the road, Emma replied, "I have plenty of doubts. To be honest, I have so many questions that I wish they'd let me do some research into her. But her reactions to our actions are really natural; she's trying to adapt to us. That's what makes me think she's way too much for me to handle. She's too perfect, that girl."

"Meaning what? It's true that the Amalgam in human form is quite impressive, but..." Theo cocked his head to one side, unable to completely understand what Emma was getting at. Compared with the golems that stood on the battlefield, Eleven was indeed quite a clever copy of a human being.

Emma had a conflicted look on her face and shook her head. "Her appearance, sure, but it's her *reactions*. Automagitons execute their duties with a certain level of self-determination. But it's more on the level of calculating the shortest route to their destination or analyzing and executing optimal movement patterns to protect targets with the greatest efficiency. I mean, the Amalgams used on the battlefield, they move optimally as infantry. The media's always trying to churn out these moving stories of how the Amalgams step out in front to be a shield for allied troops, but their movement is entirely rational, based on mission execution efficiency. Emotion's got nothing to do with it."

"But Eleven is fairly..." Theo paused thoughtfully. "It doesn't show on her face, but she gets troubled, confused."

Emma whirled around and stopped. "That's just it. Automagitons can't usually take action beyond what they've been ordered to do. But Eleven's different. That's not just some human-shaped weapon. She understands all these human emotional reactions and acts accordingly."

"Isn't she just demonstrating that she has emotions?"

"Weapons can't have emotions. The Society of Sorcerers won't allow it. It's the line that absolutely has to be maintained," she declared firmly, looking so serious that Theo was surprised.

He felt a nervous tension stinging his skin, and his throat suddenly went dry. "B-but for instance...what if it was extremely intelligent and developed emotions?"

"Not possible." Emma shook her head. "Maybe she's extracting the optimal solution from a situation analysis, and her execution is abnormally fast, so it *looks* like a natural reaction. Hmm...would you get it if I said she's like a trained dog?"

"You mean if a human being did such and such, then she's simply set to react in such and such a way?"

"Probably. Which is maybe why they're called Hounds. What d'you think?"

"Oh, I hear what you're saying, but... So she's like a well-made doll, then." Theo was perplexed as they walked toward the building they'd seen from the window. It was two houses up along the street, two stories tall, and seemed to be a currently unused office.

"You're not getting it, Theo. It's not on that level. What I'm saying is: That girl, okay, she's been trained to react how you want without you having to say anything at all."

He stopped unconsciously and turned to Emma. The expression on her face was serious.

"With no set personality, she's maybe all the more free to try and respond to demands on a level that you're not even aware of," she continued. "This is at best just an example, but if you challenged her and tried to destroy her in legitimate self-defense against an attack, she would kill you without mercy if you secretly harbored any suicidal aspirations. Which is why I'm talking to you about it now, when it's just the two of us like this."

"I don't have any suicidal aspirations," he said.

"So then I'll ask you. You ever look at her and think, 'This is an Amalgam just like the one that burned my home to the ground, so how can it be so human? If only it would run wild like that Amalgam, then I could just hate it'?"

Stunned, Theo couldn't immediately answer her. What flitted through the back of his mind were the words of Commander Guin: Only someone who knows that fear could handle an Amalgam. He couldn't have possibly meant that the Hound would detect that terror and regulate its own behavior, could he?

Emma faced Theo grimly. "Your feelings belong to you," she said quietly. "It's no wonder you hate the Amalgams. What you went through was really awful. But you can't use her as a diversion. You can't predict what in you she'll pick up on and how she'll convert that into action. You have to stick to work orders and only work orders. Got it?"

"...Thanks. Much obliged for the warning."

She looked like she wanted to say something else, but he ignored this and moved forward. The idea of him giving Eleven orders of a personal nature was absurd. He wanted nothing to do with her outside of work.

But Eleven had asked after his preferred appearance and personality. If he wanted, she would behave in the most unscrupulous, vicious ways in a truly loathsome appearance. Then he could shoot her without hesitation. Would he feel better if he did? Even though shooting her wouldn't kill her?

When he looked back, he could see Tobias and Eleven walking around the apartment building. The skirt of Eleven's uniform swung back and forth. Her light step resembled that of Theo's little sister when she showed him a new outfit.

■

Together with Eleven, Tobias walked around the apartment building, looking at the plumbing. The sound of her feet crunching the grass underfoot came regularly half a pace after his own.

"Is that a habit of yours, Eleven?" he asked.

"To what are you referring?"

"You try not to walk alongside people, yes? You always walk slightly behind them." He glanced back, and she looked up at him with wide eyes.

"From this position, I can guard against all three hundred and sixty degrees and protect you."

"Oh, makes sense." He nodded in understanding. "You can pull me back or shove me forward. Very rational indeed."

"Do you have any points of discomfort regarding the distance between us?" she asked.

"No, no, it's fine. You're very nice, aren't you, Eleven?"

She merely blinked several times. From her appearance alone, she was a docile, adorable young girl. It seemed impossible that she could overwhelm a grown man without even breaking a sweat. Tobias didn't know too much about these Amalgam weapons, so he was curious about his new trusty sidekick.

"Ohhh." He nodded to himself again. "Theo's attitude didn't put you off, did it?"

"We do not get 'put off,' and his attitude did not offer insult," she replied simply. But she quite obviously shifted her gaze away from Tobias and pursed her small lips. She looked like a child holding back what she really wanted to say, and his face slackened into a smile.

"What is it?" he urged her. "Go on and tell me."

"...He despises Amalgams. I have surmised it may have a negative effect on the investigation if I work with him."

"He really is surprisingly childish, hmm?" Tobias said. "Despite that look on his face that screams, 'Don't bring personal business to investigations!'"

She blinked her gray eyes at him several times. "There is no relationship between face and action."

"Mm. Not a whit," he agreed readily. "So. Can you shoot fire? Make yourself as big as a mountain?"

"Shooting fire is immediately possible, but I require materials and a preparatory period to enlarge myself to the size of a mountain."

"So then if enemy aircraft scramble against us, you won't be able to get really huge and shoot down the enemy machines with your flamethrower?"

"I will obey orders," she told him. "But if it is a matter of shooting down aircraft, it would be more realistic for me to transform into a bird and fly away."

"Ha-ha-ha! I suppose so. Don't worry about it. I just wanted to reassure myself."

Eleven appeared to be thinking through the meaning of what he'd said, but Tobias very transparently changed the subject.

"If something went down that shower drain, it would've had to have gotten caught in the catch basin. But how big do you think it was? If it was small enough to slip through the mesh, we'll have our work cut out for us."

"Judging from the wounds on the victim, I surmise that it was at least the size of an adult male's hand," Eleven told him.

"Well then, there's no problem. Ah, there we are! This is the lid. No key or anything, hmm?" He looked around for a tool to open the catch basin lid. But Eleven immediately got down on one knee and lifted the steel cover. Tobias had been bracing himself for the worst, but the inside of the basin was quiet; nothing but water with patches of oil floating on it. He crouched down next to Eleven to peer into it.

"You really are strong," he said. "A real champ. I thought my heart would leap right out of my chest there."

"Is this metal basket always in the catch basin?" she asked.

"It's for cleaning. The garbage collects here, so you can just toss it all in one go. If anything went through that drain, it should be here." Tobias put on a glove, pulled out the cleaning basket, and was instantly speechless.

There was none of the garbage that should have been in the basket. The side had been punched out, and one part of the shredded basket had pieces of viscera caught on it.

Eleven looked at the basket and said, "It ate what it wanted and then fled."

"I'd really prefer not to imagine such a creature." Tobias grimaced. "Eleven, do you have any ideas?"

"Judging from the opening here, it's small. At present, there is no alignment with Amalgam characteristics, so it would be best to search for a magical creature, a small automagiton, or similar."

"Right. If it's gone all the way to the sewers, it'll be hard to find. We'll go and let the superintendent know—"

He lifted his face and froze. Eleven had vanished.

Theo and Emma went in through the garage to the rear of the building. The fixtures and lighting on the first floor had been removed, and the materials sat in a pile. But time had passed without anyone beginning the renovation work—stains from the rain leaking in and other damage to the room remained untouched.

Theo shone his flashlight over the area and looked at the front door. The glass was broken, and the lock was smashed. Two sets of footprints were clear on the floor.

So someone other than the owner of the place has been in and out who knows how many times.

Emma called to him and beckoned him with a hand. He walked over to her and saw a locked storage box hidden in the mountain of materials. The box clearly wasn't too heavy. Emma managed to lift it even though she wasn't particularly buff.

"...I doubt this is all his stock," Theo said. "Maybe just the stuff he stole?"

"From the weight, it's possible it could be cash," she replied. "Either way, it's nothing dangerous, so we can call Forensics—"

Suddenly, there was the sound of the front door opening. Surprised, Theo turned and met the eyes of a man wearing a hood. The man had no sooner realized that Theo had seen him than he was running away. Theo hurried to chase him.

The man fled into an alley, kicked aside an empty can on the ground, and knocked over garbage bins as he ran. Theo desperately ran after him, but the man was extremely quick on his feet. Perhaps he was using muscle enhancements adapted from synthetics.

Like I'm letting you get away. Theo gritted his teeth and followed the man up the emergency stairs of the ancient apartment building.

Listening for the sound of a door opening and closing, he flew out onto the roof and sent his gaze racing around. He thought he'd caught up, but there was no sign of the man. Where had he gone? Theo turned his head searchingly and immediately took a hit from his blind spot. The man had hidden behind the rooftop air conditioner and shoved Theo forward, knocking him off-balance. He tried bracing himself with his legs, only to kick at empty space.

Crap, he thought as his body leaned forward, and he teetered on the edge of the roof. A triumphant smile appeared on the man's face as he turned away. Theo's feet stepped off the edge of the roof. He watched the whole thing happen as if in slow motion, and then his eyes flew open wide.

A black belt slapped the man down. Winding itself around him, it dragged the man from the roof. Before Theo knew it, something caught his arms. His shoulders hit something hard, and he felt a bloom of pain.

When he lifted his face, gray eyes were staring at him from surprisingly close up. Soft white-blond hair fluttered in the wind. Eleven was holding him in her slender arms, and she opened her thin lips.

"Are you injured, Investigator?"

"No..." He took a breath. "I'm not... What happened?"

"I caught you when you fell off the roof," she replied. "At the same time, I apprehended the man who was fleeing."

He carefully let his gaze wander. Eleven was standing on the ancient balcony railing, her grip on him firm; a mass of black fabric dangled down from that railing, from which he could hear the man's muffled moans. The arms supporting Theo's shoulders and backs of his thighs were fearfully thin, and yet they did not so much as twitch from the strain. He was immobilized until Eleven jumped down from the balcony and stood him gently on the ground.

"That was...quite outside of the norm," he said.

"No. It cleared the Hound requirement standard."

Theo felt like they were having two different conversations.

Eleven released the man from the fabric, and it rolled up into itself, returning to its original form as a military uniform jacket. The man stared blankly, scared out of his wits. Theo snapped handcuffs onto his wrists and handed him over to the police that had arrived on the scene. When he returned his gaze to the former office in the distance, he saw Emma explaining the situation to a bewildered Tobias.

Utterly exhausted, Theo sighed and took a step forward to join her. But Eleven stopped him.

"Investigator." She was so hesitant that it seemed impossible that she had just performed a daring bit of rescue and arrest theater.

He glanced back at her, surprised at the quietness of her voice.

"Was I useful?"

The question was almost too pitiable to have come from the automagiton Amalgam Hound, a specially produced, top secret military weapon.

He assumed she was joking, but her face was serious, and he was unable to ignore her earnest gaze. This appeared to be an important question to her.

When he went to answer, the inside of his mouth grew dry, and his voice was nothing but a croak. If she hadn't saved him on the roof, he would have been hovering on the border between life and death right about now after crashing into the pavement below. When he considered his attitude up to that point, it was a bit much to simply say thank you. In the end, he cleared his throat and turned around.

"…You did well." A pathetic statement, even by his own standards. And yet Eleven replied briefly, "Understood." He couldn't pick up any emotion in her level tone, but she trotted to catch up with him, and soon she was half a pace behind him.

He felt awkward, but he took her with him back to Emma and Tobias. They had just managed to unlock the storage box. All that was inside were commonly distributed drugs and some cash. None of these pills had been sold at the fight club.

"So no major discovery here." Theo sighed. "I hope we can get something out of that man."

"And apparently, there was a car coming and going from the building until recently. Let's just be happy that we have any leads at all," Tobias said optimistically before telling everyone to pack it up.

■

After hearing what the local police had to say, the detective replied with a fed-up look on his face, "Guy's name is Jacus Ghilane. Has priors. Works as a debt collector. Tested negative for drugs. We're searching his house now. Relationship with the victim's unclear."

"Nice work," Theo said. "Any developments with the victim?"

"Mm. His fingerprints were in the database. Name's Bob Derry. He's been arrested for selling illicit substances before. Ghilane looked pretty shook up when we showed him a picture of the body, but all he'll say is 'No idea.' He won't talk. Hasn't called a lawyer, though, either. You think he's the killer?"

"Can't know until we ask him. Autopsy results?" Theo asked, and the detective's face clouded over as he held out the investigation file.

"…There were wounds on his stomach like something had eaten through it to the outside. No saliva or other fluids detected. I think they used some kind of tool, but basically all we found were a few dissolved capsules. Details aren't too clear."

"Understood. We'll investigate on our end, too, so send the body to the bureau. We'll let you know what we find."

The detective and Theo thanked each other, and then Theo returned to his team. Emma lifted her face from looking at Eleven's hands with a concerned expression.

"Feels like we're just lucky to be able to question him, huh?" she said.

"Mm-hmm. They learned his name, which is a step forward, but… What is she doing?" Theo also looked down at Eleven's hands. She was holding the dial-type padlock that had been pried from the storage box and was silently trying four-digit combinations.

"She's been working on that this whole time," Emma told him. "Said if there were two people coming and going from that building, then the combination would maybe be something meaningful to both of them. I suppose she can guess the combination from the sound and feel, but…"

While they were talking, the lock opened with a *snap*.

Tobias read out the digits: "Zero-nine-two-six… A date? Theo, what are their birth dates?"

"The victim Bob Derry is December eighth. The suspect Jacus Ghilane is July fifteenth."

"It's the date exactly in the middle between their two birth dates," Eleven noted point-blank.

Theo scowled as if to ask *And what of it?* while Emma pressed her hands together.

"So what? They're meeting in the middle like two schoolgirls? They must've been pretty close," she said.

"But if they'd been that close, the suspect would have been more upset when he saw the photo of the victim." Tobias cocked his head to one side thoughtfully. "Did he know he was dead and came to collect the safe box? Like as something to remember him by."

Theo thought for a moment and nodded. "They were both released at the same time, so it's possible they knew each other in prison. Try a sympathetic approach. Eleven, stay out of sight. He'll only get pointlessly worked up."

"All right," said Tobias. "I'll go and talk to him."

Theo watched Tobias and Emma go into the interrogation room while he went with Eleven to watch the questioning through the one-way mirror. He took out the case file the detective had given him and scanned it once more.

The investigation into the victim's phone records revealed that the last contact Bob Derry had before his death was with his mother. They'd apparently discussed how he was about to come into a large amount of money soon and then return home, but what exactly that meant was unclear.

If he'd been able to earn that much money by just dealing the drug to the fight club, there had to have been something more to the whole operation. Or perhaps it was natural to assume someone had killed him to silence him after the fight club was raided by police.

Theo fell silent in thought, but then he heard a *ping* from his cell phone and left the room.

"What is it, Rocky?" he asked. "New development?"

"*Son, is the Amalgam girl with you?*" the older man asked. "*I need you to bring her to the hospital.*"

"...I can do that. Is there something she can help with?"

"There's just the one fellow without any physical changes. And he seems real strange. I can't get anywhere with him on my own, so I was hoping another Amalgam might be able to get the job done."

On the other end of the line, Theo could hear the voices of a man in pain and nurses trying to comfort him. "We'll be right there," he said before ending the call and looking back at Eleven. "Can you do anything about a fake Amalgam that's still inside a body?"

"If it has not yet been injured, yes," she replied. "There's a possibility that I may be able to extract it."

Reassured, Theo exhaled, left a message for Tobias and Emma, and hurried with Eleven in tow for the hospital. The day was about to end without him having had a wink of sleep.

■

When Tobias entered the interrogation room, Jacus Ghilane looked up with a bored expression. "Now who is it?" he spat.

"Hey there. Nice to meet you." Tobias sat down across from him. "I'm Investigator Hillmyna. Sorry about the rough treatment during the arrest. No one took your feelings into consideration, which was honestly quite rude."

Ghilane glared at him. "...The hell are you even talking about?"

"First, I'd like to offer my condolences," Tobias said gently. "You and Bob Derry were quite close. It's simply terrible what happened to him."

Ghilane stiffened from the shoulders up and then very obviously averted his eyes from Tobias and leaned back in his chair. "Guy in the grisly photos, yeah? I already told the cop. Never saw him before."

"...You were such good friends that you made the combination for the lock a date exactly between your birthday and his, though," Tobias remarked. "You sure you don't have any idea who killed him?"

Ghilane very deliberately avoided his eyes.

Tobias sighed and flipped through some papers. "You and Derry are quite far removed in age, but you were released from the same prison at the same time, hmm? After that, you both found steady work, but Derry returned to dealing drugs. Are you sure you're not just trying to deny the relationship here, given that you had walked away from a life of crime and were trying to get back on your feet?"

"Not even close," Ghilane insisted firmly.

Tobias waited for him to continue; Ghilane sniffled as he turned his gaze on Tobias. And then he was leaning forward across the table.

"The only person who ever gave me a hand inside was Bob," Ghilane began. "They took away my synthetics and forced me to live with prosthetic legs and a cane, and he was the only one who helped me out. For me, he was... I owed him my life. I thought of him like a big brother; he treated me like a kid brother."

"And what about after you were released?" Tobias prodded.

"I needed synths for both legs; Bob needed a kidney. But synths cost money, especially the organs. I scraped together enough as a debt collector, but Bob couldn't. He went back to dealing, using his old contacts. He was still a master at it. He had the money in no time and got his synth. But..."

Ghilane looked around before lowering his voice and continuing.

"The gambling den I worked for started a fight club, and before too long, *he* came along."

"'He'?" Tobias frowned. "He who? Someone you knew? Or someone Bob knew?"

"Never saw him before." Ghilane shook his head. "I got a lot of debtors thanks to how Bob's clients used to always tip me off. So I thought it'd be the usual story. But suddenly, this guy butts in, saying he wanted to hand off some merch."

Ghilane licked his dry lips nervously.

"...The guy said the drug was still in the testing stages, wasn't on the market yet. And we just went along with that. Sold the drug to a ton of folks at the fight club. I dunno what kind of deal it was, but Bob was making bank, and I got a pretty hefty cut myself. The deal last night earned me a real chunk of change, so I was drinking the most expensive stuff they had at this one place I always go to. It was only last night..." His voice shook. He wiped roughly at the corners of his eyes with his sleeve and sniffled.

Tobias handed him a box of tissues. "You saw Bob today?"

Tears welled up in Ghilane's eyes. He blew his nose repeatedly and wiped his arm across it as he groaned. "…When I went to Bob's apartment, *he* was on the phone out front. Of course, I hid, and he walked away pretty quick, so I couldn't really hear. But he said he'd 'taken care of the dealer.' And that all that was left was to deal with the fixer. I figured something was seriously up, and I went to see Bob straight away. But by the time I got there, he was bleeding from his stomach and…" A sob slipped out of him.

Tobias furrowed his brow at the new twist and closed the folder before him. "You didn't report it, then? What did you do after you saw Bob's body?"

"…I ran. I couldn't go to work. I thought I was next; I was so scared. But Bob hid the money he'd made in that building. Said he wanted to give it to his parents back home. 'Cause he'd always been such a bad son. So I figured the least I could do was bring it to 'em."

"And that's when you bumped into Theo and ran? Did you feel like you were being followed or in any danger?"

"I had no idea who was after me, so I was just running. I don't really know."

"…Thank you. All right, then. We'll get a sketch done of the man you mentioned. Mind helping us out?" Tobias asked, and Ghilane nodded repeatedly, weeping.

He left Ghilane in the care of the local police. When the sketch was complete, he stared at it, a serious look on his face. Emma's own face clouded over at the sight. The solution to this case was apparently not going to come to them wrapped in a neat little bow.

■

As they walked toward the hospital reception desk, Rocky came running over. After exchanging a brief greeting with Theo, Rocky quickly led Eleven to a private room.

Fred Wood—the only person among all the fighters who had no experience in the ring and was thus completely uninjured—was lying in a bed, clutching the sheets and moaning. Blood vessels were visible rippling all over the surface of his body.

Rocky turned to Eleven. "He was only admitted for observation, but as you can see, well… He started complaining of shortness of breath and pain about an hour ago. I can't go giving him any external wounds, so I can't give him a shot or an IV. There's nothing we can do here, you see?"

"Is the cause of the issue known?" Eleven asked.

"This is merely a guess," he replied. "But I think the Amalgam fused with his blood can't get out, and so it skipped right over that part and entered the multiplication stage. Thanks to its habit of protecting the host, there's no bleeding."

Eleven nodded. "…I understand the situation. I will remove it right away. Prepare a dish and sutures."

The doctors appeared half-disbelieving, but they quickly raced out to make the preparations. Eleven rolled up her sleeves and touched Wood's arm with her alabaster hands. He gripped the hem of her uniform pleadingly.

"It's okay," she said and gently slid her palm along his arm. Her hand shone with a pale red light, and the blood vessels that had been rippling so wildly calmed again. The fake Amalgam writhing inside his blood vessels released a similar red light and gathered beneath her palm.

"H-how are you doing that?" Theo asked, bewildered. "What kind of mechanism is this, then?"

"I'm sending a control signal and making use of the Amalgam's nature." Her face was the epitome of calm. "The Amalgams are made such that when they receive a signal from another individual, they will tune themselves to it. It will prioritize my instructions over parasitizing its host."

She peered into the struggling Wood's eyes.

"Sir. A needle opening is too small, and there's a chance that the blood vessel will rupture," she told him. "I am going to cut open your skin and take out the Amalgam without anesthetic. The wound will need to be treated, but I promise this will remove the pain you are in. Do I have your consent for the procedure, sir?"

"Anything… Anything—just please help me…" Wood stared into those endlessly cool gray eyes, desperately clinging to the girl.

Eleven immediately looked back at the doctors. "I have received his consent. I will now proceed. Please stanch any bleeding and provide sutures."

"R-right. Okay…"

Once the doctors were ready, Eleven changed one of the fingers touching Wood's arm into a sharp knife. Thin and slender, the blade easily cut into the skin where the red light was concentrated.

What oozed out from the gaping wound was not blood but a red light. *Zlrsh*. The viscous liquid that rushed out quickly enveloped Eleven's hand. That was it.

Theo stared, stunned, and carefully removed his hand from his gun.

Wood let out a cry of anguish, but the doctors calmly stepped in to take care of his pain. Eleven slowly stepped away, her eyes on the undefined mass tangled around her hand. The viscous liquid oozed sluggishly, glowing red all the while.

"I am in command," Eleven said to it coolly. "Hear me, fear me, bow down before me. Cease operation immediately."

The light abruptly faded from the fake Amalgam. Eleven reached out for the petri dish and poured the silver dust of what had once been an automagiton into it.

Rocky looked at the fake Amalgam with deep interest as he covered the dish with a lid. "Can you take care of the folks with the Amalgam on the outside like this, too?"

"No," Eleven said. "I was merely able to guide it now because it was seeking a way to escape outside the body. In cases where it has already fused with the tissue structure and is multiplying, the priority will be on protecting the host body rather than my instructions, and I will not be able to extract it."

"That so…? Ah, well, that was marvelous. You've really proven yourself, young lady." Rocky put the petri dish into a protective case and patted her head.

Eleven tolerated it, but when Rocky pulled his hand away, she fixed her mussed tresses and asked, "Investigator, was there something in my hair?"

"What's that?" Rocky arched an eyebrow at her. "When a dog does a job for you, you pat her head and tell her what a good dog she is."

"A dog?" Theo said. "Rocky, you're seriously—?"

"I mean, she's called a Hound, so I figured it's easier for the young lady to understand if I compared her to a dog, yeah?" he replied as if it was the most obvious thing in the world and went to talk with the doctors treating Wood.

Wood looked over at Eleven through the gap between the nurses and thanked her with his eyes.

She bowed to him neatly and then turned to Theo. "Shall we wait until his treatment is complete?"

"...No, let's go back to the office. Tobias should be done with the interview by now." He sighed and pressed a hand to his forehead where a headache was brewing. It was good that they'd saved one of the victims, but it looked like it was going to take a while yet to catch who was behind all of this.

By the time Theo and his team were assembled at the office, the sun had set. He furrowed his brow as he examined the composite sketch of the suspect that Tobias and Emma had put forth with serious looks on their faces.

Short hair. Eyebrows and eyes that angled upward. Prominent nose and jaw, threatening countenance. And a distinctive scar on his forehead.

It was definitely Jim Kent, the criminal consultant wanted both inside and outside the country, part of the radical faction of continentalists. He was complicit in many of the subversive activities of dissident groups and was marked as a dangerous element by investigative organizations worldwide. But this had not led to a single arrest.

Continental unificationism. While strictly speaking, this was the concept that the entire continent should be placed under the rule of one country, the enactment varied wildly depending on how each faction selected the ruling country and the target of their aggrieved anger. Theo had no idea which definition Jim Kent was operating under.

"But if there's one thing we can say at present," Theo said with a sigh, "it's that he intends to accomplish something in Delverro using the Amalgams."

"Looks like," Tobias replied, his expression serious. "After using humans as cores for the fake Amalgams, he produced something that moves while feeding repeatedly. However it plays out, there's going to be serious damage."

Emma nodded. "The whole situation changes dramatically depending on whether he's planning on attacking a person, a group, or a country. It'd be one thing if we knew the ideology he's working under, but…"

"Statistically, the most dangerous crimes domestically are committed due to religious beliefs," Eleven said. Three pairs of eyes turned on her, and she continued quietly. "When a crime originates from a simple extremist movement or destructive impulse, betrayals and other similar acts can bring about internal dissent, weakening the group. This leaves room for conversation and persuasion. But when people act in accordance with religious thought, the possibility of betrayal is extremely low, and the aggression increases."

"…You said that with the 'Glory to Roremclad' text, too," Theo noted. "Religion, hmm?"

Tobias looked fed up. "There was a cult like that. Something about how if they sacrificed the continent under unified rule to God, they could go to heaven, and heretics would go to hell. If a radical faction led by Jim Kent got involved, they would indeed make any sacrifice for the sake of paradise and commit truly abhorrent crimes."

"…I shudder at the mere thought of it. But according to Ghilane, payments were in cash, meaning we can't pin down Jim Kent's location, and the deals were done in that building and that building only. Dead end, huh?" Emma sighed heavily.

"Let's lay it out in chronological order." Theo looked back at the board. "Bob Derry and Jacus Ghilane were a drug-dealing team. Ghilane brought in the customers; Derry sold the drugs. Ghilane was the first to make a connection with the fight club management, and Jim Kent contacted them as a drug merchant in order to use that connection."

"According to Ghilane, the final deal took place the day before we raided the fight club," Tobias continued. "He took the money, went drinking, and that was the last time Ghilane talked to Derry."

"After that, Jim Kent, who normally keeps to the shadows, went out of his way to eliminate Derry and tried to get rid of Ghilane, too." Emma picked up the timeline. "It definitely wasn't a solo hit. Whatever his motivation is now, he's working for a different reason than he has up to this point."

Theo's gaze naturally shifted to the photos of Bob Derry. "Jim Kent doesn't get his own hands dirty. The cause of Bob Derry's death was not an external wound but an injury caused by thrusting outward from inside the abdomen. We have no idea what actually caused the injury, nor any likely culprits, be they creature or weapon."

"I put in a message to the Amalgam lab through Eleven, but they said that there wasn't enough information to say for sure," Tobias said. "I'd like to secure the actual specimen if we could, but it's impossible for us to search the sewers."

"The lab? R&D?" Theo turned around with a start. "I can't believe you managed to get in touch with them."

Tobias shrugged. "Eleven's basically got a free pass within the military. After all, she herself is top secret information. But for us to lean on R&D, it looks like we're going to need to collect more information."

Theo automatically glanced at Eleven, but she was simply staring at the board.

"As of right now, we've found the pills sold to the fight club and the capsule that Bob Derry took," Emma said, looking back and forth between the drugs seized as evidence. "If the pills are fake Amalgams, then the capsule should also have some Amalgam connection."

"That's the issue right there." Tobias sighed. "According to Eleven, the individual thought to have killed Derry doesn't fit the description of an Amalgam. It was either made independently just like the fake Amalgam or it's something totally different. We'll have to try to pinpoint what it actually is at the same time as we investigate Jim Kent, hmm?"

Theo and his team fell silent, left with nothing more to say in the face of the mountain of work before them. Breaking the silence that followed was the sound of banging on cubicle walls. They looked up to see Captain Paloma walking over to them.

"The papers from Intelligence are here," he announced. "Is that her? The one on the team on a trial basis?"

"Captain Paloma," Theo said. "You were told about this?"

"Mm-hmm." The captain nodded. "More or less. Can't quite believe it, though. To think there's a specimen even more advanced than the Amalgam."

Paloma stood diagonally to Eleven with as much distance as possible between them. The look on her face did not change as she quietly saluted him. Seeming bewildered, Paloma responded with a wave before quickly clearing his throat and looking at Theo and his team.

"So… What's it gonna be? Did you all come to a conclusion?" he asked. "We treating her like an investigator, or are you gonna put her in storage in the armory? Commander Guin said he left the choice up to Investigator Starling. Are you going to investigate together or, uh…? Well?"

"…I—"

"We Hounds"—Eleven's sharp voice interrupted Theo. She brought her hands to her sides to assume a formal posture—"unlike normal Amalgams, were designed with the prerequisite of carrying out missions independently. I recommend a policy of leaving me on standby in the armory and only mobilizing me when an Amalgam involved in a crime is discovered."

"…But, Eleven—in that case, there's no point in you having a human form, is there?" Emma said gently.

Eleven turned toward her and quietly replied, "There is. A human form is nothing more than proof of a high-level mimicry ability. There is no need for me to be active as a human being. Please prioritize the feelings of personnel involved and the efficiency of the investigation. You are all human beings, creatures that act based on emotion."

Theo gasped, feeling like he'd been punched in the head. He was painfully aware of Emma's eyes on him. His own attitude toward Eleven was to blame.

My whole body probably screams to her how much I hate Amalgams.

She could have just stayed quiet and awaited orders. But Eleven did not do that.

Why not? Perhaps because she had detected that Theo loathed her presence?

Detective Operations had no experience with the operation of automagitons or the like. If a recommended course of action came from the automagiton in question herself, it was only natural to go along with that plan.

Yet Tobias said, "I understand your proposal, Eleven, but that's a bit difficult in practice, isn't it?"

"Is it, Investigator Hillmyna?" asked a surprised Captain Paloma.

"Yes," Tobias replied with a smile. "It is true that she on her own has far and away more power than all our arts rejectors combined. But assuming she arrives on the scene once she gets the mobilization order and supposing we're facing an Amalgam of a size you'd see on the battlefield, she'll have to take care of it with this body. She might be able to change form at will, but it apparently takes even her time to prepare to enlarge herself, and we might have to provide backup. In which case, rather than having her in the armory, I believe it's both more practical and more efficient to have her on the scene with us, playing it by ear to handle things."

"Any obstacles to investigating together?" Paloma asked. "She appears to communicate just fine."

"Naturally, there are no issues there," Tobias responded. "She even saved Theo when he went after a suspect and was very nearly injured."

"Tobias, that's—," Theo reflexively argued, but the pressure of Tobias's smile forced his mouth closed again. Memories of being lectured by that smiling face in their academy days came back to him. He leaned back against his desk awkwardly.

Paloma looked baffled, but he switched gears with a sigh and turned toward Emma. "So then. What's your opinion, Investigator Canary? Seems like your extra member there's giving the team a leg up."

"…Given that we don't know how to deal with Amalgams, I would also be glad to have her tremendous fighting power on our side. But I also understand where Eleven's coming from. I leave the decision to our team leader." Emma glanced at Theo and stopped there.

Eleven watched Theo carefully. There was no malice on her face; her expression was simply one of waiting.

Not letting this pass unnoticed, Paloma said, "Investigator Starling, let's talk in my office. I have some files for you."

Theo silently followed him. He could feel the eyes of not only Emma on him but also the other investigators as he entered the captain's office. Paloma lowered the blinds to obstruct their view and sighed.

"…Five years since you lost your family, is it?" he asked. "You've managed to pull through it admirably."

"Thank you, Captain Paloma," Theo said.

"Considering what happened to your family and your hometown, you must have a hard time accepting an Amalgam into the unit. But given that we're dealing with the unprecedented matter of Amalgams, she's obviously a real asset."

"…You're exactly right, sir."

Paloma glanced back at him, a troubled look making its way to his face. "We don't have any experience operating Amalgams. She herself has proposed a course of action, but Investigator Hillmyna's comments are quite right, too. Taking all that into consideration, where do you come down as team leader? How do you think you can use her and protect the people from Amalgams?"

Theo let out a long sigh. He chased all extraneous thoughts from his head and focused solely on the facts.

Automagitons were loyal to orders. Theo had the authority to give orders. He would be the one controlling her.

The case they were currently investigating involved the criminal consultant Jim Kent and Amalgams of unknown origin. Given that they didn't know who they were dealing with, the power of a Hound was indispensable.

Theo was an investigator with the Criminal Investigation Bureau and the leader of the special Amalgam crimes team. His duty was to protect the people from dangerous criminal Amalgams and reveal the truth as soon as possible.

Personal feelings could not be a part of this. He would consider the situation with a cool head and make a rational decision. In the back of his mind, long red hair flitted past.

When his sister, who had been a number of years younger than him, learned that he was joining the Criminal Investigation Bureau, her blue eyes had shone with pure joy.

"Wow! So you're going to be everyone's hero now."

"I will include her as an investigator," Theo said. "She'll go out into the field with us, and I'll have her deal with any Amalgams we discover immediately. This way is more certain, and I can monitor for any strange movements."

"...Safer in all kinds of ways than having her out there alone. All right. Let's get you those files."

Theo watched Paloma move to his desk and clenched his hands into fists. This was right. The rational decision.

Heather... This is...the right thing, isn't it...?

His stomach hurt. He gritted his teeth, and in the next instant, he was faltering at the volume and weight of the files thrust at him.

"C-Captain Paloma, are these really all necessary?" he asked.

"Mm-hmm. Transfer forms for her transferal to DetOps, and since human ID is required for an investigator, you'll need to fill in the forms required for guarantor of identity. They classed her as parts over in Intelligence."

"Parts?!" Theo's eyebrows shot up. "Not even as weaponry but as *parts*?!"

Paloma nodded. "Submit all the paperwork to me. This tome here is the Amalgam Hound operation manual. Commander Guin said to take a look at it if you have any trouble. The contact info for the Hound development team's on the front of the manual. You're supposed to get in touch with them if you run into any problems with her."

"...Roger that..."

"I'll handle the rest on my end, so you can go now," the captain told him. "Take tonight off. A string of all-nighters is not going to do you any good."

Staggering under the unexpected weight of papers and documentation, Theo left the office.

Tobias looked at him in surprise. "I thought you were talking with the captain. Where'd all that come from?"

"When I said I was adding her to the team, he handed me papers for her transfer, identification, all that," Theo replied, dropping the heavy load on his desk. "The manual's just incredibly thick."

"Oh, makes sense, I guess. Since she's an automagiton, you'd have to vouch for her identity, huh?" Emma nodded, convinced, and then cocked her head to one side. "So. Who's going to be Eleven's guarantor, then? I'm a sorcerer and all. Want me to do it?"

"But Theo's the one with authority over her, so isn't he ultimately responsible for her?" Tobias protested.

Theo pulled out a form and ran a pen across it. "It's just on paper, at any rate. I can do it. Although age and income-wise, Tobias might be the better fit... But I'd feel bad if your partner got the wrong idea and thought it was a romantic thing."

"...How very considerate of you. Appreciate it." Tobias smiled wryly and leaned back against his desk. "So then we can put your address down, too."

"Is the address of the Delverro office not allowed?" Eleven asked, standing in front of the board.

"There's no way the papers would go through with something like that on them," Theo told her. "And where would you live, exactly?"

"The cleaning-supplies closet or the parts warehouse. It is possible for me to be on standby there outside of working hours," she said, as if this was the most obvious thing in the world. It was no surprise that she would come up with an idea like this since she had been handled as parts in the Intelligence Service.

Theo pressed a hand to his head, and Emma gently wrapped an arm around Eleven's shoulders. "Listen, Eleven. You're joining our team as an *investigator*. Not as parts."

"Does that have any relationship with my standby location?"

"It absolutely does! No investigator commutes to work from parts storage!"

"Now, now. You've been on standby before during missions, right, Eleven?" Tobias asked in a deliberately even tone. "And you've worked with people before, too. So how did you spend that time?"

Eleven blinked. "I remained on standby until my next order, maintaining the desired form with the desired personality memorized. My standby location was often a place far from human presence such as transportation containers and storage rooms."

"I see. Then it seems we'll have to take a different approach," he responded. "You'll be working as a DetOps investigator, so you'll have plenty more contact with other investigators and citizens. You'll have to act as human as possible in front of people. To that end, you'll need to be on standby in a place where a person would live."

"My address will not have any effect on the other investigators nor on the general population," she protested.

"Even so." Tobias twirled a finger in the air. "If there was a dorm, it'd be a different story, but the Delverro branch doesn't have one. Sorry, but the most natural thing might be for you to stay with Emma or Theo."

The problem was which house she should live in.

Emma pressed a hand to her cheek. "I suppose it would make sense for her to stay with me since she's a girl. But Hounds have excellent mimicry abilities, so what if we got her to be a boy and stay with you, Theo? I mean, the neighbors will be curious regardless."

"No," Eleven said. "I already have a form that conforms most easily with human society. There is no problem."

"Oh yeah? Show us," Theo demanded, lifting his face from his papers.

Eleven's body melted into black fabric and came apart at the seams. The fabric twisted up into thread and became a belt before curling up and hardening at the foot of the board. While the three investigators watched to see what would happen, this lump gradually took shape, changing into a dog with pointed ears and a nose and fluffy white fur and a tail. The midsize dog sat with its paws politely before it and looked up at Theo.

"This is the optimal solution for blending into human society," Dog Eleven said.

"But you're a *dog*!" Theo protested.

"I am a dog," she agreed. "Over the long course of history, a dog by the side of a human being has never been deemed a problem worthy of concern."

Watching the white dog that was Eleven open her mouth and speak people words made Theo's head hurt. He lifted her up and inspected her stomach and paws. Her white fur was soft and resembled the color of her human-form hair. The feel of her as he held her up, the skeleton, the toenails—it was all very canine.

"...You're a dog," he said at last. "Absolutely and completely."

"If I am in this form, I can adapt to human society without issue," she told him.

"No, but we're talking about as an investigator. Why would you go turning into a dog for an investigation?"

"I thought that identification was required because of my human form, and that the issue would be resolved if I was not human."

Suddenly, Theo heard the sound of a camera shutter, and he hurriedly looked up.

Emma was holding up her cell phone, and before he knew it, she was snapping more pictures.

"Hey!" he cried. "Quit that! No photos! Emma!"

"Hold up—don't move!" Emma commanded. "Eleven's so cute. Look this way!"

Still held by Theo, the white dog turned her snout in Emma's direction. Listening to the cry of delight and the repeated shutter sounds that welcomed this, Theo closed his eyes in annoyance. The soft fur in his hands shifted, fluffy against his fingertips. When she changed positions from time to time, the soft fur would touch his jaw or neck.

A dog... When I was little, I was so jealous of my friends who had dogs.

Theo had never had pets. And while he did feel rewarded by his job, it was also exhausting. How soothing would it be to have a fluffy white dog like this at his house?

Just as he'd had the thought that it was surprisingly doable, the soft sensation went away. When he opened his eyes with a gasp, Eleven, once again a girl in a military uniform, was standing against the wall, averting her eyes from him.

"...I withdraw that proposal," she said. "Human form is more appropriate for an investigator than that of a dog."

"Y-yeah... I suppose it is..." His voice held an echo of regret that was greater than he himself was aware of.

Seemingly satisfied having taken her fill of photos, Emma put her cell phone in her pocket and said with a smile, "H'okay. Now that we've had our fun, we need a decision. Given that the person in charge of her and the guarantor of her identity are one and the same person, I think the best plan is to put Eleven at Theo's house. It'll be easier for intelligence services to get in touch with her, too, which is good. I might be a sorcerer, but Amalgams are not my area of expertise. I won't be any help."

"That said, though..." Theo felt some resistance to the idea of a teenage girl in his house, of an Amalgam there.

Eleven looked back and forth between him and Emma while Tobias

asked with a smile, "Eleven, you can take that dog form at any time? Can you turn into an even bigger and fluffier dog?"

"Yes," she answered. "Anything the commander prefers."

"How lovely that the Amalgam, the most powerful weapon on this planet, would also make a good therapy animal. Maybe I *do* want you at my house," Emma said, grinning at Theo with Tobias.

Theo clicked his tongue. "Fine. I'll take Eleven. For safety's sake. And absolutely *not* because of the dog."

"Yeah, yeah. Let's just go with that story."

"...Do you have any remarks, Investigator?" Eleven asked, and all three humans turned to stare at her.

"What?" they replied in unison.

Eleven blinked several times, and the humans unconsciously looked at one another. The first to speak was Emma.

"Now that I'm thinking about it, you don't call people by name, huh, Eleven?" she asked. "Is there a reason for that?"

"It's merely a habit as a Hound," she said. "Notation is prioritized over individual call signs."

"Well, your name is just the number eleven and all." Tobias nodded, seemingly convinced, but Emma pursed her lips unhappily.

"We're in the same unit. We're going to be spending a lot of time together. So let's call each other by name. Okay, Theo?"

"...I mean, I'm fine with that," he said, not entirely on board. "There are times when it'd be better not to call attention to the fact that we're investigators."

Tobias laughed and nodded again. "Theo himself is saying so. How about it, Eleven?"

"I understand. Tobias, Emma, Theo." Eleven spoke their names with palpable awkwardness.

Seeing this, Tobias flashed a strained smile while Emma said, "Look at you! Good girl!" as she patted Eleven's head happily.

Theo had an abrupt realization and asked Eleven, "They treated you like parts in intelligence services, and you have no identification. Do you have anything along the lines of personal effects?"

"No, I do not," she told him. "I mimic the specified clothing and use the provisions supplied."

"I'm impressed you managed to make it up to now. A military facility—they would have an arts rejector placed at the entrance, yes? Has your mimicry even been canceled?" Tobias asked with a hurried air.

Eleven blinked before replying quietly, "I was instructed to pass through an entrance for personnel only, so my mimicry was never forcefully removed. Even in the event that my mimicry had been removed, I would return to the clothing that was in my factory settings."

"Oh!" Tobias clapped his hands together. "So then you wouldn't suddenly be naked or anything like that. That's good, you being a girl and all."

"No. Weapons do not have gender. I simply carried over the practice from the Intelligence Service and am mimicking the women's uniform—" Eleven abruptly cut herself off. Emma was hugging her very tightly.

Theo watched with Tobias as the scene played out, while Emma lifted her face, a severe expression on it.

"No clothes?!" she cried. "This is serious! Why didn't you say so to begin with?!"

"No. We Hounds are fine with mimicry, so—"

"What are you talking about?!" Emma said. "Having food, shelter, and clothes is the very fabric of life itself! A Hound doesn't need food, and we've solved the shelter part, so all that's left is clothes!"

"Those are human needs—"

"What would suit you? I think you'd look good in practically anything! Which stores are open at this hour…?"

"Theo, please stop Emma. Theo."

The force of Emma's embrace was too powerful, lifting Eleven's heels off the ground. The girl begged Theo for help in a faint voice, but he gently shook his head.

"Accept your fate," he said. "Once that switch is flipped with Emma, she won't quit until she's satisfied. And the captain did tell us to take tonight off. Let's go relax and get back to the investigation tomorrow. I just hope we can get some information on any Jim Kent sightings."

"We might also want to hope that Emma's shopping spree ends soon, too." Tobias got a faraway look in his eyes, but Theo had already acquiesced, stuffing papers and the Amalgam manual into his bag.

He averted his eyes from the problem of the Amalgam coming to his own house and followed Emma out of the office. He felt Eleven's gaze on him as she walked, half dragged along, but there was nothing that he or Tobias could do. All he could do was bring the car around.

■

As soon as they pulled up at the large shopping center, Emma took Eleven and made a beeline for the ladies' clothing stores while Theo sat down with Tobias on a bench in the rest area and let out a long sigh at last. He opened the Hound manual, thinking to at least get an overview for the time being.

"...Right from the first line, it's 'The Hound is normally only given orders,'" he said with a frown.

"Well, I don't suppose they'll protest a dress or two," Tobias replied. "Emma's having a good time anyway."

"I can't tell if she's trying to welcome Eleven in her own way or just blowing off stress."

"Isn't it wonderful, though, that we have the luxury of shopping for nice little outfits?" Tobias mused. "I mean, it's really only been this last year that we haven't had to worry about air raids. Maybe it's just temporary, but this peace now is marvelous."

Theo glanced up. Tobias was watching Emma and Eleven with a tranquil expression. So was that what this was? Theo leaned back on the bench and looked out at the mall.

All the stores were littered with slogans that were no doubt very particular to this time and place: NEW LOOKS FOR A NEW PEACE, TIMES ARE TOUGH; YOU DESERVE THIS!, FORMAL WEAR FOR THE PEACE MEMORIAL. This shopping center itself had only just finished repairs and reopened at the start of the year. Life was finally moving forward again, and the economy was recovering, which maybe explained why the faces of the customers coming and going were bright, and the shops were filled with energy.

"...Peace memorial, hmm?" Theo said. "Speaking of, that's next month already."

"To be honest, I have no idea what next year will look like, not when I can see the number of fires just waiting to be lit. So best to have the ceremony this year when we're at peace and everyone has all this hope. For the sake of the people we've lost, too." Tobias's voice was thick with emotion as he clenched his synthetic left hand.

What if Theo had been blown to bits in that mortar attack? What if Tobias had been crushed under that collapsing building in the air raid? They would not have been sitting there now. Tobias in particular had just barely made it out alive after saving his parents during that air raid; he'd had to have his left arm amputated. Theo shuddered when he thought about how he might otherwise have been offering flowers to Tobias at the peace memorial.

"Now, then." Tobias recomposed himself, and his expression grew troubled. "The issue at this point is Kent. He's the one dealing these drugs."

"...A pill that parasitizes you with a monster and another that kills you with a monster," Theo said. "Real end-of-the-world style."

"True, we might be taking the first steps up that staircase." Tobias nodded. "This is where I'd really like to hear from an expert. If these drugs are merely an experiment, then Kent's going to want more data, and we're going to see more damage."

Hearing the word *experiment*, Theo felt a little pinprick in his memory. "Considering it from that angle, then Kent will be more focused on the latter—the specimen raised in the human body that ate its way through the stomach and escaped. Does he want to mass-produce Amalgams himself?"

"I really can't see him being able to control a process like that, but maybe that's the point in the end? Ugh, I do *not* like the sound of that at all. If he's distributing these drugs via the usual routes, it's only gonna go deeper and deeper." Tobias's concern was spot-on.

Theo cradled his head in his hands. There was no doubt that they were in a race against time. And there was one other thing that was worrying him.

"The military and R&D have kept the Amalgam technology top secret," he said. "If there *are* Amalgams on the loose out there that even Eleven isn't aware of, then we have to assume the technology was leaked. If Kent didn't know what a real Amalgam was like, he couldn't produce anything that resembled it. Someone in R&D turned traitor?"

"We should look into anyone who left the lab within the last few years," Tobias agreed. "I'd actually like access to the lab as well. If it's an inside job, we'll probably have trouble getting in, though."

Their faces as they talked quickly grew too serious for the mall's laid-back atmosphere. Theo flipped through the pages of the manual half-heartedly and prayed for Emma and Eleven to be done shopping soon.

■

Emma walked through the racks of clothes, picked up a piece she liked, and held it against Eleven's shoulders. Cute face, adult air, pale hair and skin, gray eyes—she wanted to make it all shine. Before she knew it, she was humming to herself and carefully examining all the clothes in each shop.

"Eleven. What clothes have you worn so far?" she asked. "Is there anything you especially like or hate?"

"I have no likes or dislikes," Eleven replied. "I have worn clothes that enhanced specified personalities."

Emma returned the blouse in her hand to the rack and looked back at Eleven. She was actually looking around the shop, but at the customers not the clothes.

"...What's this 'personality' you keep talking about?" Emma asked curiously. "How far do you 'become' a person?"

"Behavior patterns, word usage, physical responses to stimuli, relationships, countering changes. Expressions of emotion, interpersonal distance, and habits while conversing are perhaps the most important."

"That's… Should I take that to mean you have a large database of human beings inside of you? And then you select characteristics from there matching your requirements and behave in that fashion?"

"Yes. That is not mistaken."

"Mm-hmm, mm-hmm. So the ability to analyze, memorize, and recreate is part of your high-level mimicry, then." Emma let her gaze roam, picked up two completely different blouses, and held them up to her own shoulders. One was navy with a white collar and straight sleeves, while the other was white and embroidered with a bowtie collar and puffed sleeves.

Eleven looked back and forth between Emma and the blouses.

"So if I was going to buy one, which one would it be?" Emma asked. "Tell me which one and why."

"The navy one," Eleven replied immediately. "You would avoid anything with significant air resistance that interferes with your Society of Sorcerers cape. Above all else, you have determined that clothing with too many decorative elements and curving lines that are often adopted for dolls and patterned after girl children do not suit you. That is all."

Her response was mechanical, but she was staring up at Emma's face searchingly, no doubt observing to see if she had hurt Emma's feelings.

Emma smiled automatically. "Whoa! That's really something. I do actually tend to avoid that sort of thing, but how did you know?" She put the blouses back and began picking out clothes for Eleven again.

"There are a number of women's clothing stores in this mall, and at the third one, the clerk said hello to you, and you replied in kind," Eleven continued, walking a little bit behind her. "I was able to discern immediately that it was a store that you frequent. The design of the clothing there was business-oriented, the prices were relatively high, and the quality was also high. The collars and sleeve openings were the barest minimum. This was evidence that you select clothing that is durable and easy to move in, since you must work with guns as an investigator, but that is also unlikely to provoke a response in people, given that you have contact with all types of citizens."

"Good eye." Emma nodded. "I'm impressed. And?"

"...When you select clothing for me, you prioritize clothing with decorative elements, but at those times, the words *sad* and *miserable* apply to your expression, although only for a brief moment."

Emma had only asked for her own amusement, and now she looked back at Eleven in surprise. When Eleven met her eyes, she averted her own and grabbed on to a nearby rack of clothing. She was too clumsy in the way she tried to laugh it off. "That's the look I had on my face?"

"You want these things but will not select them for yourself," Eleven explained. "Many human beings have a similar expression on their faces when they think this way. Thus, my analysis was that you have decided they do not suit you."

In fact, she was exactly right. Emma grabbed the dress Eleven was touching. White and smoky blue, with a beautifully draping, voluminous knee-length skirt and plenty of ruffles peeking out from under the hem. Dark blue ribbon tie at the base of the wide, round collar, cuffs and hem decorated with brilliant embroidery. The sort of adorable outfit that Emma never bought.

"...I loved this kind of thing when I was a kid, you know?" she said. "But I grew faster than the other kids, and the sizes for these outfits don't run too large, so I couldn't fit into them anymore. After that, I went the adult route and set my sights on clothes that suited me rather than stuff I liked. I could start buying this stuff now, but it doesn't go with the clothes I already have. It would just take up space in my closet. About the only cute element I could add is a blouse collar."

"...If I mimicked the clothing, it wouldn't take up any space," Eleven told her.

"Honestly! What are you even talking about? Hee-hee! You're a funny kid. You're more than enough the way you are." Emma laughed at the unexpected proposal. They didn't need to go out of their way to specify a personality; Eleven was perfectly fine as Eleven.

Looking at the dress, Emma abruptly noticed that it came in a wide range of sizes. She grabbed two and held the smaller smoky blue up against Eleven and the larger wine red against herself. She thought the richer colors would suit the girl better, but the pale blue went very well with Eleven's cloud-colored hair.

"...How about we buy matching outfits in different colors?" Emma said impulsively. "To commemorate our first meeting, bring us closer."

"Will your closet allow that?" Eleven asked.

"It can handle one more outfit, I think. Now, let's get you some clothes!"

Emma went along picking up things that would work on Eleven, even if they wouldn't on herself. She wanted to get some things for everyday life, work, and lounging around. Eleven would also need shoes and accessories. Emma never imagined the day would come when she was picking out clothes for an automagiton. And such an adorable girl, at that.

"Are there any materials that get in the way when you're transforming?" she asked Eleven. "You change together with your clothes, right?"

"There are no elements that interfere with my mimicry abilities. All materials transform in tandem with me."

"So then I can focus on design and silhouette? Hmm. Might be good to pull together some more grown-up things."

"...Emma, are you having 'fun' right now? There is no 'sad' or 'miserable' on your face."

"Mm. This is fun," Emma agreed, smiling from the bottom of her heart, happy to welcome Eleven as her colleague—even if this colleague was a weapon. "After all, you're going to be wearing these clothes and working with us!"

■

Theo noticed Emma and Eleven returning from their shopping trip, then closed the manual and shoved it into his bag. Emma had two large paper bags hanging from each arm and a satisfied look on her face.

"Aah, it's been ages since I went shopping for clothes like this!" she said. "That was a great time."

Theo frowned slightly. "Isn't that a lot? There's only *one* Eleven, you know."

"Oh! Three of these are Eleven's. One's for me."

Theo looked down at the bags in amazement, but unable to say anything, he contented himself with giving a little snort. Eleven's facial expression told him nothing about what she was thinking, as usual, but the way she took the bags from Emma was polite.

"I so needed this break from the investigation," Emma told them. "Although I do hope something cracks open tomorrow."

"Well, we're up against someone who slipped through the net intelligence services cast," Tobias replied. "It'd be a huge help if we could find some eyewitnesses."

"All we can do is keep looking," Theo said. "Nice work, everyone. Try to take it easy tonight."

This was the perfect moment to say their good-byes. Theo returned to his own car alone and then noticed quick footsteps keeping pace with him. "Oh, right. So about your room…"

"If you would allow me a space to deposit the clothing, I will go on standby in a location and size that will not interfere with you," Eleven told him.

"…No need for the weird concern. I have an extra bedroom. You can use that."

"Understood. Thank you very much."

It grated on him that she tried to be thoughtful, but he would no doubt have been equally annoyed if she'd taken it as a given that she would get her own room. He tsk'd to himself and started the car. *This is a real trial, if I do say so myself.*

His house was a little ways from the Delverro branch of the Criminal Investigation Bureau. Neither he nor Eleven spoke during the drive. The silence made Theo uncomfortable, but there'd been nothing about conversing with a Hound in the manual—although he'd only skimmed it—and he didn't know what to say to get things started.

They slipped through the entrance to his apartment building and headed for the elevator, where they ran into a resident on his way out for the night shift as a security guard.

The man raised an easy hand in greeting. "Hey, Theo. You just getting home?"

"I am. And you?" Theo asked in reply. "I feel like you're working more nights lately."

"Well, you know." The man shrugged amiably. "You saw the whole 'goat mask gang' thing on the news, yeah? Folks're tightening up security 'cause of them, so I got more shifts." He dropped his gaze. "Oops! You got someone with you. Who's this, then?"

Theo automatically turned his eyes toward Eleven. She bowed her head politely. They were far apart in age, and they definitely didn't look like they were related. It was only natural his neighbor would be curious.

"Mm." Theo was at a loss for words. "She… Uh, she lost her family in the war. I'm a distant cousin, so I'm taking her in."

"Huh, so she's— Ah no, I'm sorry. You just let me know if there's anything I can do to help."

"Thanks. You take care, too." Theo watched the man walk off.

Eleven also thanked the man with her eyes. "Are there guidelines for interacting with residents?" she asked.

"Guidelines…" Theo thought for a second. "Awkward avoidance could actually arouse suspicion. Just chat with them as appropriate."

"Roger. I will add that to my behavior guidelines."

Their conversation ended with this mechanical response from Eleven. Holding back a sigh, Theo pressed the elevator button more roughly than usual. He arrived at his apartment still in a foul mood.

As soon as Eleven entered, she observed her surroundings. Theo had given the living room only a lick and a promise when it came to cleaning, seeing as Tobias and Emma were about the only visitors he had, and he now hurried to grab a garbage bag.

As he tossed empty beer cans and takeout containers into it, Eleven offered, "Allow me to help you clean."

"I'm fine," he told her. "You go put your new clothes in the closet. That's your room there. Mine's farther down the hall. The door next to the kitchen's the bathroom. If you've got all that, then go."

"Understood. If you'll excuse me." Eleven went into the bedroom as instructed.

Theo picked up any messes he could see and then gasped with realization: There was no need for him to clean his house for a weapon, was there?

"What am I doing...?" he scoffed and set the garbage bag in a corner of the kitchen. He clearly hadn't figured out how exactly he was going to handle this girl.

When he peered into her room, she was taking clothes out of the shopping bags and putting them away neatly in the closet. Because this was the only place in the apartment that was properly cleaned, there was no dust, the curtains and bed linens were all fresh, and not a single smudge marred the surface of the mirror.

In this room decorated in aging flowery wallpaper and romantic lace curtains, Eleven in her military uniform seemed out of place. Theo saw the ghost of someone else where she stood. His little sister would always fix her long red hair in the mirror and check that her collar and hem were straight before whirling around toward him.

"Is it really acceptable for me to use this room? When will its original owner return?"

At Eleven's quiet question, Theo came back to himself. She had finished putting her new clothes away and was now looking at him. The question was not malicious; it was only natural that she would ask. In addition to the fact that the decor very clearly did not match his own personal taste, there was also the dining table in the kitchen with two chairs across from each other. It was clear at a glance that two people had originally lived here.

He shook his head. "Oh...there's no one using it now. Don't worry about it."

"But the fact that I am in this room corresponds to your 'displeasure.'"

"What? My displeasure?" Theo was shaken.

Eleven continued. "Your face shows 'disgust' that I am in this room, and your 'loss' grows stronger with me here. For the purposes of mental health maintenance, I thought it perhaps necessary to take measures."

"I never said a single word to that effect." He automatically left the room, baffled. His heart throbbed and ached.

It was his own fault for seeing his little sister in her. Emma had warned him time and again, and he hadn't taken her seriously enough. That was all.

Eleven followed him out of the room. "I will respond to your preferences. Please specify an appearance and personality."

"I *told* you I have no preferences," he snapped.

"It is possible for me to reproduce your desired form and behavior. I can estimate the age of the user from the interior decorations and damage to the furniture, but if you share with me a specific image, I can recreate it more accurately."

She pressed her hands to her chest, and her form shimmered like a heat haze. The skirt of her military uniform grew longer and changed to a soft orange color while Eleven herself grew a little taller and her hair stretched to her waist, reddening—

"Stop it!" Theo shouted before he was even aware of it.

Like smoke clearing, Eleven's form returned to that of the girl in the military uniform. She didn't say anything, but her gray eyes were clear as though they penetrated deep down into the unknown depths of Theo's heart. He very much could not meet her gaze.

He pressed a hand to his forehead and averted his eyes. "Sorry for yelling. But if I want to tell you something, I will actually tell it to you. That was my little sister's room... I was just remembering her. It's got nothing to do with you."

"Then why am I here?" Her voice was monotone, but he felt something stronger in the timbre of her words.

He lifted his face to find her staring earnestly at him. The same way she had right from the start, all this time.

"I am a weapon, Theo. Please clarify the operational guidelines. Please say what you mean. Why do you not state your preferences when you clearly have preferences?"

He was irritated by the constant repetition of this exchange. "I told you, I don't— Huh?" He felt a sudden buoyancy and looked up at the ceiling.

In the next instant, he fell backward onto the sofa. For a second, he couldn't breathe, while in the corner of his eye, a sword flashed. Quickly drawing his gun, he froze in place, a cold sweat breaking out on his forehead.

At almost the same time as he thrust the barrel of the gun at Eleven, the sword that her right hand had turned into closed in on his windpipe. She looked down on him with abnormally calm eyes.

"What the hell are you doing?!" he shouted. "It's one incomprehensible thing after another with you. And now this?!"

"It would have been best for me to do this at the very beginning," she told him. "If you are unable to put your emotions into words and maintain control of them, then it is best to simply engage with weapons."

"Enough already! I don't know what you've picked up on, but—"

"Every time you hear the word *Amalgam*, 'terror' and 'hatred' appear on your face. You wear an expression that human beings often have when looking at targets for elimination. Are you not aware of it?"

He adjusted his grip on his gun. He didn't know what Eleven was up to here, but the blade pressed against his throat didn't so much as twitch. He had to proceed with caution. He swallowed hard.

"Are you not going to shoot?" she asked. "That's quite impressive."

A tremor bled into his hands. The barrel of the gun shook noticeably, and seeing this, Eleven continued.

"It would appear that your magnificent sense of justice applies to all those in human form... Is that why? Your little sister is no longer in the form of a human being, so she has been removed from the targets for justice."

The blade disappeared, and a girlish, slender hand pressed to her own chest.

"Your poor sister," Eleven said coolly. "Simply due to the intervention of an Amalgam, she loses her life, is abandoned by her older brother, and remains unavenged. What were her last words? A prayer to God, begging for her life? Or cursing her fool of a brother who couldn't even protect her—?"

Theo shuddered in fury. Before he knew it, he was grabbing her lapels and pressing the barrel of his gun to her throat. He panted through gritted teeth. "Don't you *dare* mock the dead! You're just a weapon; what the hell do you know?!"

"What will the dead protest?" she asked. "You use the fact that she does not speak as a convenient foundation for your justice. You crucify your sister with your justice."

Each of the icy words roiled in his stomach. He felt like the maelstrom of burning anger inside him would erupt through the top of his head. He clamped his jaw shut so firmly, it creaked in protest. This girl had no idea how his sister had died, no idea how Theo had dealt with the death of his family. She simply assumed she knew everything from his facial expressions and behavior, acted like she knew better.

What would a weapon—an undying doll—know about her, about my family—?

Theo set his finger on the trigger as if to blow her head clean off. He locked eyes with himself transformed in his fury as reflected in her gray eyes, which were quiet and unchanging.

He felt like a bucket of cold water had been dumped over his head. His shoulders heaved up and down as he panted raggedly, and he took several deep breaths before forcing his stiff hand to move and shifting the barrel of the gun away from Eleven's throat.

He'd had his fist clenched so tightly, the blood drained out of it. When he opened his hand, it shook. He pressed it to his forehead and sat down on the sofa. At the edge of his field of vision, he noticed Eleven's shoes taking one step and then another toward him.

"...You got a rise out of me just by playing the *Amalgam* and *sister* cards, eh?" he groaned.

Eleven stopped moving. "I prioritized the selection of expressions that would induce anger. Did I not meet your expectations?"

There was none of her earlier icy attitude in her words now. He exhaled at length. She probably didn't know why his family had died.

Nevertheless, she'd managed to goad him into nearly shooting her—a response to some "request" that he'd locked away in the depths of his heart.

"...Don't go trying to fulfill requests I haven't even spoken of with shoddy provocations," he told her. "It's annoying."

"Isn't it more precise to say that you *cannot* speak of them rather than you have not? You didn't explicitly state it, but I understood from the moment we met at the bureau that someone you cared about died in connection with an Amalgam."

Theo reflexively lifted his face and looked into her eyes. It felt like peering at the surface of a lake on a clear winter's day.

"'Grief' appears on your face with a high frequency," she continued. "You look at me with the same eyes that you would turn on the person who killed your loved ones. From that 'hatred' and 'grief,' it was simple to reach a conclusion. My analysis was that you sought the resolution of that 'hatred' and compensation for the 'loss.' Haven't you wanted to enact your revenge and be free of this anguish for some time now?"

She looked at him intently, and her gaze became frightening. Theo pulled back, and Eleven pushed forward in response, putting her knees on the sofa and wrapping a hand around Theo's and the gun it held. As if to make sure that the barrel absolutely did not move away from her chest.

"It's true that I cannot die. But I can perform you my death until you are satisfied. How shall I die? What can I do to lift the darkness from your heart?" Eleven pressed him quietly, dispassionately.

Before he knew it, almost all the strength had drained out of the hand on his gun. Eleven was the one tightly gripping it now—along with his hand that was holding it—in both of her own hands.

"Please ask for it. Please order it. Please make me useful."

The look on her face was earnest. He even saw a hint of desperation in it. He felt a sudden pity at how hard it would be to be a top secret weapon. She had been doing this forever, picking up on people's desires, being operated. As a weapon of war, as nonconsumable equipment.

Theo gently removed her hands from the gun, pushing them away lightly, and returned the weapon to its holster. Just as Rocky had noted, her fingers were cold. Her hands were those of a girl and much smaller than Theo's own.

"...I understand your nature," he told her. "But I don't want that. I want to keep on being the investigator my sister was proud of... I'm not taking revenge now, after all these years. I know it's not...what she would have wanted."

"Then your 'suffering' will not end."

"My suffering ending won't bring back the dead," he said frankly. "In which case, I want to be a person my family can be proud of."

Eleven blinked and responded a heartbeat later. "Then I cannot be useful?"

"You're an investigator with the Criminal Investigation Bureau, and a top secret anti-Amalgam weapon. Fulfilling my own personal requests is not within the scope of your duties. Go take a shower. And then do whatever you'd like." Theo pushed her toward the bathroom. Her shoulders under his hands felt slight.

■

Eleven changed into the navy-blue dress that Emma had bought for her and reflected on Theo's words.

Fulfilling Theo's personal requests is outside the scope of my duties...

A commanding officer had never said anything like that to her before. Had he gone over the operation manual? She returned to the living room to reconfirm his intentions, but he wasn't there. She determined from the slightly ajar door and the footprints on the carpet that he was in his bedroom and then looked inside.

Theo was lying on his back on the bed. Perhaps he had laid down and fallen asleep right away; he'd taken off only one of his shoes, and he was still wearing his tie. She knew that when human beings slept, they wore comfortable clothing and covered their form with a blanket. She looked around to see if there wasn't an appropriate covering, and her eyes stopped on the photographs hanging on the wall.

A family photo taken on a mountain that was lush with green trees. A picture of the brother and sister in front of the Criminal Investigation Bureau academy gates. And a group photo of new recruits clad in brand-new uniforms, all with different expressions on their faces. All these pictures showed a younger Theo. The family photo was the oldest. The siblings were still young children. This photo alone was faded with water stains here and there, and it looked to have been ripped up and taped back together.

The photos hung in a place where they could be seen from both the desk and the bed.

This is the injury, Eleven intuited. Each of these pictures was a wound for him.

It was best not to touch a wound. Especially an unhealed one.

She picked up the throw blanket on the chair and laid it across Theo's torso.

"…Good night, Theo," she said to the sleeping face that could hardly have been described as peaceful. Her voice, pitched quiet enough to keep from waking him up, was even quieter than she had expected.

CONFIDENTIAL

Chapter 3
The Style of the Inhuman

AMALGAM HOUND
Criminal Investigation Bureau:
Special Investigation Unit

When he'd talked to his parents about going to the Criminal Investigation Bureau academy after graduating from high school, it had turned into their first-ever argument. He'd raced out of the house, and the one who came to call him for dinner was his little sister, Heather.

"Theo," she said. "Mom and Dad are just worried about you. I mean, investigators do a lot of dangerous jobs and all."

"Whatever." He sighed, still sulking, and she laughed. Not caring about dirtying her orange skirt, she sat on the ground next to him.

"Hey, so even if you can't graduate from the academy, and you don't get to be an investigator—even if you're not some kind of genius, that'll never change the fact that you're my brother and I'm proud of you."

He could still vividly recall the way she looked in the evening sunlight. Heather smiled bashfully.

"I mean, you've always been my—"

Theo's eyes snapped open. He shifted his gaze away from the familiar ceiling to the clock, which showed a time much earlier than when he had to get up for work. He'd apparently fallen asleep as soon as he laid down.

He sighed and rubbed his eyes. It had been a long time since he woke up from anything other than a nightmare. He got to his feet, and a throw blanket he had no memory of using dropped to the floor. Likely

Eleven's doing. Hot on the heels of yesterday, he was filled with a complicated mix of emotions as he folded up the blanket and left the room.

The instant he opened the door, he froze in place, his eyes growing wide as saucers. The garbage he'd tossed half-heartedly into a bag had been neatly separated, there was not a speck of dust in the living room, and the books on his shelves had been arranged by genre. Every nook and cranny of the kitchen had also been polished, and the scent of coffee wafted through the air.

"Good morning, Theo." Eleven emerged from the kitchen wearing an apron over her new clothes.

Theo closed his eyes and counted to ten. He was unnerved when he opened them again and saw this wasn't a hallucination. "…What is all this? What's going on?"

"I went out to get the paper, and I ran into the lady who lives three doors down." Eleven pulled out a chair. "Please sit." Aware that this whole thing had him so shaken his brain wasn't functioning properly, he obediently sat down in the chair.

Eleven continued as she returned to the kitchen. "She taught me that meals are foundational for human beings and should be cherished. Thus I am implementing that starting today."

"…So you're better with my neighbors than I am?" he asked.

"Her teenage grandchild lives far away, and she was very happy to see me. She said it was like being with her own grandchild."

Theo was wordlessly opening and closing his mouth as a plate and mug were deftly set out before him. Fragrant coffee and an energy bar: This was not the usual morning table setting.

"I prepared breakfast today with what was in the apartment. Please enjoy." She removed her apron and stopped moving when she sensed his gaze on her. Her gray eyes were so much like the surface of a lake that they reflected the morning light coming in through the window and appeared to shine brightly. "I assumed that you were a coffee drinker, but was it for guests?"

"Uh, no, I just never dreamed that a Hound would be making breakfast for me," he explained. "And it looks like you cleaned up as well."

"I finished the cleaning during the night. I will report to you the damage to appliances and cookware at a later date."

"That'd be... Mm. Thanks." He felt like this was the first time he'd ever eaten an energy bar when he wasn't pressed for time. He picked it up and took a bite. Same flavor as usual. The dry texture sapped his mouth of all moisture.

"Is there any issue with me making myself of use in this manner?" Eleven asked.

The energy bar turned to lead at the bottom of his stomach. Hounds did not sleep. After he'd half passed out last night, she had continued thinking about how she could be useful to him, and this was apparently the conclusion she had come to.

"...Theo. Is something the matter? Is there an issue with the energy bar?"

"No... Did *I* make a mistake? I mean, as the commanding officer of a Hound?" Theo asked, surprising himself.

Eleven blinked, and after a moment of silence, she replied, "The commanding officer determines operation policy. You cannot make a mistake." She blinked slowly again. "However, I will take some time to adapt. That is all."

"...Well, I guess that makes two of us. I'm not used to this, either." He told her—albeit not proudly—that he hadn't actually managed to go through the entire tome of a manual.

She merely responded with her usual quiet "Yes." But even though her face was as expressionless as ever, he saw it softening a little. Or maybe that was just him hoping. He cleared his throat, ended the conversation, and finished off his strange breakfast.

■

Nothing in particular changed at the Criminal Investigation Bureau with the assignment of the specialized automagiton Amalgam Hound. Emma and Tobias were already there when Theo stepped into the office.

"Good morning!" Emma greeted them brightly, and then her eyes lit up as she caught sight of Eleven's outfit. "That really does look good on you. I'm so glad! Well? How's it feel?"

"Good. There is no hindrance to my normal movements or mimicry. Thank you very much, Emma." Eleven was wearing only a casual jacket over the outfit she'd worn at breakfast. The entire ensemble highlighted her slender physique.

"Then I chose right." Emma nodded, satisfied. "I wanted to get both that ease of movement and something with a grown-up feel."

"It looks great." Tobias also smiled. "The military uniform suited you, too, but this is the bureau, after all! I think you've got the perfect balance here—not too casual, not too stiff. Theo, why don't you quit wearing suits all the time and try something a little more laid-back every once in a while?"

"...I don't get casual wear," Theo replied. "Suits are easier."

"Your tastes have always been behind the times," Tobias noted. "You're better off in a suit."

"What do you mean, behind the times? I'll have you know this is a standard, traditional style."

"Investigator Starling!" a loud voice called, and Theo nearly jumped in surprise. He looked back over his shoulder to see Paloma poking his head out of his office and beckoning him with one hand.

Theo hurriedly pulled some papers from his bag. "I have to give these to the captain. Sorry—would you go ahead and teach Eleven the ins and outs of work here? I fell asleep as soon as I got home last night and didn't manage to explain much of anything."

"We got this! C'mon, Eleven. We do a whole lot of paperwork here." Emma happily headed toward the shelves of documents.

Eleven glanced at Theo, and when he nodded, she quickly joined Emma. It seemed that the girl absolutely had to have his permission or an order from him.

"...I'm glad you're all right," Tobias said. Theo automatically froze. "I thought one or both of you might not make it into work today."

"...Are you being serious right now?" Theo shot him a glance.

"I'm worried. About the both of you." Tobias winked with an

affected air and laughed. "Better get in there already." He began paging through the case file.

Theo was not entirely done with the conversation, but he hurried toward the captain's office anyway before Paloma could call him again. Tobias was indeed more experienced, and he had also taught for a time at the academy while Theo was there. Still, had Theo done anything to give him cause to worry like that?

...No. Oh—right. Maybe.

Just as Eleven had seen his hatred and grief, Tobias was also a careful observer of people. As the oldest person on the team, he must have viewed the situation between Theo and Eleven as relatively precarious.

Eleven hadn't said anything about what happened the night before, maybe because Theo himself hadn't brought it up. He hadn't been lying to her when he said that he wanted to make sure he made choices that would not cause shame to his little sister and his parents. But he also couldn't deny the existence of the hatred he'd shoved into a box and locked away in the depths of his heart to that end.

When he stepped into the captain's office, Paloma put the phone call he'd just received on hold with a quick "Hang on a second" in order to prioritize dealing with Theo.

"You get a good sleep last night?" he asked as he accepted the papers Theo handed him. "You don't look so hot."

"Mm, oh…" Theo shook his head. "It's nothing, really. I've just got some things to think about."

"And what's that? Amalgams? Or is it the case?"

Theo sighed. "It might be both."

Paloma furrowed his brow, set the papers to one side, and turned back to Theo with a questioning look.

"Given that we suspect Jim Kent's involved, finding him will be our top priority," Theo explained. "But we're talking about a man who can keep out of sight of even intelligence services. I have my doubts as to whether we'll find any eyewitnesses."

"Hmm… Jim Kent." The captain nodded. "Picking up his scent is going to be a bit of work. And?"

"Um... Captain Paloma, have you ever thought about revenge?" Theo himself was aware that this was an odd question.

But Paloma simply murmured, "Revenge?" and looked out the window. Outside, the city of Delverro was rebuilding and recovering as fast as it could. "Gotta admit that I have. In a job like this, you meet all kinds of victims. Times I've hated the perpetrators, others I've been mad at the kinds of circumstances that would drive a person to kill. But I don't go seeking revenge. It's not mine to take. Even if something were to happen to my own family."

He sighed heavily and picked up a framed picture. For the first time, Theo noticed that it was a photo of three generations of a large family taken in front of a big house in the countryside.

"Listen, I believe a person's actions absolutely have consequences. And that's what God's there for."

"I didn't expect that from you, Captain," Theo said. "I thought you were more, er...cynical."

"Setting my job aside, most things'll end up working themselves out. Especially when you get to be my age." Paloma smiled slightly, set the picture down, and picked up a brand-new investigator badge and handgun. He looked up at Theo again. "What we do in the Criminal Investigation Bureau is catch the serious criminals—the ones who are too much for the local police to handle—and maintain the peace for the citizens. You know only too well just how hard it is to keep people safe. Despite that, you chose to have an Amalgam out in the field. She might be in human form, but that girl's a military weapon. People are going look to you to be responsible for her actions. You've got no problem with that?"

Theo understood immediately that this was his last chance to walk away. Even so, he took the badge and gun. "...I made the right decision as an investigator."

"So long as you're sure. Now go on, get out of here. I've got people waiting on me." With that, Paloma picked up the phone, and Theo left his office.

When he returned to his own desk, Emma had a file in one hand and was explaining something enthusiastically to Eleven, who every so often peppered the sorcerer with questions. But Eleven immediately stood up and raced over when she noticed Theo.

"Investigator badge and handgun for you, Eleven," he told her and hung the badge around her slender neck. "Don't lose them."

"I won't. Thank you very much, Theo." Eleven touched the badge curiously.

"Now you're a full-fledged investigator," Tobias said with a smile. "And this is purely out of curiosity, but do Hounds even use guns?"

"Occasionally," she replied. "It is also possible for us to transform into guns, but taking performance and power into consideration, an actual gun is more precise."

"Huh, makes sense. I suppose so." Tobias nodded to himself. "The main Amalgam weapon is an actual military issue weapon, after all."

It was a quiet morning. They spent it looking for information on Jim Kent, but they weren't able to pin down where he went after he left the murdered Bob Derry and the apartment building. They had Jacus Ghilane in custody, so they didn't need to worry about an attack on him for now, and they spent the time peacefully, with no new developments.

After lunch, they were doing paperwork as they waited for a report from the local police when the phone rang. Nearest to it, Tobias picked it up.

"'Ello! You've got Delverro Detective Ops here." The grin on his face disappeared abruptly, and he began taking notes with an urgent look. "We're on it," he told the person on the other end and hung up.

He turned to the others. "Request for backup. The goat mask gang is holed up at Pallonen Bank with a bunch of hostages. They're armed. Status of two security guards is unknown."

"Pallonen Bank?" Theo repeated, quickly grabbing his jacket.

But Emma stopped with a dubious look on her face. "Bob Derry had an account there. It's the nearest bank to that apartment building."

"Talk on the way. Let's move." Theo led his team out of the office. There were hostages; they didn't have a second to spare.

Leaving Tobias and Emma to their car, Theo sped with Eleven toward the bank in question.

"Any Jim Kent sightings there?" he asked over the wireless.

"**None,**" Emma replied. "**Reports of people with similar builds but no one got a look at any faces.**"

"**Whole thing seems odd,**" Tobias chimed in. "**Pallonen's small. If they were after cash, it'd make sense to hit a bigger bank.**"

"I'm gonna lose it if Jim Kent and the goat mask gang are connected," Theo groaned.

"Is this gang well known at the bureau?" Eleven asked, finally fastening her seat belt.

"**Right,**" Tobias said. "**Sorry, Eleven. We haven't explained yet, have we?**"

"It's not a huge case," Theo told her. "Men in goat masks have been robbing banks across the country lately. People are definitely talking about it, but it's more on the level of curious gossip. I'm not surprised you haven't heard of them in intelligence services."

"**But there's just no way they're not coordinating with one another somehow,**" Tobias interjected. "**A bunch of people randomly deciding to go rob some banks in goat masks? Not a chance. We suspect they have some common objective, but all the investigations have basically gone nowhere. Maybe the only commonality is that they all need money.**"

"...It *is* odd," Theo agreed. "Balaclavas would be easier to get a hold of and less identifiable. The masks are so conspicuous."

Sirens blaring, Theo and his team raced over to Pallonen Bank, a small facility that started out as an individual moneylender nestled among other small companies and shops. The squadron of police cars parked in front of the bank was much more imposing than the unassuming bank building. Police tape blocked off the area, but a large crowd of onlookers had already gathered. It was chaos on the ground.

Theo parked his unmarked police car a little ways from the crowd and pushed onlookers aside to make his way to the officer on the scene.

When he flashed his investigator's badge, the municipal detective gave him a frustrated look.

"Any changes?" Theo asked.

"None." The detective shook his head. "They're using the hostages as a shield, not moving, not responding to our attempts to negotiate. We want them to at least let the paramedics in, but we're getting no answer. Special forces already have the place surrounded."

"How many gang members inside?"

"We've confirmed three. Which matches the report originally called in."

Theo accepted a pair of binoculars from the detective and peered into the bank. Three men with guns had hostages held in front of them and were looking this way. They all wore the same goat masks, and the hostages not being used as shields had been herded together behind them. If they fired on the gang members, there would definitely be casualties among the hostages.

"…Shall I handle the situation? It is possible for me to go inside alone," Eleven said, her voice pitched so that only Theo could hear.

He held her back with a hand as he looked at the robbers and the hostages through the binoculars. "No one's holding a gun to the hostages, but they still seem deathly afraid. A lot of time has passed, people are injured, and the robbers' backs are turned to them. And yet no one's resisting. Which means there's some other threat in there. Could be dangerous to provoke them accidentally."

"But there doesn't seem to be a fourth robber," Tobias pointed out. "The hostages are all looking down and not moving. The robbers aren't looking at each other, either."

This was indeed strange. Theo turned the binoculars downward to take a good look at the feet of the hostages and the robbers. Polished leather shoe tips and the mark of a well-known brand. The moment he saw these, he started running.

Parting the crowd with the panicked voices of Emma and the detective behind him, Theo hurried back to his car. Eleven was already there, opening the door.

He skipped thanking her and grabbed the wireless. "We're in front of the bank! Special Forces, did you confirm any vehicles departing the location?!"

"This is the shield rush squad! We have seen no vehicles!"

"Sniper squad here. Also a negative on that one!"

"Theo! What on earth is going on?!" Tobias ran over, Emma in tow.

"They're getting away!" Theo roared at them. "What robber wears luxury-brand shoes? They switched places with the hostages!"

"That's— So then, you don't mean, the reason the hostages are afraid…?!" Emma's eyes flew open the same moment an explosion rang through the air. The shock of it easily reached Theo and his team. The bank windows shattered out into the street, and plumes of black smoke rose from the flames.

The wireless in Theo's hand jumped to life.

"Urgent! Calling all cars! Vehicle thought to contain the perpetrators has charged the line! Requesting emergency backup!"

The team grew pale and leaped into their cars. Theo yanked his seat belt across his chest and set his unmarked patrol car into motion.

"The vehicle is a black Carmen! License plate alpha, Mike, five, seven, Romeo, Yankee! Heading north on Alderta Avenue from bank rear entrance!"

"Roger! Car six-two in pursuit!" Theo slammed his foot on the accelerator.

Eleven finally put on her seat belt and said, "If they are proceeding north on Alderta Avenue, then is their destination likely Main Street?"

"No." He shook his head. "Too much traffic there at this time of day. If they're trying to get away, they'll take Yellow Hill Road." He activated the emergency light on the roof of the car and flicked the siren on as he pushed the vehicle forward. He swerved around civilian vehicles and made a sharp right immediately before the light was about to change when a cry rose up from the wireless.

"Theo! Don't play the hero!"

"Quit whining and go after them! If they get away, we've got nothing!" he yelled back.

The wireless chattered constantly with updates on the situation at the bank. He was worried about that, too, but he nevertheless urged the car to move faster.

"Theo," Eleven said, cool in contrast to Theo's panicked frustration. "Confirmation of the vehicle license plate ahead. Distance, two hundred meters. A black vehicle currently turning between a blue and a red vehicle."

"Good job," he told her, impressed. "Escape vehicle confirmed, driving west on Yellow Hill Road!"

"Roger. We'll head it off."

Theo narrowed his eyes and stared until he caught sight of the blue and red cars along with the black Carmen recklessly changing lanes. He gritted his teeth, overtook a taxi, and steadily closed in on the Carmen. He clicked his tongue. Late on a weekday afternoon, the traffic was already heavy.

"We can't let them get away from us. It'll be a disaster if they merge onto Thaley River Road."

"Thaley River Road corresponds to the streetcar route," Eleven said.

"Mm." Theo nodded. "Who knows what the damage'll be if they collide."

The black Carmen weaved left and right as it raced ahead. Maybe the driver was having trouble. Theo was about to push his foot down even further on the accelerator when Eleven cried out, "Theo! Brake!"

This was the first time she'd ever yelled. It briefly diverted his attention to the scene before his eyes—one he couldn't immediately comprehend.

A truck was charging straight at the getaway car as it veered around the other vehicles on the road. The black Carmen and the truck both swerved at the last second to avert the collision.

But now the truck was heading directly for Theo.

The truck driver's face grew pale, so close that Theo could see it drain of color.

* * *

Instinctively, Theo slammed on the brakes and yanked on the steering wheel. Eleven opened the passenger-side door, grabbed on to the car frame, and threw herself up onto the roof. The vehicle tilted hard to one side on two wheels as it squealed into a sharp turn. Truck and car slipped past each other, side mirrors scraping. Theo felt himself float for an instant. When he next took a breath, his car had plunged into a tree on the sidewalk.

The airbag deployed from the steering wheel and knocked the wind out of him. Eleven quickly undid his seat belt and dragged him out through the passenger-side door.

"Dammit," he groaned. "Thanks, Eleven."

"Not at all. Are you injured?"

"Mm... Doesn't seem like it. What about the black Carmen?"

"It remains in motion."

"Goddammit!" Theo cried and pulled out the wireless as he wrapped an arm around his sharply aching ribs. "This is car number six-two. Unable to continue pursuit due to a collision. All vehicles, maintain pursuit of the getaway and take the perpetrators into custody."

"Roger. In pursuit."

He heard a clear voice in response but not over the wireless. By the time he looked back with a gasp, it was already too late.

Using the hood of Theo's car as a springboard, Eleven leaped over the truck and onto the roof of a passing car. The slender lines of her silhouette receded as if she was in flight.

"Hey! Eleven!" he shouted. "I didn't mean *you*...!"

He left the cars that pulled up to the scene to deal with the aftermath and started running down the sidewalk on Yellow Hill Road.

■

Leaping from car roof to car roof, Eleven eyed the distance between her and the getaway vehicle. The target's movement was erratic, and if the driver noticed her approach, they would discharge their weapons, despite the risk of hitting a civilian. She quickly finished her

calculations. She couldn't allow herself to be reflected in their mirrors in order to get close enough before they counterattacked.

Eleven sent her eyes racing around the area and leaped up. She maintained visual contact with the getaway car as she jumped from streetlamp to streetlamp, and after calculating the vehicle speed and distance, she arrived at the optimal point of contact.

She jumped down with all her might. *Skreeenk!* The soles of her shoes crashed into the railing of the pedestrian bridge. She made her small physique dance up into the air at a speed greater than the acceleration of the vehicle passing directly beneath the bridge.

And then she landed on the roof of the car with the full force of her weight, the metal squealing and groaning in protest.

She heard a man speaking through the glass window and metal frame. As could be expected from the upset and confusion present in the man's voice, his steering was chaotic, and the vehicle swerved unsteadily across the road. Ignoring this, Eleven laid down on the roof and dropped her head to face the driver's side window. She beat on the glass with her investigator badge.

Three men were inside the vehicle, masks removed and wearing casual clothes.

"This is the Criminal Investigation Bureau," she told them. "Please stop the vehicle immediately."

"Wh-who the hell is that?!" one man screeched, pure terror on his face. "A monster?!"

Eleven rapped on the window again. "Driving any farther is dangerous. Please stop the—"

"Shut it! You can go to hell, monster!" the man in the passenger seat spat as he readied his gun. He fired three times without even waiting for the driver to lean back.

Eleven raised her hand and plucked the three bullets out of the air. "I repeat: Driving any farther is dangerous. Please stop the vehicle immediately."

"Wh-whoa! Whoa, whoa, whoa! Shake that thing off already, dude!" The man in the back of the car kicked the driver's seat over and over.

The driver looked back and forth between the passenger seat and Eleven as he gripped the steering wheel, his face pale. He showed no sign of stepping on the brakes.

Eleven checked the vehicle's direction of progress. At present, ninety kilometers an hour. Probability of collision with vehicles merging from side streets was 72 percent. She did some calculations using the streetcar schedule and the prescribed speed to ascertain that the likelihood of impact with the streetcar that had just departed the station was 64 percent. The distance from the vehicle to the rear was just over one hundred meters.

Eleven determined that now was her only opportunity, and ignoring the moaning of the men in the car, she stuck her face in through the window.

"I will force the vehicle to a stop," she said as she caught another two bullets fired at her. "Please brace yourselves for impact."

"What the hell is this thing even talking about?! C'mon, just shoot her already, you idiot!"

"Look, I'm shooting her! But she keeps stopping the bullets! I mean, you're seeing this, right?!"

"Ten seconds until impact. Please assume defensive positions." Eleven leaped up in the direction they were moving and landed on the road. The men screwed up their faces and screamed. She didn't give them the chance to yank the steering wheel to one side or the other. She quickly dropped down low and threw her arms out in front of her.

The screech of metal filled the air. The ground shook with the impact. The vehicle's back end bounced up with the bumper as the fulcrum. The men inside were plastered against the windshield, and the tires spun in vain until they eventually came to a stop.

After absorbing the impact to a certain degree, Eleven set the car down. The half-destroyed black Carmen shrieked as its tires hit the road, and white smoke drifted up around it. The men in the car stared with wide eyes, motionless.

Eleven forced open the locked door and looked at them. She let go of the bullets she had crushed in her hand, and they clattered to the ground.

"You will accompany me as suspects in bank robbery, bodily injury, property damage, and other criminal acts."

She could hear weeping and teeth chattering from inside the vehicle. The driver's cargo pants had very obviously changed color, and the smell of ammonia wafted up. Dazed and no longer willing to put up a fight, the three men shrank back into the car to try getting away from her. They were still sitting there, frozen, when Theo arrived on the scene.

■

The suspects aggressively demanded to be taken into custody the instant they saw Theo, and all three were placed in cells to be questioned in turn.

Theo left that to Tobias and Emma, dragged Eleven into the bureau office, and shut the door before turning around to face her. "You went too far," he told her, getting straight to the point.

Eleven blinked slowly before replying, "Is there a problem?"

"Well, obviously. Your pursuit was so terrifying that a grown man pissed his pants."

"Is that a problem?" The gray eyes looking up at him were so entirely sincere that Theo was the one who flinched. "Excluding the driver, they were in an offensive and aggressive state. They were subjects for immediate suppression. In fact, while they were in a state of terror and fear, they were obedient and docile."

She had indeed apprehended the criminals without injuring them and had avoided any damage other than the explosion at the bank. But Theo couldn't ignore the fact that she had leaped from car to streetlamp and stopped the vehicle by force.

He ran a hand over his forehead with a sigh. "All right, then, let me ask you: You couldn't have apprehended them in a safer manner? What was the point of deliberately scaring them?"

"That is our design concept. We are made in the form of people, and we do things that people could never do. People see this and lose their will to fight. I obtained results perfectly in line with that concept," she stated coolly, the look on her face matter-of-fact—although it was the same blank expression as always. She kept her eyes firmly fixed on Theo's.

He groaned despite himself. He felt like he was taking a crash course in the mind of a weapon.

Her abilities to carry out orders, to pick up on things quickly, to coolly analyze and make decisions to achieve an objective were nothing more than one function created to annihilate, suppress, and control all enemy troops. Even away from the battlefield, if it was to achieve her objective, and it was the quickest, most optimal method, then she would take that path as a weapon.

Theo frowned. He'd thought that he could make this work if he kept a certain distance from her. But he was wrong. Even if she did stand there awaiting orders from him with the innocent face of a girl. Just like he couldn't forget what had happened to his family and his home, in the end, Eleven also couldn't change what she was beneath that thin skin. It was like he was keeping a monster as a pet.

He forced himself to swallow the futile words that tried to push their way out of his throat and started again. "Eleven. This is not a war zone. Our job is to protect the citizens and bring criminals in alive. Though I suppose compared to the work you've been doing so far, it's a bit of a lukewarm job."

"Work has no temperature," she objected.

"It does," he said. "Those bank robbers were regular people until yesterday, and right up until the second they committed their crime, they were citizens to be protected. Our job is not to make them freeze in fear nor burn with murderous rage. We arrest them alive and make them pay appropriately for their crimes in order to bring peace to the victims and their families. Don't treat people like enemies. Be…close to them."

Theo exhausted his supply of words, but Eleven only blinked lazily.

Her gray eyes slowly turned away from him, and finally, she said, "No human being would feel safe with a weapon 'close to' them."

Theo was momentarily speechless.

"It is possible for me to analyze their mental state, mimic the appropriate 'closeness,' and execute this order," Eleven continued in a small voice. "But there is no empathy or sympathy in that. It is merely action. That is our limit. The idea of being close to people is not included in our design concept. Which is why...I cannot."

"You *can*," Theo told her. He set his hands on his knees and leaned forward. Eleven lifted her face and stared back at him so that he was looking directly into her gray eyes for the first time. "Listen. Have you forgotten how easily I drew my gun when you provoked me? Or who made me breakfast? And who was it that shouted out a warning and saved me from colliding with the truck? You actually look at people and respond in line with what you see. You're *already* being close to us. Am I wrong?"

Eyes clouded with ice widened faintly and then softened slightly. She lowered her lids as if to try and keep him from noticing, but eventually, she opened them again. "I will add 'be close to people' to my study items. I appreciate your continued guidance."

"Mm. You got it." Theo stood up and exhaled at length. It didn't look like he was going to be able to make this work well with a mere skimming of the manual after all. This Hound weapon was too complicated for that.

He looked toward the interrogation room, and his eyebrows slid down into a frown. The explosive at the bank had destroyed the back entrance and the front door, but because the hostages had been some distance from the bombs, none of them had been killed. However, the two security guards had been shot, and by the time the paramedics got to them, they had already breathed their last.

"...This was the first offense for the three men we arrested," Theo said. "But they were strangely skilled in their work."

"Perhaps bank robberies have been standardized?" Eleven suggested.

"Perhaps. If we take a look at the security camera footage, we might—"

A white blur abruptly raced across his field of vision, and the office door was thrown open.

◼

Tobias brought the most docile of the bank robbers into the interrogation room: the driver, a man who kept looking around nervously. The youngest of the group, he was so timid that it was hard to believe he would have had anything to do with a criminal act like this.

Tobias looked over at Emma, and after a quick conversation with just their eyes and a few hand signals, he leaned against the wall while Emma sat down opposite the man. The man jumped even at the sound of the chair scraping against the floor, looking thoroughly cowed.

"Don't be so scared," Emma said reassuringly. "I just want to talk to you…Grey."

When she said his name, the man—Grey—timidly lifted his face.

"Your partners both had guns, yet you weren't carrying anything," she continued. "But you went into the bank together, and all the people who traded places with hostages had guns, didn't they? What happened to your weapon?"

"I—I…had a model gun," he stammered. "Just me… And I couldn't use it, so…"

"Is that right?" Emma nodded understandingly. "So then I bet you were pretty surprised when the other two shot those security guards, huh?"

Grey bobbed his head up and down and ran his shackled hands through his hair. "I—I didn't know. Th-they said there'd be no k-killing. But they—!"

"So you didn't know? Who suggested doing the armed robbery, then? And who figured out the plan?"

"I—I can't. I can't tell you. The master said I can't say anything."

"The master?" Emma repeated, and Grey froze in place. Sweat

beaded on his forehead, and he shrank into himself, trembling. Before they knew it, he was rocking back and forth in his chair so violently that the chair itself creaked in protest.

He began to curse himself. "That's why I'm no good," he repeated over and over again.

Emma hurriedly got to her feet. "Grey, calm down. No one's blaming you. Today was just a day when a lot of things happened. Isn't that right? You got a real scare when you were driving away, too, huh?"

"I—I was so scared." He shuddered. "Where is she? She dropped down from the sky, she..."

"She's not here. No one here is going to hurt you. This is a safe place, Grey. You're safe here," Emma said gently as she held him back with a hand.

Grey took several deep breaths and relaxed slightly. As the squeak of the chair and the clatter of his handcuffs grew quieter, he began to meet Emma's eyes.

"...There we go, Grey," she said approvingly. "Can you tell me a little more? I mean, blowing up the rear entrance and escaping from the bank was a pretty spectacular way of doing things. Why didn't you try to sneak away?"

"...H-he likes putting on a show... N-not me. Mike..."

"So you were just the driver, hmm? Pretty amazing that you got your large vehicle license. Is that why they asked you to do it?"

"No." He shook his head. "I— People tell me I'm a great driver. So I—I said I'd do it. Myself."

"The person in the driver's seat's got to have nerves of steel, though," Emma noted. "Weren't you scared?"

"I didn't think about that. I—I figured it'd all be okay if I stepped on the gas and got us out of there..."

Tobias narrowed his eyes as he watched Grey. The man grew more eloquent and relaxed when they got to his area of specialization. Emma looked up at Tobias and nodded. She wanted to get the same thing out of Grey now that he was in this more comfortable state.

"Hey, Grey?" she said gently. "Weren't you scared to rob a bank?

And you weren't expecting anyone to be killed. That had to have been a surprise."

"...I—I don't think it was scary," he insisted. "I decided that...I wouldn't. I mean, it was necessary..."

"Necessary?" She furrowed her brow slightly. "What would you have to muster up your courage like that for? Because the master said so?"

"...Yes. The master...is welcoming an angel. So I-I'm not scared. I-I'm not!" Grey's eyes flew open abruptly, and he leaped to his feet, kicking the chair back.

Tobias and Emma immediately drew their guns.

Grey clenched his hands into fists and started shaking all over. "This is a h-h-holy war! Everything, wealth—give it all back to God! Everything is...m-meaningless in the face of paradise! O-our paradise will be...the foundation to welcome th-the angel! Glory to Roremclad!"

The moment he shouted this, a mouth shot up from inside his own throat and swallowed his head. A jet of blood dyed everything red from the walls up to the ceiling.

Tobias gaped, unable to believe what was happening before his very eyes.

Crack. Krrnk. Grey's head was chewed to pieces, becoming a shapeless mess on top of his neck. Taking its place was a silver substance shining with a dull luster.

The irregularly shaped something stretched up from Grey's neck with a slithering sound, and silver scales began to cover it until eventually it took on the form of a snake looking down on Tobias and Emma. Mechanical red eyes glared at them.

"Grey...?" Emma said, her face drained of all color. "What the hell just happened...?"

Grey's body remained motionless; only the snake lunged forward. Emma reflexively pulled the trigger of her gun, but the snake's charge didn't stop. The empty darkness of its gaping maw closed in.

Tobias immediately threw out his left arm to protect Emma, but then a slender arm slammed into the snake's mouth.

Eleven stood in front of them, her arm thrust out at the grotesque snake.

The snake wriggled and squirmed in irritation as she held a hand over its jaw. But Eleven did not retreat a single step, instead clutching the snake more tightly. Its jaw creaked.

"I am in command. Hear me, fear me, bow down before me. Stand down in terror of me," she announced, almost terrifyingly quiet, her voice sounding like peace itself as a sound.

But the snake did not flinch. Instead, it produced another head from Grey's neck with a shivering noise.

Despite the fact that the air was still, Eleven's hair fanned out around her. Her gray eyes burned red.

"Stand down," she repeated.

The snake's two heads let out a strange cry, and all four of its eyes shone red. The mechanical beast showed no sign of giving up.

But Eleven dug into its jaw even further, and one of the snake's heads rotted away. The remaining head shrieked and rose to attack just as a magical bullet shot through it. The creature yelped and flinched, white smoke seeping out from between its scales, until it went limp.

Eleven immediately pressed closer and pierced Grey's throat with the knife of her right hand. The blade's fine, sharp tip stabbed into a red jewel. When the gem shattered, the silver snake turned a dark ashen color, dropped back against the neck of the collapsed Grey, and fell quiet.

Tobias exhaled the breath he didn't know he'd been holding and finally looked back.

Breathing over his shoulder, Theo lowered his arts rejector and sighed heavily. "No one's hurt?"

"No." Tobias shook his head. "Thanks, Theo. You too, Eleven. Can't believe you got in here so fast."

Eleven looked up from where she was kneeling next to Grey. Her eyes had already returned to their usual gray. "Of course," she replied quietly.

"...I'll call Forensics. You three wait here." Theo slung the gun over his shoulder and left the interrogation room.

Eleven watched him go and then abruptly stood up and raced over to Emma. "Emma, what's the matter? Are you ill?"

Tobias turned around to find Emma leaning against the wall, pressing a hand to her chest, her face white as a sheet. Eleven touched her arm with a hesitant hand, and Emma finally came back to her senses.

"Sorry. I'm just a little shaken up," she said weakly. "I think it was actually Grey himself when we were talking. But then he was eaten from his own throat...and that Amalgam appeared. That was... Was it really just a fake? Or was it an Amalgam that took human shape like a Hound?"

"Unlike us, that was a human body from the neck down," Eleven told her. "You were indeed speaking with the man himself, Emma. The Amalgam likely broke through his body and came to the outside at some kind of signal."

"Makes sense..." Emma nodded to herself. "Even this close up, I couldn't tell. They ought to revoke my sorcerer's license."

"No, you are not to blame, Emma," Eleven said. "I couldn't detect it, either, until immediately before the change."

"H-hang on just a minute here," Tobias hurriedly interjected. "Until Grey had his head bitten off, he was human to you, Eleven? You couldn't detect an Amalgam...one of you. Is that what you're saying?"

"My hypothesis is that the Amalgam was in a dormant state until it began to act," she replied. "Therefore, I also would not be able to detect it."

"In other words, an Amalgam was lying in wait in his throat... And it just *appeared*...?" Emma muttered, dazed, and covered her mouth. "Is that even possible? I mean, an Amalgam... We're talking automagitons. It's hard to make one the size of Eleven, and yet this thing was miniaturized to the point where it could hide *inside* a human body?"

Tobias pressed a hand to his forehead. He really did feel like he was losing his mind.

■

"And so," Theo said with a frown when the four of them were assembled in the office, "with no outward changes, the moment he cried, 'Glory to Roremclad,' the Amalgam materialized from inside his body, and Grey died. Is that about right?"

"If we're talking about what we saw, yes," Emma replied. "Maybe there was some kind of trigger in his throat."

"If there was a mechanism in his physical body, Rocky'll find it," Theo said. "In the autopsy."

Emma didn't reply, seemingly lost in thought. Tobias opened his notebook.

"At the very least," he began, "this means Grey's not the ringleader. For one, he had no interest in the crime. But he had a guide, this 'master,' and he told himself the bank robbery was necessary. Given that he was using words like *holy war* and *paradise*, religion's a part of this just as we'd initially wondered. Although we don't know if this 'Roremclad' is the name of a religion or the god he believed in."

"…A new religion? Or maybe a cult. I don't like the sound of that." Theo sighed. What kind of paradise awaited a religious group that allowed drugs, murder, and bank robbery? They couldn't let their guard down. Whatever this cult was, it might take even more radical action. "We should be careful questioning the other two."

"True." Tobias nodded. "Grey was so meek, I never dreamed he'd react that strongly."

They both fell into thought, and Emma abruptly spoke up.

"He helped with the bank robbery, but he didn't think his partners would kill the security guards. I have a hard time believing he was just pretending to be so shook up. I don't think he would have been able to accept a suicidal act, no matter how this 'master' might have sweet-talked him."

"…So are our bank robbers unaware of whatever it is that's set up inside them? When it's producing that teensy Amalgam?" Tobias scowled. "This is no joke."

Theo groaned and looked back at Eleven. "How does it look to you as the Hound who dispatched the Amalgam?"

"My assessment is that it is an extremely early model compared with the Amalgams introduced in the war." Eleven picked up a red fragment in an evidence bag: the core that she had destroyed. "This is indeed an Amalgam core. My sensors—what you would call your sense of smell—determined this. However, a core this fragile is an object from the research stage and was not introduced into actual battle."

"...It *is* pretty small, hmm?" Emma said. "So you're saying the Amalgams used on the battlefield are something different."

"Yes," Eleven agreed briefly. "In addition, this Amalgam did not obey a signal from a Hound. In general, the Hound has command authority as the highest-ranked individual among the Amalgams. This is for security purposes. But this Amalgam was different. We were produced through different means. It prioritizes something other than the Hound."

"Is the ranking of an individual that important for automagitons?" Theo asked, and Emma nodded firmly.

"The commanding officer's got top priority, but they're not always in a position to give instructions, y'know?" she said. "So a lot of automagitons have another chain of command set in advance. The norm for soldiers is the pyramid command structure, and it's the same for Amalgams. There always has to be a leader."

"Ohhh." Theo grew pensive. "So instead of a herd of animals, it's more like, you know, the relationship between the sheep and the sheepdog and the shepherd? The sheep are led by the sheepdog, and the dog acts on human orders."

"I think that's a pretty apt comparison," Emma replied. "But it's weird. The fake Amalgams parasitizing the fighters at the fight club obeyed Eleven's orders, right? I guess that means they were different specimens?"

"That is the issue at hand." Eleven blinked and looked down at the core. "This is nothing more than conjecture since we have no sample other than the Amalgams generated by the pills. Could it be that the experiment saw success and the result was this concealed Amalgam?"

"The military and R&D are gonna be up in arms about the origin of that core..." Tobias cradled his head in his hands.

An Amalgam's core was the rare mineral fortunite. Everything about it, from excavation to use, was overseen by the military. What if the mineral was being diverted to outside parties? What if there was a traitor within the military? Theo's stomach hurt at the mere thought of it, and he screwed up his face into a deep scowl.

"...We'll contact R&D," he said. "But at present, all we can do is gather what information we have. Either way, until the results of the autopsy are back, our only option is to talk to the other two suspects..."

"I'll go," Tobias offered. "But I want Eleven to come with me."

Eleven blinked slowly and looked up at Theo, seeking his permission. When he nodded, she quietly came to stand beside Tobias.

"...Thanks, Eleven." He smiled at her. "We don't know the exact mechanism yet, but I think it probably doesn't activate until they say the whole phrase 'Glory to Roremclad.' I know you can shut them up before they finish saying it. Can I count on you?"

"That is not a problem. I will deal with it promptly."

"I'd expect nothing less. All right, then, let's get going. We're absolutely going to wring some leads out of those two chuckleheads." The smile was already gone from Tobias's face as he turned on his heel.

"Don't go out on any limbs, though," Theo said with a sigh. "Emma, let's go hear what Ghilane has to say. Given the situation, he's our only material witness. He might know something."

"Roger that," she replied. "I want to pin down Jim Kent sooner rather than later. The way things are, who knows how much damage we're looking at...?"

They had Ghilane brought from holding to an interrogation room. He sat down, shackles clanking, and leaned forward toward Theo and Emma.

"Did you find out who killed Bob?" he asked.

"We're currently looking for him, but we need your help," Theo told him. "Did Bob Derry ever mention the word *Roremclad*?"

"Mm." Ghilane nodded, remembering. "That's the hospital, yeah? The place where Bob had his synth surgery."

"...Was there any change in Bob after he went to this hospital?" Theo asked, and Ghilane frowned.

"I tried not to pay too much attention to it," he said slowly. "Dunno if it's 'cause he got his synth and felt like he had some breathing room or what. But he started dealing a whole lot more and saying all this weird stuff. That's when I really got to worrying. Stupid shit like 'This city's gonna be a battleground, so you gotta get out.' Or 'The guys at the fight club are failures spurned by God.' But he really meant it. That's why he was hustling to try and get back to his hometown quick."

With synthetic internal organs, patients had to have regular check-ups at the hospital for a certain period of time for observation. Ghilane recounted to the investigators what Derry had told him while he was an outpatient. But he didn't know where the hospital was.

After talking with Ghilane for a while, they thanked him and left. Theo went through what they'd learned, looking at his notebook.

"...Bob Derry was rejected for surgery at the hospital he'd intended to go to. He was arguing with someone at the synthetics shop when he met a man who said he was a doctor. Derry then had the surgery at Roremclad and was an outpatient there. The synthetics he got were illegal from an unauthorized dealer, so no normal hospital would want to court the risk of treating him. This Roremclad place went out of their way to save him and made him a believer. Although it does look like Derry did try to escape."

"Then these are the kinds of patients Roremclad needed...?" Emma stared at the investigation documents with a serious look on her face. "So that no matter how guilty they might end up feeling, they can't go to the police? Or because they need the internal synthetics? They use a general anesthetic for those surgeries, right? Do they pull some kind of trick while the patient's under?"

"...We'd best check for synthetics in our bank robbers, too." Theo sent Tobias a quick message. After seeing the brief reply Roger, he shoved his cell phone into his pocket. "Tobias can look for clues about Roremclad. We're going after Jim Kent. Bob Derry was first marked by him, yes?"

"Mm-hmm," Emma told him. "Maybe someone saw the deal with Kent."

"Right." Theo nodded and hurried off with Emma in tow.

■

After sending a quick reply to Theo's message, Tobias sat down in front of the gang still whining about their innocence across from Eleven. Voices that cried out in surprise in the holding cell instantly fell silent, and the two men, Mike and Butch, shifted awkwardly where they sat on the bench.

"Well, to be honest, you know, I don't particularly care whether you did it or not," Tobias told them. "I know you've got this marvelous master guiding you, and I think your organization's message is very noble."

"…So then why are we having this conversation here?" one of the men—Butch—asked suspiciously.

"This is the only place we can talk." Tobias smiled at him. "The interrogation rooms are always recording video and sound, after all."

The two men looked at each other.

"I was really moved, too, by the idea of continental unification," Tobias continued. "From what I could see with Grey, it seems pretty difficult to learn directly from the master. So I figured you guys could help me out." He noticed the men's eyes straying to Eleven. "Oh, you don't have to worry about her. She's only loyal to her duty. Diligent, a good kid. She's not a threat to you."

"…This reeks," Mike spat.

"Well, I can't really help that, can I? I mean, I work for the Criminal Investigation Bureau, and here I am trying to join your group. I'm deeply impressed by the Roremclad ideals, but I'm under tight watch. So it's a real pleasure to meet some kindred spirits in this way."

Butch shot a glance at Mike. It seemed that Mike was higher up the food chain. Tobias turned toward him, his smile widening.

"Look, this whole bank robbery—you needed to do it for the holy war, right?" he said. "Real brave stuff."

"You got that outta Grey!" Mike snarled. "He's a wimp, that one. A total coward!"

"Now, now." Tobias held up his hands in protest and smiled amiably. "He was surprisingly faithful to Roremclad. And if he'd told me everything, well, I wouldn't have had to come all the way down here, would I?"

"See, Mike?" Butch said reassuringly.

Mike sighed. "Whaddaya wanna know?"

"Right." Tobias paused thoughtfully. "Maybe how you two encountered Roremclad. They don't do public-facing work, right? I haven't been able to make direct contact myself, in fact. So how'd you find them?"

"…They came to us as a charity. We owe 'em our lives," Mike replied quietly.

Butch nodded and picked up where Mike left off. "The three of us used to work in this factory. But the place shut down all of a sudden, and we were tossed out on our asses. That factory did a real number on our throats and lungs… No way we were gonna find new jobs. We were stuck."

"…Your throats and lungs?" Tobias repeated. "From what I can tell listening to you speak, though, you sound perfectly healthy."

Butch shrugged while Mike answered, fed up.

"Was a real shithole. We were making paint and the guts for fusion bullets, but they were stingy SOBs when it came to equipment. They just vented all the dust and exhaust fumes, showered us in the stuff. Our throats bled; we used to cough our way through the workday—some guys even coughed 'emselves to death."

"We were lucky, y'know? 'Cause we got out of that factory before we died. But while we were living on the streets, one of the guys who survived it all with us, he died," Butch recounted, his eyes misting over.

"That's when the master and them from Roremclad found us. They got us a doctor, gave us food, new clothes. On top of that, when we told the master about our situation, he offered to get us synthetics for our throats and lungs. Said it wasn't our fault."

Mike turned his face away and snorted. "...Sure, I was suspicious at first. I mean, it was too good to be true, y'know? But after the operation, I really did feel better. So we decided we'd do whatever it took to thank the master. If he came calling, we'd answer."

Tobias nodded. It was all coming together. No wonder even the obviously timid and weak Grey would feel compelled to rob a bank.

"So that's how the robbery came about?" Tobias asked.

"The master said it was a good shot across the bow in the holy war," Butch said. "So we were happy to help."

"Damn straight!" Mike agreed. "It was the best frickin' job. Our gracious Roremclad."

"Yeah? Maybe I could get you to take a look at this picture, then." Tobias opened his case file and showed them a photograph. The smiles on their faces froze in place. They stared at Grey with his head eaten, rigid in death, hands clutching at his chest.

"...Hey. The hell is this?" Butch whispered. "Grey... Grey is..."

"Was it you?! Did this monster here kill Grey?! Goddammit!" Mike leaped to his feet, enraged, but Eleven checked him with one hand and forced him to sit back down.

Butch shuddered as he looked anywhere but at the picture of Grey. He inhaled sharply. "Dear Lord, angels, please save me! Glory to Rorem—"

His shriek of despair was abruptly cut off, leaving only the creaking of vertebrae rubbing together.

Eleven squeezed Butch's neck with one hand and covered Mike's mouth with the other as she pressed him up against the wall.

Tobias hadn't even seen her move.

"...Sir. Please remain quiet. If you speak any further, you will die,"

Eleven announced softly, holding both men in place with about the same effort of holding back a curtain.

Butch turned beet red and slapped at Eleven's arm as he nodded repeatedly. The instant she released him, he doubled over, coughing violently. Mike slid to the floor, his back against the wall and his face drained of all color.

Tobias thanked Eleven and returned to the photos in his folder. "'Glory to Roremclad,' those were Grey's last words. The instant he spoke them, a monster leaped out of his throat and ate his head, killing him."

Butch trembled while Mike shook his head lifelessly. "You're lying. The master… He said the angels would save us if we were ever in real trouble…"

"Hell no… I dunno a thing about that…," Butch moaned. "I mean, that's a monster…"

"I can show you the video," Tobias told them. "I want you two to see Grey's last moments."

Both of them were shaking, their faces white as sheets, but Eleven yanked their arms mercilessly and dragged them into the interrogation room.

She really is a strong one, Tobias thought as he walked behind them with a crooked grin.

When he showed them the video, Mike dropped to his knees and started praying, and Butch vomited into the bag that Eleven had brought.

Tobias crouched down beside Mike and handed him a notepad and a pen. "Tell me the names of your comrades and the place where you had the surgery. The same mechanism is set up inside of them, too."

Now drained of all vitality, Mike took the pen and notepad and started writing with a shaky hand.

■

Theo and Emma talked to one dealer after another until one of them cocked his head to the side.

"Ah, Bob Derry? He started doing real well all of a sudden," he said. "So this woman kept pestering him to lend her some money."

"Do you know what their relationship was?" Theo asked.

"Business associates. Before she got busted, she used to pick up some guy, get him blind drunk, make him do drugs, and then when he was really hurting for them, she'd turn him out and get him selling. That was her way. Marie or Mary or something, I forget her name. But I know where she lives. Above the bar."

Theo and Emma thanked the man and headed toward the bar in question. The place was locked up tight with only a handwritten sign on the door that read CLOSED INDEFINITELY.

With no other option, Theo turned toward the second floor. Of the three apartments up there, one door had mail spilling out of the postal slot: a mountain of dunning notices all addressed to Molly Young.

"...Seems she was in a tight spot financially," he remarked.

"It's no wonder she'd be hitting up old acquaintances." Emma smiled uncomfortably and pressed the buzzer. She rang it several times, but there was no answer.

"Oh my. Officers?" a voice called out to them.

When they turned around in surprise, an elderly woman with a cane was walking toward them.

"Are you looking to speak with the young lady who lives there?" she asked.

"...I'm sorry," Theo said. "May I ask who you are?"

"I live next door. Is she causing trouble again? She *is* a handful, hmm?" The elderly woman sighed as though at her wits' end, perhaps only too accustomed to police visits.

"Ms. Young doesn't appear to be home," Emma said. "Excuse me for asking, but you wouldn't happen to know where she went, would you?"

"Mmm." The woman nodded slowly. "I suppose it was yesterday? She was dressed to the nines. Just lovely! I asked where she was going, and she told me her big sister was getting married. Said they were having a party at her sister's shop, closed to the public. In such high spirits, she was! Grinning ear to ear. I had to smile myself."

"Is that right?" Emma smiled along with her. "Do you know the name of the shop?"

"Kate's Cakes, a little bakery. Lovely place, truly lovely."

"We appreciate your assistance. We'll go and take a look, then." Theo jotted down the name of the shop and left the apartment building, the elderly woman watching them go. He turned to Emma and said, "Do you think the sisters are close?"

"No, not a chance." Emma shook her head. "Taking her MO into consideration, the only thing likely on her mind was picking up a customer at the wedding... Although I hope nothing actually happened to her."

They headed toward the shop in question, and the situation there surpassed their worst fears.

A sign out front said PRIVATE PARTY along with a welcome board. The store itself didn't appear to be locked. It hadn't been cleaned since the wedding party.

Theo and Emma drew their guns and cautiously entered the premises.

Showy decorations, all flowers and ribbons. Dolls modeled after the bride and groom. Music playing endlessly. A broken showcase, overturned chairs and tables, tablecloths stained red.

And a total of nine men and women flat on their backs, covered in blood.

While Emma was identifying the dead, Theo advanced into the kitchen, weapon still drawn. All he found, however, was an open refrigerator door. But there was blood streaked along the walls and floor toward the back door. He moved forward, careful not to step in any of it, and exited the shop. From what he could see, the blood trail ended at an open manhole.

He clicked his tongue and called Forensics before going back inside where Emma was looking at a piece of paper on the head table.

Noticing Theo, she flapped the page at him. "There was a program. Looks like the party was last night."

"So the old woman was right," he said. "But this is just…"

The bride and groom lay on the floor next to each other, holding hands, eyes closed. Their stomachs were ripped open, and their beautiful outfits were dyed red.

The party attendees also bore grievous injuries to their stomachs. But two of the bodies were different. One was a man, the other a woman. Both had been largely gnawed at from the neck down, nothing but skin and bones left. As if a herd of animals had descended upon them.

While waiting for Forensics to arrive, Theo looked around the inside of the shop, and the message board caught his eye. The party attendees had written little notes on it to the couple starting their new life together. There were the usual words of celebration, but the name of a support group for people who used synthetic organs also made a frequent appearance. This seemed to be where the couple had met.

"…Bob Derry had that gaping hole in his stomach, and his kidneys were synthetics," Theo noted.

From what he could tell looking at the messages, seven of the attendees had been support group members. The same as the number of corpses with holes in their stomachs. He had a hard time believing this was a coincidence. He left the arriving Forensics team to Emma and called Rocky.

■

When Tobias arrived at the location he'd gotten from Mike and Butch, he looked up at the building with a grave expression. "Eleven. You sure this is it? Really?"

"Yes." She nodded. "There's no mistake. Although it doesn't appear to be a facility for medical treatment."

Most of the buildings around them were abandoned factories. They stepped inside this one through the open shutters, but it was just a large, empty space.

"...True, nobody's likely to pay any mind if you just cart surgery equipment into an empty factory," Tobias said.

"Outside of machinery, what is necessary to embed synthetics?" Eleven asked.

"Basically the same as what you'd have for any general surgery. Except that the equipment and the storage case used when implanting a synthetic are specially made. And I guess electrical consumption jumps way up during surgery. Taking that into consideration, the contracted ampere-hours of a factory might be just right."

There was nothing left in the factory, so left with no other choice, Tobias went around to question the neighboring residents. He asked about the factory during the period when Mike and the others had their surgeries, but the residents had been told that renovations were being done after the factory shutdown, so they hadn't thought anything of the noise or movement of materials in and out. They couldn't remember any specifics from that period.

"So this was a bust." He sighed. "Can't get a hold of Mike's or Butch's friends, either. Dead end."

"Haven't we gained something simply from learning that they were moved for their surgeries to a building with a large amount of contracted electricity rather than a hospital?" Eleven asked. "It's very clear that these surgeries were carried out illegally."

"I suppose so. Let's take this as a win, then," Tobias said, picking himself back up, but then he frowned when he looked at the message that arrived from Emma.

■

Seven of the nine bodies they'd discovered at Kate's Cakes that had suffered grievous injury to their abdomens had used internal organ synthetics, albeit for different organs. The two who had been eaten entirely were the groom's older brother and Molly; unlike the others, they had not used synthetics.

According to the autopsy, no drugs or anything similar had been detected, and the wounds of the seven synthetics users were very similar to Bob Derry's. But they were completely baffled by the wounds on the groom's older brother and Molly. As before, no traces of saliva were detected. When they examined the contents of their stomachs, they found that everyone except the older brother and Molly had drunk the same sparkling wine. An inquiry revealed that it had been Molly who bought the wine.

Eleven bodies deemed to have been killed by Amalgams. Just looking at them covered and lined up in front of him, Theo felt a chill run down his spine.

Rocky started speaking, a tired look on his face. "The silver lining here is that more bodies mean more discoveries."

When Theo turned toward him, he removed the covers from the bodies of Bob Derry and the groom.

"...The size and shape of the wound perfectly match the damaged synthetic," Rocky said.

"First I'm hearing of a damaged synthetic," Tobias commented. The synthetic shown enlarged on the screen was indeed shattered. "Different structure from my own. I guess it's gotta be a lot tougher to replace an organ."

"Mm, naturally." Rocky nodded. "Synths intended for external wear prioritize a lightweight construction, which is in turn less durable, with the assumption of replacement. But the internal-organ types are basically never replaced. The power source is a mechanism in the person's blood. An organ's gonna end up constantly cycling blood, after all."

"...But then why are they broken?" Emma cocked her head to one side, curious. "Because they're in a place where they could be broken?"

Rocky crossed his arms as he leaned back against the wall. "Because after the vic's stomach was ripped open, an Amalgam was born."

"...Your evidence?"

"Pills, capsules, the cooperation of the young lady who's an

Amalgam herself. And thanks to these folks who died after being eaten by an Amalgam from the inside, I've no shortage of materials to work from," Rocky said and looked over at a body a ways off. The covering over the head area of that corpse sank to the floor. The name tag that read Grey seemed pointless.

"The pills used at the fight club," Rocky continued. "We talked about how they fused with the blood, yeah? Well, I discovered that right before Grey died, all the blood in his body was sucked up by his head. There's a real strong connection between the Amalgam and the person's blood. The issue is what they're using the blood for. So I had the young lady take a look for me."

He pulled up four images.

"These are all of her issuing an operation order. The left is the core—the pill and the blood fused. In the center, we've got the core recovered from Grey. And then these two on the right are of my blood added to a core."

"Only the core that was given blood is moving... Is it making the cells multiply?" Emma asked, looking disturbed.

Eleven blinked slowly. "The core recovered from the fighter and the core recovered from the bank robbery have ceased functioning. But they recovered function temporarily as a result of introducing human blood, and I was able to confirm that they caused the cells to multiply up to a certain fixed number. The cores are crude with low function. However..."

She paused uncharacteristically, and Theo furrowed his brow.

"It's bad enough that they can be restored as Amalgams," he said. "Is there something more?"

"...The Amalgams' greatest strengths are the fact that we do not require supplies or rest along with our powerful regenerative ability. But even without those functions, if we receive nourishment, even a core of this level can operate as a threatening weapon."

"Well, to put it another way," Rocky said, a grim look on his face. "When you mix a single Amalgam cell, a crude core, and human blood, it indiscriminately devours whatever's around it to give rise to a growing monster. Not to mention we don't know the total number at present."

Emma swallowed hard. "Can automagitons go that far? I wonder if R&D's got a handle on this."

"Most likely, they discarded this model because it needs supplies," Tobias replied. "So why all the fuss about it on the outside now after all this time? This must've upset R&D—wherever it leaked out, whatever superhuman dug it up. But why are the synthetics broken?"

Rocky groaned. "Indeed, spot on. The Amalgam parasitizing the fighters at the club—it was equipped with a blood circulation function. To keep the host alive, mm? I discovered that this circulation references the internal organ synth. And the issue with the internal synth—well, it's got a huge output."

"...I suppose that's only natural given that it's taking the place of an organ," Theo commented.

"It makes use of that, yeah," Rocky told them. "Inside the human body, the Amalgam can't grow too large. The young lady and I discussed it, and our hypothesis is that it stands by in the abdomen or the throat—the places where it's easiest to break through—usurps the power generation structure of the internal synthetic, and makes its way out of the body. The synths of all our victims were drained of power."

Theo, Tobias, and Emma were at a loss for words in the face of this impossible information.

"Hang on a second." Emma's visage grew pale. "You didn't find any capsules in the bodies from the cake shop, right? So you're saying it's advanced into a form so small that human beings wouldn't notice it and could be forced to ingest it?"

"More or less," Rocky replied. "We recovered some wine from the shards of glass, and we're currently conducting a detailed analysis."

In the silence that fell over the morgue, Eleven abruptly turned toward Theo. "The situation is a fight against time. We should ask the experts in R&D for their opinions."

"Mm." Theo frowned and then lifted his head. "Oh... It doesn't matter if it's confidential information. As long as we have you, we can make it work, yeah?"

"Yes," Eleven agreed. "The knowledge that Emma and I possess with regard to Amalgam incidents is obviously insufficient. I thought it would be a good idea to send R&D the bodies and the information from the investigation and ask the opinions of the doctors there."

"You and I will go, then, Eleven?" Theo asked. "Tobias and... Emma, what's wrong?"

Emma lifted her face with a gasp, yanked out of her thoughts. "Something Rocky said is bugging me. If the Amalgams went after prey, what would they eat? Organic material? Are they any requirements?"

"It is possible to feed on anything as long as it is not a substance that would dissolve the physical body," Eleven replied concisely.

"I see." Emma scribbled something down. "If the Amalgams are preying 'indiscriminately,' like Rocky said, then I just wondered if there'd be any harm we're not picking up on. Maybe we can find some reports of property damage or something."

"...Makes sense." Theo nodded. "It could be that they've been on the move for a while, and there's only the fuss now because of the dead bodies."

"It's nothing more than a guess at this point," Emma said. "I'll try tapping some friends and see if I can pick up on anything. What about you, Tobias?"

"Right." He thought for a second and then waved his notebook lightly. "Maybe I'll follow the synthetics thread. Roremclad was operating without a license. I'll ask narcotics if they can chase down the trail of drugs being sold to places that aren't hospitals and the like. And I want to check into the shop where Bob Derry got his synthetics."

"True, they were fighting," Theo said, remembering what Ghilane had told them. "So a shop selling illegal synthetics?"

Tobias nodded. "You need a license to sell synthetics. The fact that an unauthorized shop had any in stock means there's an engineer selling to places directly without going through the administrative authority. Roremclad is probably tied up with this engineer. I think they saw that Bob Derry would be rejected for surgery and they set up shop."

"That would make sense." Theo paused thoughtfully. "It's late. We'll call it quits for today and get back to the investigation tomorrow when we're fresh. I'll share information on the bodies with the night shift and get them to call us if there's anything."

"Sounds good. Okay, then. Nice work today, gang. You too, Rocky," Tobias said amiably.

Rocky sighed and rolled his shoulders. "Haven't seen this many bodies outside of war or natural disaster. Quite the thing."

"Sure is...," Theo said. "I'd really prefer not to see any more of them."

Utterly exhausted, he got into his car. *Home*, he thought and rested his head on the steering wheel.

"...Eleven. Do you remember what food there is at home?"

"There are energy bars, jelly beverages, and crackers," she told him. "In addition to several bottles of alcohol and mineral water."

"...Of course." He groaned. "I guess it's the grocery store before home. How much can you carry?"

"If you have no preference with regard to method of carrying, it is normally possible for me to transport up to the weight of a passenger vehicle."

Theo let slip a hollow laugh, and he started the car. She really was so much like a monster.

■

Eleven got out of the car and picked up the weighty bags one after another. She had no issue carrying them, but with her current physique, they blocked her field of view.

"Oh boy," Theo murmured as he also got out of the car. "This was maybe a bit too much even just to stock up. I mean, I'm the only one doing any eating or drinking."

"This is the ideal amount to purchase for shopping once every two weeks, and it is less than the average meal size for an adult male," Eleven told him.

"That so?" He moved to take some bags from her. "Oh, right. Can you eat things?"

"It is possible," Eleven replied concisely. "I merely have no need to."

"Okay, then. Here. A snack. The store gave us a free sample." He popped a candy on a stick into her mouth.

She rolled her tongue around it and detected an artificial sweet flavor and a fragrance. She determined the flavor to be lemon. "You also require sugar, Theo."

"The clerk gave it to 'the young lady,' so you eat it." His cell phone beeped a new message at him. "Sorry. You go on ahead."

Eleven followed his instruction and headed from the parking lot to the front entrance. It was the first time she'd been given food as remuneration, and she crunched and chewed up the non-dissolving candy. Even if eating was not required, she did at least know how to do it.

Normally, when she absorbed materials, she did not break them up into small pieces or scrutinize their structure. But she deliberately spent time on the digestion of this item, despite the fact that she could absorb it in an instant. Would people call this "valuing"?

While she was thinking, the small elevator arrived, and Eleven swallowed the stick and stepped inside. She pressed the floor button with her elbow just as a man came running up.

"Wait!"

He pushed his way in just as the door was on the verge of closing, told her his floor, and turned a smile on her, his shoulders heaving. She would have categorized it as a smile with the objective of friendliness rather than an insincere one for politeness' sake.

"Sorry. Thanks," he said, panting. "Haven't seen you before. You live here?"

"Yes. I moved here recently."

"You did? Well, nice to meet you. I'm Jamie."

"It's a pleasure to make your acquaintance," Eleven replied.

The man was somewhere in his late teens or early twenties. From his musculature, he must have been more of a track-and-field person than a martial artist. She judged him to be not a danger and turned to face the elevator door.

"Ah, um," the man said from where he stood beside her. "Mind sharing your name?"

"It's Eleven. Excuse me." The doors opened as she stated her name, and she got out on her destination floor.

But the man held the door and called out to her, "So, uh!"

When Eleven looked back, his cheeks were flushed and his pupils wide. These indicated his "interest" and "good will" toward her.

"It's just, you're so pretty, y'know?" he said. "I was curious what kind of name you'd have. Your hair sparkles like stars, and, um, I think you look like an angel. So, uh… I don't mean that in a weird way, sorry."

"No. There is no issue," she told him. "Don't concern yourself."

"Oh," he said. "Yeah? Okay, as long as you're good, then. G'night, Eleven."

"Good night," she replied briefly, and the man finally let the elevator door close to ascend to the higher floors. Eleven pondered this encounter as she returned to Theo's apartment, not understanding the man's intentions.

"My goodness, Elena!" The woman who lived three doors down caught sight of Eleven and called out to her. There was "worry" on her face. "Aren't you loaded down! You all right? Can you even see where you're going?"

"My name is Eleven, ma'am. I'm very good at carrying things. There is no issue."

"My, is that right?" The woman looked her up and down. "So you're a strong one, hmm? I'm sorry to have stopped you, then."

"It's fine. Have a nice evening."

The woman stepped forward with her cane and departed for her daily stroll. Walking quietly beside her was the large dog who guarded her. Both of them waiting on their masters, Eleven exchanged a greeting with the woman's knight with her eyes and returned to the apartment.

At mealtime, she asked Theo about Jamie, but he didn't know him.

"How shall I deal with him in the future?"

"You can just make small talk as long as he's not a danger," Theo told her. "You're the stronger one, and if push comes to shove, just make him understand that without actually hurting him… You're attractive. This sort of thing's bound to happen." He brought a spoonful of tomato soup to his mouth. On his face were "loneliness" and "longing."

Eleven replied with a simple "Okay." She could not ask him if this was about his little sister.

CONFIDENTIAL

Chapter 4
Loveless Monster

AMALGAM HOUND
Criminal Investigation Bureau:
Special Investigation Unit

When Eleven ended the call, she returned the cell phone to Theo. "The doctor shares our sense of urgency," she said. "I may enter the laboratory with one guest. No time was specified, so we can prioritize the investigation."

"Great. That's good news. Emma's apparently learned something, too, so we'll head to the office first." Theo set his dishes in the sink and left the house in a hurry.

There was someone already in the elevator when it arrived. A man around college age, he lit up with a smile when he saw Eleven.

"Morning, Eve."

"Good morning. It's Eleven."

Theo frowned at how smoothly the man ignored him, then proceeded to place himself between the man and Eleven. This was no doubt the "Jamie" Eleven had told him about.

Jamie paid Theo no mind. "Is 'Eve' too simple?" he asked Eleven. "I couldn't think of a nickname for *Eleven*... Something like Ellie or Elena or Levvie might be more chic. Maybe you'd like one of those better?"

"I have no preferences with regards to nicknames," she told him. "Please feel free to call me what you wish."

"Oh! Sure! Then I'll call you Eve, okay?"

Eleven's response was not in fact friendly, but Jamie seemed undaunted and responded with delight. He waved as he headed toward the parking lot, but Eleven didn't so much as send a glance his way.

"...He's quite smitten with you," Theo remarked. "You really only met for the first time last night?"

"Yes. I cannot guess the reason why he would be smitten with me."

Theo was indeed curious, but if she said she had no idea, then that had to be the end of it.

"He's fallen for a real handful of a woman." Theo sighed and shook his head, got into the car, and headed for the Delverro branch of the Criminal Investigation Bureau.

The situation at the bureau was the same as ever. But Theo's face clouded over when he stepped inside. Emma and Tobias were peering at files with serious looks on their faces.

"Seems like you've got something," he said. "And it doesn't appear to be good news."

"Mm. Morning, Theo. It might actually be nothing, but it keeps bugging me." Emma held out a small collection of cases put together by the Delverro municipal police's public safety division. They were all lost item reports, missing person investigation requests, and damage reports, none of them solved.

The damage reports in violent incidents involved victims both male and female, and perhaps because the incidents had taken place at night, no one had seen the perpetrators. There was also a report of an injured pet dog.

The lost items were things like a rug set outside in the yard in preparation for moving house or a decoration with blue gems. From the situation, one could only assume that someone had walked off with them, but neither the someone nor the item had been found. And when they compared the investigation requests and the photos provided by the families, the only commonality seemed to be that the missing person was a skinny man of a similar age; their appearances were all different. Facial hair, skin, eyes were all different colors.

But the period during which these damage reports were submitted was at most a year earlier, with the newest being from a week ago, and the locations of occurrence were broadly concentrated in three areas.

"...This indeed might be an issue," Theo said. "And this?"

"I'm sorting them all now. I want you to have a good look at this," Emma replied. She stuck pages with rough human silhouettes drawn on them onto the board, followed by the damage reports. Theo scowled as he watched them go up one by one.

Collected at the top were photos of dogs and several injured women with curly hair, a missing person with distinctive chestnut-colored curls, and a long rug. Gathered beneath these were a blue gemstone, a missing person with distinctive blue eyes, and missing persons with similar mole placements on their arms and legs.

A man with curly chestnut hair and blue eyes rose up from the collage of police reports.

Tobias looked back at Theo. "Emma noticed this, so we talked to the victims again," he said, his face serious. "The curly-haired woman—someone suddenly grabbed hold of her hair, yanked her backward to the ground, and made off with her hair and her scalp. The dogs with the long coats: They had scars like they'd been bitten by a large beast. And then...there's this."

Tobias placed another photo on the board—a photo of victims discovered at a confectioner. Their bodies were half eaten.

"According to the documentation from these cases, the shape of the wounds and the lack of any saliva all match up. It can't be a coincidence."

"...So the Amalgams have been on the move this entire year?" Theo asked.

"Pretty much," Emma said. "How about it, Eleven? You think they're Amalgam prey?"

"Amalgams normally do not have a mouth. We Hounds also simply reproduce the mouth shape in order to take a human form. But that does not mean that we cannot eat anything. We absorb materials, and we are able to convert these into our flesh. We incorporate them whole."

"Whole," Theo and Emma said in unison. They couldn't picture what this might look like.

"For instance." Tobias picked up his empty mug. "What would happen if you were to incorporate this, Eleven?"

"I would press it into my abdomen where the contact area is greatest and incorporate it, to make it a part of my body."

"...Meaning you don't normally chew things up," Theo said. "You swallow them whole without digesting?"

"The earliest Amalgams did chew and digest like animals," she replied. "But there are no records of any cases of a prey item escaping alive."

Eleven's declaration seemed to be extremely important information. Theo stood up from the desk he was leaning against and walked over to the board.

"In other words, we can assume this was all done by Amalgams. It wasn't that they were trying to eat, but rather... Did they just want that one part? The hair, the blue thing, just those parts."

"So then it can't actually be..." Emma's eyes narrowed. "They're only collecting parts they need? They're not trying to hunt or attack, they just really want to build this guy?"

"If that's the case, the timeline of the cases maybe makes sense." Tobias tapped one of the reports with a finger. "After they stopped attacking people and animals, we got a string of missing persons. Maybe they figured out that it's faster to take the whole person with similar parts rather than simply collecting the bits that look like what they need."

"So then they should be gathered together somewhere," Theo said. "The fact that we have victims with the same features might mean that the bodies decompose so they can't keep them for long, and they need to restock. It's not clear what their aim is, though."

Eleven abruptly turned to look at Theo. "What could motivate them to try to create a person?"

"...Right." Theo nodded. "Filling in the gaps of their losses maybe. They want a replacement for someone who's died?"

Tobias furrowed his brow, but Emma answered before him.

"I guess. You see this with serial killers, too, where sometimes, they can't lay a hand on their actual target, so they take out their urges on other people. Hate, love—depends on the person."

"Love and hate are strong emotions, and their targets can't be so easily changed," Theo said. "Even so, they seek out a replacement?"

"They do." Emma nodded. "In some cases, the person is dead, but some killers will practice on someone who looks like their person to build confidence before they approach their real target. In love, in murder. Not a pleasant topic, though."

"I see." Eleven nodded briefly and looked at the man displayed on the board. "So then we need to look for the person who is seeking a replacement for this man."

"The Amalgams themselves wouldn't be looking for him?" Tobias asked.

"That's not likely. Amalgams cannot 'fixate.'" Eleven rejected the idea smoothly. "Amalgams have no emotion. Although they can act as though they do, this never goes beyond the realm of imitation. Love and hate are born in those who face death. They cannot exist in us."

Tobias looked saddened by this, and Emma patted him on the shoulder.

"They're weapons," she said. "They might look like they're moving on their own, but you gotta assume someone outside's behind the wheel. If we could at least find out who this man is, that'd be something to go on."

"...Right. I suppose so." Tobias sighed, shifted gears, and picked up one of the missing person investigation requests. "Okay, then. Why don't Emma and I go through the list of missing people and look for a synthetics engineer? Whoever's doing this would have to be pretty knowledgeable of both synthetics and Amalgams."

"Agreed." Emma nodded. "What about you guys, Theo? Think you can make it to the R&D lab today?"

"Eleven got us an appointment. We'll head over there now." Theo left Tobias to Emma and quickly marched out of the office he'd only just arrived at.

Tobias had relied on Eleven for this job, but he hadn't been treating her as a weapon, so the shock must have been all the greater for him. Theo was a little concerned himself.

"Say, Eleven? What would you do if I died?" he asked while they were waiting for the elevator.

"I would not let you die."

Her voice was so firm, it stunned him. Surprised, he glanced at her, but her face was the same expressionless profile as ever.

"I would not let you die," she repeated quite forcefully. "Ever."

"...You wouldn't, huh? That's...comforting." He was shocked and could only reply in the most conventional way. Were her words themselves not a fixation? That declaration was so unshakable that it seemed impossible for an emotionless Amalgam.

■

A two-hour drive from the city of Delverro was a building halfway up the mountainside, hidden among the trees. Thanks to its superior military camouflage and defensive walls, it had never once been exposed to enemy attack: Fort Ray, a bastion of knowledge as the army's top R&D facility. It was said to be the largest research city in the nation of Adastrah, where magic and science joined hands and developed in lockstep with each other.

As instructed by Eleven, Theo stopped the car in front of the gates. They were inspected by soldiers with guns and given ID badges. Once Eleven was finished filling out forms, the soldiers saluted her and unlocked the gate. The metal doors opened heavily, and Theo carefully urged the car forward. The atmosphere was palpably tense.

"...That's a military lab for you," he remarked. "Pretty tight security."

"There will be three more inspections," Eleven told him. "Are you confident of your ears' semicircular canals?"

"An inspection to test my semicircular canals? What on earth are they looking for?"

Theo stopped the car where he had been told to and soon came to understand the meaning of Eleven's words.

While they were still in the car, a semispheric shutter had no sooner closed around them than he was pressed back against his seat with incredible force and moved forward with the car. When the roaring died down and they got out of the car, they had to sit on chairs in the lobby in front of the elevator. His seat together with him on it were swallowed up by a sphere, and he got to experience what it was like to be a towel spinning around in a washing machine. After he somehow managed to get into the elevator, he was subjected to intense g-force as he was whisked down to the lower floors.

Theo was ready to vomit, but Eleven went through it all without complaint.

"...Are those tests required?" he demanded. "Come on. Are they *really* necessary? They're not just harassing us?"

"To ensure security, we examine people from all three hundred and sixty degrees," Eleven explained. "Please understand."

Feeling like his head was no longer quite right from all the pressure changes, Theo stepped off the elevator. The floor they'd arrived at was a quiet place with only a front desk and a lounge area. The news was displayed on a monitor on the wall, the quiet murmur of voices from the television taking the place of ambient music.

Theo saw Eleven take a step forward and so he trailed after her. The person at the front desk quickly greeted them with a smile and a "Hello."

"Authorization and guest registration," Eleven said quietly.

"Of course. You'll need to be scanned. Please go right ahead."

As instructed and led by Eleven, Theo got up onto a round pedestal. There was the gentle *whoosh* of air jetting around them, and they were put into a glass case. A green light illuminated his body. He had the curious sensation of being stroked by something lukewarm; he felt nauseated and pressed a hand to his chest. Skin, internal organs, blood vessels, nerves—the light thoroughly, neatly palpitated everything until it reached the top of his head, and he was finally freed.

The scanned information was tied to a voiceprint and a name, and Theo was given a guest pass into the building.

"Please note that this guest pass is only good for this date. Please continue straight ahead. And once again, welcome to Fort Ray." The receptionist smiled at them and indicated a path with one hand.

When they slipped through the automatic door, the lobby behind them was replaced with a featureless wall that shone blue. The door of the cylindrical room was circular, and there were no windows; instead, the room was illuminated by slender beams of light that popped on as they passed below them.

"…What's this?" Theo asked, looking around.

"Inspection illumination to control the functions of magical weapons. It's the final safety check. Please cooperate." Although the light would have had an effect on her as a magical weapon, Eleven remained calm, so Theo stayed patiently in place until the lights stopped. Eventually, the exam was perhaps finished; the lights went down, and the door opened.

When Theo followed Eleven through it, he found himself speechless, overwhelmed by the scene that awaited him there.

A large, circular atrium. It continued both up and downward for what seemed like forever. In the center, blue jellyfish carrying gondolas swam around leisurely. The jellyfish drifted freely to and fro, with people sitting in the gondolas on the creatures' backs.

"Eleven, what…are those?" Theo asked, completely baffled. "They're not *real* jellyfish, are they?"

"They are gondolas specialized in vertical movement," she explained. "I was told that the designer was a jellyfish aficionado."

At her urging, Theo got into one of the gondolas. The jellyfish reacted to the weight of his person by luminescing faintly. When Eleven inputted the lab number, the jellyfish deployed its hood and drifted upward.

If Theo had correctly interpreted all the shaking and jostling and turning that he'd experienced thus far, then they should have been deep underground. But as they passed floor after floor, he could see the bright light of the sun, a peek of the night sky, out-of-season sunflowers swaying in a breeze, and storms of snow and flower petals filling the air just one corridor away from each other. It was a chaotic and beautiful space.

"...This is quite the place, hmm?" he said. "Each floor has its own weather, climate, and time zone."

"It was designed to allow for research in the optimal environment," Eleven replied. "The same climate and season as outside are experienced in the residential area. There are also educational facilities and commercial spaces. The fort was intended to be complete in and of itself."

The glow of the jellyfish dimmed when they reached their destination. Out of curiosity, Theo placed a hand on its tentacles and felt a soft jelly body against his palm, just as he'd imagined. He was impressed. *To think that it's artificial...*

Eleven led Theo through an inorganic white corridor. CLOSE-COMBAT AMALGAM LABORATORY was engraved on the doorplate. When Eleven placed her palm on the authentication screen and Theo held up his pass, the white door opened automatically.

On the other side was a greenhouse overflowing with life, as if to belie the inorganic corridor. The white window frames were exquisitely decorated, and on the other side of the glass, birds were singing beneath rays of brilliant sunlight.

In the center of it all, a small elderly man in a wheelchair was peering through glasses at some documents. When he noticed Theo and Eleven enter, he took off his glasses, leaned back in his chair, and turned to face them.

"Welcome, Investigator Starling. I'm Tokinos, the director of this facility. Apologies for taking some time to reach my conclusion. I appreciate you sharing your information with me."

"Thank you for your cooperation, Doctor," Theo said. "Now, about the case at hand..."

"No mistake, you're looking at Amalgams. Come. I will tell you some secrets." Tokinos turned his wheelchair around and moved down a corridor that led deeper into the greenhouse. Theo and Eleven followed him as he glided his wheelchair forward.

Beyond the automatic door was another totally new world, a study. The desks were all clear, and there was no one around. Tokinos sighed and settled in at the desk farthest back. Urged on by Eleven, Theo sat down in a chair in front of it, and Tokinos began to speak.

"I've kept all discussion of the current matter from everyone else in the facility. I say this to let you know that I'm determined to get to the bottom of this information leak. I'll cooperate in any way you need in order to prove my own innocence as well."

Theo nodded. "Thank you very much. To get right into it, what is your expert opinion of these Amalgams we're dealing with?"

"Small potatoes. But for that reason, they can be mass-produced. One thing is certain: You've got quite a difficult case here," Tokinos said resolutely and tapped at a nearby device. A number of photos of Amalgams at various stages were shown on the screen on the wall.

"First, as a prerequisite: Whatever functionality an Amalgam might have, it has to have a core. This is the key source of power. If its core is destroyed, the Amalgam cannot be reactivated."

"So then the reason the parasite Amalgam dies with the host is because it's lost power?" Theo asked. "Because it's produced through the fusion of blood and materials in the pill?"

"Exactly. It's also a trait deliberately cultivated to prevent Amalgam recovery by enemy forces," Tokinos explained briefly, and his face grew stern. "Even so, the real issue is that someone is producing Amalgams by deliberately using the human body as a chrysalis. It's been quite some time since I've seen this type myself."

The photos on the screen were fairly old with low resolution. The specimens displayed there looked like larva that had crawled out of their cocoons without making it to the butterfly stage.

"This is an extremely early Amalgam, you see. It required little power to operate, but it needed to feed. The wounds on your victims strongly resemble the chrysalis after its emergence."

The next slide was two shots—an Amalgam moving from sphere to chrysalis and then emerging from the chrysalis.

"The motive force used for synthetics was originally an Amalgam growth stimulant," Tokinos continued. "Because the output for internal organ synthetics is particularly large, they likely used them to power the rapid development of the Amalgams."

"I see…" Theo looked at the images. "We only hypothesized that they were using the power of the synthetics. I had no idea this power had actually been used as a growth stimulant before. Do the people and synthetics engineers know this?"

"I doubt it." Tokinos shook his head. "It's a by-product of Amalgam research. If the origins of this power source were made known, people might pull at the thread of the manufacturing methods of Amalgams themselves. The military's kept this under wraps for a long time."

Tokinos cleared his throat lightly, seeming tired.

"The troublesome fact here is that anyone can manufacture this type of Amalgam as long as they have the materials. Another sticking point is that they won't obey orders if they don't have a strong relationship with the creator, as parent and child. They are quite hard to handle."

"They're weapons, and yet they are born in cocoons and have parent-child relationships?" Theo asked curiously.

Tokinos chuckled. "It's not like the parent of a living creature. A stable specimen is used as a parent to produce the Amalgams to increase production. The parent splits its core and raises this piece as a child, thus multiplying. In this case, the priority in the control relationship is the parent over the commanding officer."

"So then…," Theo began. "We should be looking for this parent specimen and the human being giving the orders."

"Precisely." Tokinos nodded firmly. "Hounds have a detector that can pick up Amalgam cores. But because the Amalgams in this case have split their cores and shared them with their children, that signal will be terribly weak. Eleven will also have difficult pursuing them unless their location can be narrowed down to a specific area."

"It's that bad?" Theo frowned. "What kind of abilities does this parent specimen have, then?"

"Basically the ability to split its core. You're safe to assume it has remarkably low functionality."

"Then mimicking a human being and blending in with the citizens is..."

"I can definitively state that wouldn't happen." Tokinos shook his head. "Hounds are the only ones who can continuously operate in human form. Even regular Amalgams can't. The issue is, where is it? And who holds command authority?"

Tokinos scowled as he pulled out a stack of papers.

"The core you recovered from that bank robber was indeed made of fortunite. I believe that the military, top management, and all of us here at the lab are suspects. This is all the data we have on every researcher, engineer, and administrative staff member currently attached to the facility. I assume you can put this to use?"

"Thank you," Theo said. "If you'll excuse me, I'll just take a look at it and see what you've got for me." Theo flipped through the headshots, but he didn't see a man with chestnut-brown curly hair and blue eyes. He lifted his face with a sudden thought. "Dr. Tokinos. Did you include people who've retired or passed away in these documents?"

"No. When people retire or die, their personal data is deleted... Wait. I should have photos, though." Tokinos put on his glasses and pulled out a thick book. A photo album. He turned several pages and then held the album out toward Theo. It was a group shot of some engineers.

"Daniel Penley." Tokinos tapped one of the engineers. "He died in a production line accident. Our only accidental death. He was still young with his best years ahead of him, so I remember it well."

"...Who identified the body?" Theo asked.

"A colleague working on the same line." Tokinos pointed to a man in glasses with curly chestnut hair. "The face was burned beyond recognition, but the body was identified as Daniel based on the earrings and glasses he always wore, and a death report was submitted."

"And what is the possibility that the body was faked by an Amalgam?" Theo looked squarely at the doctor.

Tokinos scowled like he'd swallowed a bitter pill. "I can't say it's zero. Not given the reason why we're here now." He leaned back in his wheelchair, utterly exhausted.

◼

Tobias got out of the car with a sense of déjà vu. It seemed like he just had no luck lately.

The address he'd gotten from the manager at the synthetics shop was home to a house with a garden on a quiet residential street. The window frames and roof had a distinctive, charming exterior, affording him a glimpse of the owner's tastes. But the garden was overgrown with weeds, the hedges had been left to run wild, the flower beds were buried in dead flowers, and mail was spilling out of the mailbox. It was easy to see that the owner had not been home in a long time.

According to the manager, the engineer who had made Bob Derry's synthetic was a man named Penley. The manager had been buying from him for about two years, but for the past year, a woman in a deep hood and a long skirt had delivered the merchandise. He said their last transaction had been two weeks earlier.

"It's been left to waste, but it is still just a regular house, huh?" Emma said, gazing up at it. "Doesn't look at all like a synthetics workshop."

"...If we turn up nothing here, too, I might actually start crying," Tobias replied and approached the front door with Emma. They pressed the intercom, but there was no answer and no sound from inside. He slowly drew his gun.

"Mr. Penley? We're from the Criminal Investigation Bureau. Are you in there?" Emma called out, yet this also got no reply.

Tobias thought about kicking the door in, but first reached out for the doorknob. His sense of alarm deepened at the fact that it seemed to be unlocked. He let go and watched as Emma took it and quickly pushed open the door for him. He stepped into the house, gun at the ready.

There was no one inside. The floor and furniture were covered in dust, undisturbed. It looked like the place had been empty for a long time. No signs of any criminal activity. Everything in the room struck Tobias as pretty standard, right down to the many photos of a loving couple hanging on the wall. The pair had been together from childhood until university graduation, gotten married, and moved into this house and were now somewhere else.

As far as he could tell from the stack of bills, payments for this past year for anything and everything were extremely overdue. The residents hadn't suddenly abandoned the house, either. There were no dishes in the sink nor any food left out, and the place, while very dusty, was quite tidy. There were no letters among the many items in the mailbox, and the photos were only of the couple; he couldn't see any friends. From the fact the bills were addressed solely to *Joe Penley* or *Nina Penley*, it was clear that they were the only occupants.

As Tobias was checking the living room and kitchen, Emma called out to him from the hallway.

"I examined the bedroom and the bathroom, but there was nothing." She put her gun back in the holster at her hip. "I guess they put everything in order before they left? But there were medical devices for home use in the closet. Looks like either the husband or the wife was sick."

"Right… And what about the last room there?"

"It's the only one that's locked. Can you open it?"

"I'll give it a go. If it's not a specialized lock, I'll have it open in a jiff." Tobias rolled up his sleeves and headed toward the room at the end of the hallway. He opened the cover of his synthetic and produced a lock-picking tool. He was able to undo the simple lock in a few seconds.

Warily, they opened the door to find a study with nothing but dust and the musty smell of old books. But one wall was covered with so many scribbled scraps of paper, it looked almost black.

"What the…?" Tobias muttered, gaping.

The notes were so faded from the sun that he couldn't tell when they were made. They were all handwritten, in terrible penmanship, and—as if reflecting the mental state of the person writing them—the grammar was a mess while the content itself was nonsensical. Tobias was able to pick out words here and there, though he couldn't make out if these were love letters or an essay or even complaints.

But even he could see the incredible tenacity revealed in these notes.

There was no sense of coherency to them. If some were personal memos, others were synthetics blueprints. The key words that stood out were *immortal* and *rebirth*. The whole thing seemed to be a plan to replace an entire body with synthetics. The notes were filled up with words on top of words, making the text incredibly dense. In one area alone, however, was a blank space that felt almost pure.

The center of the wall of text was occupied by a portrait of a young woman. It was without a doubt the woman Tobias had seen in all the photos: Mrs. Penley. *Nina* was written in cursive at one edge of the portrait, and below this was what appeared to be the signature of the artist. The background was indistinct, a wash of soft colors, but a beam of bright sunlight shone down on the beautiful wife as she looked back at the artist with a smile. What had he thought? What had he written while looking at this portrait?

The words surrounding the portrait were passionate: his dream of spending an eternity with her, his regret that this would not happen because of her illness, his hatred of the world, his firm resolve to stay married to her for life whatever he had to sacrifice. Etched out on this wall was the utter and complete love he carried in his heart for his spouse Nina.

Emma cocked her head to one side as she stared at the portrait with Tobias. "The manager said it used to be a man who came in with the synthetics, but then this last year, a woman started coming. As far as I can tell from these notes, though, it was this lady in the painting here who got sick—terminally ill. Nina. The Amalgams were collecting

parts for a man with chestnut hair and blue eyes; Nina's blond with green eyes. It doesn't add up."

"...The handwriting's all the same," Tobias remarked. "One person wrote all of these. The handwriting of the title of the portrait and the signature also seem to match up. Joe or Nina, with this knowledge of synthetics... If we had their yearbook, we could figure out where they went to school. Let's go see if we can't find something like that."

They split up and searched the house, but they didn't locate anything that would give them clues to the pasts of Mr. and Mrs. Penley. However, Tobias did notice that there were a number of letters to Joe from a certain Tom MacKenzie, who appeared to have been the priest at the Penleys' wedding. He had written a letter of congratulations on their marriage, saying that they could count on him for anything. The last letter was dated a year earlier.

Tobias wondered who exactly this MacKenzie was and then noticed that Emma had come back. He turned to her.

"Looks like they had a workshop called Penley Lumber Industries," she told him. "Owner's Joanna Penley. If it's still open, we might find someone to talk to."

"Let's go check it out. Maybe we should meet up with Theo and Eleven there." He jotted down the address of the workshop, and they left the Penley house behind. He felt a faint shiver at the dissonance between the happy couple's home and the obsession that filled the locked study.

"...So Joanna's nickname is Joe," Tobias said. "You think it was Joanna and Nina living together?"

"The photos were of a man and a woman," Emma replied. "From the look of the house and the furniture, I doubt they had any other family living there. If she was selling illegal synthetics to make a living, she could have just taken 'Joe' as a pseudonym."

They hurriedly jumped into the car and drove away.

■

When Theo got the call from Emma, he spoke with her briefly and then quickly turned back to Tokinos. "Doctor. Was Daniel Penley married?"

"Mm." Tokinos nodded. "But she died not long before he did. She was terribly ill, couldn't even handle the transfer to Fort Ray. As I recall, she was admitted to a local hospital."

"Do you remember what he was like around the time his wife passed away?" Theo asked.

Tokinos frowned sadly. "He was terribly depressed. It seemed like he was trying to forget by throwing himself into his work. When he heard she'd taken a turn for the worse, he hurried to the hospital. But she had already been put into a clean room by the time he got there, so he could only care for her through the window. It's not hard to imagine how lost he must have been."

"So they were close? As a couple?"

"Yes, quite close... If only we could have treated her at Fort Ray at least."

"...This is very helpful," Theo said. "Thank you so much."

"Not at all," Tokinos replied. "Do give me a call if there's anything else."

Theo shook the doctor's hand and was about to leave the lab when he noticed Tokinos trying to look into his eyes. Theo stopped. Tokinos set his thin hands back down in his lap, turned his wheelchair, and called out to Eleven.

She silently walked over to him, and he took her hand.

"I know you could never mistake what you need to be protecting," he said to her gently, as if speaking to a small child. "But allow me the foolishness of praying for your safety. You are our pride and joy, our most advanced Hound."

"...Thank you very much, Doctor," Eleven replied. "I have memorized that."

Their good-byes were brief. Tokinos saw Theo and Eleven off with a "Good health to you" and closed the inorganic door.

Leaving Fort Ray behind, Theo asked Eleven as he got into the car, "Did something happen with Dr. Tokinos? He seemed worried."

"…I was once brought in after losing my entire body, so he is 'worried,'" Eleven told him.

"Your entire body?" Theo stared at her. "Even though you're a Hound?"

"Yes. One time, on the battlefield. My core was intact, so my recovery took place within the expected time period, but the doctor…" She paused. "Perhaps the expression is 'It pained him.'"

"I suppose it would. That sort of thing would be unbearable for the parent who gave birth to you." Theo clicked his tongue. This made a strange kind of sense to him, especially since Eleven had taken the form of a slender girl. Tokinos had already seen this daughter-like figure come in with serious injuries; it was only logical that he would worry.

"The doctor is the type of human being who prioritizes memories of failures rather than successes," Eleven commented.

"…Well, that's something he and I have in common, I guess. I tend to forget the missions where I succeeded." Theo remembered only the relief of succeeding in the mission and the discomfort of the transport home. He would forget the type of drinks he shared with his comrades but remember the fact that they had laughed together. They were maybe dead somewhere. He felt a pain in his heart and cleared his throat. "At any rate, about the only thing I remember clearly is the Alkabel campaign."

"If you are referring to the large-scale battle in the city of Alkabel, then wouldn't that mission be classified as a success?" Eleven asked.

"If you look at the big picture, sure. But too many people died."

"…That is not your responsibility, is it, Theo?" Eleven said dispassionately. "I heard that reinforcement troops were delayed."

"No." He gave her a pained smile. "Our diversionary mission was a success, and we let our guard down. Even though it was only natural to expect an attack. The whole thing was awful. I mean, the kid who saved me was blown to bits protecting me."

They came up on a curve in the mountain road, and he decelerated carefully into the turn, gripping the steering wheel with a sour look on his face.

"Even if you 'regret' that your comrade died," Eleven said, "wouldn't the soldier who saved you have been 'proud' of saving you?"

Never dreaming that she would say something like this to him, Theo shifted his gaze to the passenger seat. Eleven turned her face toward the windshield, leaving him unable to see the expression on it.

"Couldn't you say the same thing?" he finally asked.

"It is nothing more than imitation. If it pleases you, that is the most important thing."

Was the fact that she sounded more mechanical than usual her way of hiding her embarrassment? Theo had a strange feeling come over him—almost impressed but also like things were strangely off-kilter as he pressed down the accelerator and continued forward.

The address of the workshop that Tobias had sent was farther west than Fort Ray, unfolding at the foot of the mountain. The area had been a collection of factories since before the war, and it was now slated for redevelopment. As they drove, they passed large construction trucks and spotted several sites with stockpiles of materials or buildings being torn down.

Tobias and Emma were waiting for them at the entrance of an old factory in the middle of this industrial zone. Due to the number of one-way streets and narrow roads, they would be investigating on foot from that point.

"Penley Lumber Industries is supposedly in here somewhere," Tobias told them. "Although the address is so old that we don't know the exact location."

"That's not a surprise. This area's had a lot of redevelopment," Theo replied. "Eleven, can you sense the core?"

"Please wait a moment." She leaped from the fire hydrant to the streetlamp and raced up to the top of a chimney. She spun around once like a weather vane, jacket flapping, before jumping back down. "The signal is still extremely weak, but I was able to perceive a direction. If we approach the building, I will be able to identify it."

"Great." Theo nodded. "You and I will go on ahead, then. Tobias, Emma, you keep an eye on our rear."

A surprisingly large number of factories had fallen out of use long ago. The team moved away from the buildings toward the mountain, and the area grew increasingly deserted. The sound of their feet on the gravel felt excessively loud.

Eventually, Eleven stopped in front of an old factory. Who knew how long it had been left to sit there? The windows were broken, the metal was rusted from wind and rain, and the external stairs were lying on the ground. The sign had also fallen off and was half buried in the dirt. It looked to have originally been a sturdy building, but the magnificent chimney was covered in vines now, and tree branches poked through windows into the factory.

"This is where the core signal is. There is no mistake," Eleven said, and Theo looked back over his shoulder. Tobias gazed up at the building and frowned.

"...Definitely doesn't look like anyone's living here, hmm?"

"Let's take a look around," Theo suggested. "Eleven, you stay on guard here. Call me straight away if anything happens."

They split up to check the area around the factory. None of the nearby buildings were in use, and the land under many of them was up for sale. A mountain road ran behind the factory, and Theo could see signs of a car having come and gone from the garage. The car in question was covered in mud, and the key was sitting in the ignition. Theo tried starting the engine, but it turned out to be out of gas. There was even mud on the driver's seat.

"What do you have to do to get a car this dirty...?" Theo was stumped. He turned the key back to the off position and moved away from the vehicle. The factory's rear entrance had apparently been used as the main entrance; there was a nameplate on the post that read Penley. There were no security cameras, and all the doors were locked. He peered inside through the broken windows, but from what he could see, there was nothing other than stopped meters and equipment left to degrade over time. He could see no sign of anyone having been in there recently.

Hearing footsteps, he turned around to see Emma and Tobias jogging over to him.

"The road's blocked by trees and mud," Emma told him. "Probably from the landslide during the storm last week."

"I've got nothing here, either," Theo replied. "There's no way people were living in there, not with the state the place is in. And the car and the driver's seat are covered in mud."

They went back around to the front, and Eleven glanced back at them from where she was obediently keeping watch.

"Eleven, can you tell from the core signal where in the building it is?" Theo asked.

"From this distance, I would guess that it is perhaps in the basement."

"…All right." Theo nodded. "Emma and Eleven, you go check out the building. Tobias, you're with me in the basement."

Emma and Eleven quickly assented, but Tobias looked dubious.

"The basement?" he asked. "How exactly are you planning on getting in there?"

"I saw an entrance for sewer maintenance over there," Theo told him. "We can get in through there."

"Bleh!" Tobias screwed up his face. "Are you out of your mind? A sewer way out here is absolutely going to be disgusting!"

"Quit whining," Theo snapped. "We know it escaped through the sewers. It's worth checking out."

Tobias's scowl grew even deeper, and he offered up a prayer to God. Meanwhile, Emma turned back to Eleven and smiled.

"Okay then, how about we start from the ground floor?" she said to Eleven. "We can probably get in through a broken window."

"No. From the section that I've been able to confirm, I surmise that the living area is the second floor. We should start the investigation on that floor."

"On the second floor…? But the external stairs are broken. Either way you look at it, we'll have to go in on the first floor."

"The balcony damage is insignificant. I have determined it possible for entry. Let's go, Emma."

Emma gaped at her, but before she had the time to shriek, Eleven had scooped her up in her arms and hopped up lightly. She kicked at the trunk of a large tree and leaped directly to the balcony on the second floor.

Theo and Tobias were forced to watch, stunned.

"...Wanna join them instead, Tobias?"

"Nah..." He sighed and started walking alongside Theo. "My horoscope today said to keep my feet planted on the ground."

■

Even after they landed on the balcony, Emma's heart would not stop pounding. "That...was a surprise... Eleven, you really are... incredible..."

"The balcony door is open. There is no sign of anyone." Eleven paid Emma's mental state no mind at all.

Fine. Right, okay. That's the kind of girl you are. Emma pulled herself together and went inside with Eleven.

The balcony led to a living room with a sectional sofa and a coffee table. There were some books and knickknacks on the bookshelf, but these had decayed together with the furniture. The kitchen she could see past the counter was also covered in mold, and the food was all rotten. There were no footsteps in the thick layer of dust.

"...No intruders for quite some time, hmm?" Emma said, looking at the photos on the wall. "They seem like a close family. I wonder what happened."

On the wall, an old photo of the Penley couple was squeezed in among pictures of a young Daniel, Daniel's graduation, and Daniel and Nina's wedding; between pictures of an elderly father and elderly mother, there was a picture of Mr. and Mrs. Penley. Everyone was smiling in all of them, standing quite close together, and it was clear they got along well.

"...Did three people live here?" Eleven asked.

"No, there's only one set of dishes in the sink," Emma replied. "The son and his wife lived somewhere else. I guess whoever lived here suddenly passed away from illness or something. Everything's been left the way it was. Doesn't look like anything's been cleaned up."

They went around and looked in the other rooms, but just as Eleven said, there was no sign of anyone in the place. In fact, it seemed that the last time people had lived here was in the long distant past. But when Emma looked toward the end of the hallway, she pulled out her gun. There were muddy tracks leading in and out of the room right by the stairs.

She cautiously opened the door and immediately coughed at the overwhelming rancid stink that hit her like a wall. "That is some smell…"

"One body," Eleven said coolly. "Judging from the photographs, it's the mother."

Emma covered her mouth with her sleeve and peered inside.

The bedroom/study was decorated in a variety of floral patterns. There was a rotted corpse on the double bed. Looking at the hairstyle and the rings, Emma agreed that it was indeed the mother from the pictures.

"…I can't believe you're fine with this stench, Eleven," she said.

"I can detect the elements in the air, but I do not have standards to judge whether a smell is good or bad."

There was an empty water jug and a package of open pills on the bedside table, leading Emma to intuit that the mother had had a chronic illness. Within the woman's reach were a half-finished novel and a family photo. She had no doubt fought her illness with these as her mental supports, but the illness had nevertheless taken her in the end. There was no sign of injury to the body.

The muddy tracks on the floor from the bedside table out toward the stairs caught Emma's eye. She crouched down and peered at the dirt. The grass mixed in with it was still green. Someone had been coming up the stairs to this bed fairly recently, with mud stuck to their shoes. But there were no footprints; the marks looked more like something had been dragged away.

"…Theo said the car was covered in mud," she mused. "There was that landslide last week and all. I guess something happened."

Emma and Eleven split up to investigate the desk. It was small, but there was a pile of letters; perhaps letter writing had been the woman's hobby. Among the many exchanges with friends, there were just two letters from Daniel Penley. The first was a wedding invitation. The second was to tell her that he was returning to his old home with his wife. Emma cocked her head to one side. By the time the letters had been sent, the wife Nina was already dead.

"...Daniel went so far as to fake his own death and leave Fort Ray," Emma mused. "We know that he went back home after that. But Nina was already dead at that point. The only one who lived here was the mother Joanna. There's no sign of the couple here... How does that work?"

"Having lost Nina, Daniel would be an appropriate candidate if a person was going to build a human being with the motivation of obsession due to love," Eleven said. "But the parts the Amalgams are looking for belong to Daniel."

"He was such an amazing engineer that he got hired at Fort Ray," Emma noted. "If he learned about Amalgams and the tech behind them while at the lab... He couldn't actually have brought Nina—"

Clang! She heard pieces of metal hitting the ground. Not on the first floor—somewhere farther off. In the back of her mind, she saw Theo and Tobias off investigating on their own.

The next instant, Eleven was running. She flew out of the room, leaving only an afterimage of pale hair.

"Eleven! Wait! Eleven!" Emma gripped her gun and started after the girl, but then her eyes landed suddenly on an oil stove in the room.

■

With Tobias in tow, Theo headed into the basement through the sewer maintenance entrance. Perhaps it had been some time since the sewers had been used; the water had completely dried up, and weeds were growing in the dirt that remained. Parts of the sewer had collapsed, and there were places where the sun shone in.

"...What a relief," Tobias said with a sigh. "No stink, no mess."

"You're still going on about that?" Theo rolled his eyes. "Honestly."

"It's important," Tobias protested. "It's connected to investigation efficiency."

Theo clicked his tongue, turned on his flashlight, and stepped forward. Despite the fact that there was plenty of greenery, there was curiously not a single insect around, which was somewhat disturbing. And then he noticed a stench in the air.

Blood. The stink of blood and dead flesh.

Having advanced to the end of the sewer, he shone his flashlight ahead of him and frowned as he stared at the mountain of dead flesh there, so ravaged that he could no longer tell whether it had once belonged to people or animals.

On the crumbling asphalt, he could see trails of blood between the mountain of corpses and the waterway that grew thicker and thinner and overlapped with each other. A good number of round trips. For a long time now.

He signaled Tobias with his eyes and cautiously entered the factory basement through a doorframe that had lost its door. They stepped into the electrical room where a fixed route along the floor was clear of dust, as if something had been dragged though the space.

Theo unlocked the door and stepped into the corridor on quiet feet. Eventually, he came out in one corner of the factory.

All the lumber-processing equipment had been removed, and the space was filled with precision machinery for the production of synthetics, an operating table and any number of diagnostic devices, plus endless machine parts. A workbench filthy with blood was buried under blueprints and synthetics prototypes.

"With all this, it'd be pretty easy to start a synthetics factory, hmm?" Tobias said quietly, surveying the area. "And do the surgery to implant them."

"...Mm." Theo nodded. "And no one would bother you way out here, either."

They advanced into the factory with extreme caution. *Krrshk*. Theo heard something scraping. But the place was deserted. In which case…

Theo and Tobias aimed their flashlights and guns toward the sound at the same time. And froze in place.

Before them was a woman pale with illness, carrying a terrifying mass of flesh in her slender arms. Noticing the light, she slowly turned around. She was covered in mud, and half of her face was hidden by hair so white it looked painted in ash. But even so, Theo could tell that this was the same face as in the portrait and the photographs, although its former beauty was gone from the gaunt visage. She stared in surprise and hugged the mass of flesh to her with arms that were nothing but skin and bones.

The mass had a form that could only be described as indescribable. It was as big as a grown man, and the swelling protrusion with strips of hair was likely the head; it had several eyeballs embedded in it. The body had no defined shoulders or neck. Instead, several arms grew from the soft and flabby flesh. The thin lines popping up on the surface were probably veins. With legs that stretched out from the stomach and back, and arms extending from the waist and chest, there was nothing human about its shape. At the ends of the fleshy mass was something like fabric, and a thing that was apparently a mouth floated about as it muttered and grumbled. Outlining the mass was a layer of uneven, curly chestnut hair.

"Are you...Nina Penley?" Theo worked hard to keep his voice even.

A smile blossomed on the woman's face with its prominent cheekbones. "It's been so long since we've had guests. Right, Daniel? Danny, my beloved," she—Nina—said happily to the lump of flesh.

It was like something out of a nightmare. Was she really saying that this fleshy mass, which seemed to be nothing more than human parts pushed together into dirt, was Daniel Penley? Several arms flailed and waved, and Nina laughed brightly.

"You're happy, too, hmm? Say, dear guests, how about some tea? How many sugars?"

"...Sorry, but we're from the Criminal Investigation Bureau," Theo said. "We wanted to ask you about the abduction of a man who shared features with Daniel Penley, including curly chestnut-colored hair. Could you explain what all this is?"

Still smiling, Nina cocked her head, revealing the side that was hidden by her hair. Theo shuddered. Her left eye and the area around it were nothing but a dark emptiness like broken porcelain.

"I mean, I needed him," Nina said, the smile never leaving her lips. "One day, I woke up to the most wonderful morning. I'd been in such terrible pain, and suddenly, it was all okay. But then Daniel got weaker. Poor little Danny, he worked so hard, but he couldn't get anywhere. And one day, he couldn't move anymore."

Theo stared at her. "Did he die?"

"Of course not!" she protested. "He fell into a deep sleep—that's all. He just needed a new body, like I did. I really wanted to get a new body for Danny the way he got one for me, but I had to make the synthetics all by myself... The children gathered so many bits for me while they fed. Things that could take the place of Danny's body. Thanks to them, Danny's— See? Back to his old self!" she declared brightly, taking one of the hands stretching out from the lump of flesh. "Danny was always so busy. He said he needed more eyes and hands, so I added lots of blue eyes and hands that are a little tanned. He's not too great at walking, so I got a bunch of legs so it's easier to support him. And see how his mouth wanders off wherever? That's 'cause he can be pretty awkward at talking. He's terribly shy."

She traced the lips that flowed along the outline of the fleshy body with a finger held out like she was holding a teacup.

"He looks a little different from before, but that doesn't change the fact that it's the same old Danny I loved. He's a big baby, hates to be alone. Hee-hee! Such a cutie! He said he wants to be with me forever!"

Her happy smile grew wider, and she hugged the mass. Several hands stretched out toward her and moved in an unintelligible fashion as if to hug her closer or peel her off.

Tobias covered his mouth at the grotesque sight and paled as he took a step back. Theo also felt the urge to vomit and cleared his throat.

"...You have children?" he asked. "It would be rude of us not to say hello to them. Is it just the two of you here now?"

"You're quite the gentleman. Thank you." She beamed at him. "But I'm sorry—the children have all left home. The pastor said that when they've grown big and strong, children should leave their parents' nest. He said to let them go."

"So then you've been here with Daniel Penley all this time?" Theo confirmed, and Nina cocked her head to one side, frowning.

"I wonder. When I first got my new body, I was at our old house. But then Danny got sick, so his mother invited us to come and live here. It's been just the two of us for about a year now. I'm glad we came. Mother is such a lovely person, and she helps with Danny's work, which makes things easier."

"...And where is his mother now?"

"Sleeping. I promised to make her the best tea when she wakes up again. So I go check on her every day, but she just isn't waking up."

"You don't think she might be dead?" Theo asked.

"Why would she be? Mother is sleeping with the most *peaceful* look on her face. She's having wonderful dreams." Nina turned back to him with a bright smile. She didn't grasp a single thing about the current situation. She was unable to comprehend the state that Daniel and this "Mother" were in, but she was still somehow proficient enough to maintain her broken world.

"Nina," Theo said cautiously. "Can you tell me more about Daniel's condition...?"

"Danny can't move on his own. So I'm taking the place of his heart. See?" She slid a hand from the fleshy body to her own chest. Her skin split where her fingers touched it and opened up to reveal a steaming heart contracting and expanding, pumping blood around the body. It looked very real, making the case that the bizarre mass of flesh in her arms was indeed alive. A whittled-down red gemstone glittered inside her chest like a transparent drop of blood. This crystal had the glitter of the fortunite that was the core of the Amalgams.

Nina closed her chest and hugged the lump that she insisted was

Daniel close to her with both arms. "Ahhh, I'm so happy. Once Danny's doing better, I just know I'll be even happier. But he hasn't been talking all this time, so I've been lonely. Danny, I want to hear you say, 'I love you.'"

A shudder ran through the fleshy body. No—it was Nina's long hair swinging back and forth. She looked at Theo with clouded eyes and noticed his own blue eyes. She laughed.

"I still haven't heard him say, 'I love you.' Which means that this isn't enough yet, right? So please, give me your eyes. Those perfect blue eyes!" Nina cried out in a high-pitched voice, her hair puffing out around her.

In the next moment, something slammed into Theo's side. Stumbling off-balance at the unexpected impact, he reflexively turned around.

The long hair was a sea of knives stabbing into Tobias's left arm. The blades that pierced his synthetic threw Tobias into the air. He slammed into a pile of materials, which tumbled down around him.

Theo fired his gun immediately to cover him, but belying her slender porcelain-doll frame, Nina did not flinch at being shot.

"Tobias!" Theo roared without taking his eyes off Nina. "Answer me! Tobias!"

He heard the dry rattle of a pipe rolling but got no answer. *Now what?* Sweat sprang up on his forehead. The acrid scent of gunpowder smoke and burned flesh wafted through the air. Nina ripped out her hair and extended it into a new blade. Her smile was tender in form alone.

"Don't be scared," she cooed. "It's all right. I'm good at this. It won't even hurt—"

Flash.

A sword swung down and split Nina in twain from the top of her head. The two halves of her stunned face fell to either side, and there was red everywhere.

* * *

Theo lifted his head in surprise as Eleven dropped down to stand before him. Her left arm had transformed into a sword gouged deep into the concrete. Keeping Theo behind her, she barked, "I am in command. Hear me, fear me, bow down before me. I will permit no further operation."

"...What an unpleasant voice." Both halves of Nina's mouth moved in unison, shouting her resentment. "I hate that voice. You want to force me to obey you and take away my one and only?"

Nina glared at Eleven with her remaining eye—a green eye burning darkly with hatred.

"This is a first," Nina snarled. "What is this? What is calling to me? The only ones who can lead me are Danny and the pastor. Don't talk to me. Don't control me!"

"You are an Amalgam. There is nowhere for you to go," Eleven stated flatly. "Ma'am, please quiet yourself."

"No. No, no, no!" Nina shrieked. "I want to be with Danny. We're going to a paradise where there's no suffering!"

"Did the pastor tell you that?" Theo demanded. "Did he tell you that you could go to paradise if you made a body for Daniel?!"

Nina screwed her face up as she desperately clutched the lump of flesh. "The pastor said so when the children were born. I did something wonderful—I worked hard so I could be with Danny, and now we'll be welcomed into paradise as angels!"

"Did you really believe that?" Theo asked. "Exactly how many people have you killed for Daniel?!"

"I don't know. I don't know, I don't know—I don't care!" she shrieked. "Go away. Get out. Don't take him from me!" With some strength still left to her somehow, she turned her blade on Theo.

Without taking a single step, Eleven severed this blade and stomped on it.

Liquid abruptly came raining down on a frozen Nina. She opened her eyes wide in surprise. "What's this? Tea?"

A particular smell wafted through the air. Kerosene.

"Emma, please go ahead," Eleven said.

Theo automatically turned his eyes upward and found Emma breathing hard, katahr in her hands. She brandished it to fire a Magirus Shell into the kerosene pooling around Nina. A red light scattered and began burning ferociously. Fire magic. It could not be extinguished without similarly magical water.

"Ahhh, ahhh, no, this is—!"

Crying out, Nina scrabbled to hold on to the fleshy mass closer to her as it turned to dirt and melted through her fingers. Cracks raced outward from the corner of her eye. In the time it took to blink, she was engulfed in flames, her screams loud enough to shake the factory itself.

Black smoke. Hoarse cries. Nina reached out a hand from inside the conflagration. Her pale fingertips turned to ash and danced up into the air.

Theo couldn't help but see his little sister in this.

The stench of burning flesh filled the room, and he staggered backward, pressing a hand to his mouth.

Eleven took his arm to support him and stared directly at him with her gray eyes. "Are you all right?"

The world flipped on its axis. Gray eyes opened so wide they threatened to fall out of her head.

The sound of explosions. Of brick collapsing. His sister's screams. Audio hallucinations rattled in his skull.

With the outstretched hand reaching nothing, his vision abruptly went black.

■

When he opened his eyes, the first thing he saw was a white ceiling. He sat up in surprise, causing Eleven in the chair next to him to blink. She quickly stood up.

"Theo, please move slowly at first. You lost consciousness."

"...Where are we? What's the sitrep?" He closed his eyes in defense against the way the world shook.

Eleven slowly pushed on his shoulder. When he gave in and fell backward, a pillow that she had likely propped up there gave him support.

"This is the bureau's medical office. The Amalgam Nina was completely burned up. We sent the ashes and core to the lab and filed a report. Joanna's body was brought in for an autopsy. Tobias is receiving treatment at the hospital, and Emma is with him. His life is not in danger, but the damage to his synthetic is severe, and he was badly beaten. The doctor judged that it would be difficult for him to return to the investigation today."

"…Mm. That's fine, then. Let's have him stay there." He retrieved his cell phone from the jacket hanging on the bedpost and sent Emma a message. This small action exhausted him, and he let out a long sigh before pulling on his jacket and getting out of the bed. "This pastor and the children Nina were talking about…"

"A letter that is thought to have been from the pastor has been submitted for handwriting analysis," Eleven told him. "The local police searched the sewers, but the conclusion was that pursuit was impossible. The whereabouts of the 'children' are unknown."

"…Thanks for getting me up to speed." He pulled open the curtain partition while Eleven folded up the blanket and returned it to the sofa. He didn't remember seeing a blanket like that in the medical office before, and he cocked his head to one side. "Where'd that come from?"

"The medical office staff said, 'Here, take this if you're going to wait,' and lent it to me."

He looked down at his watch and realized that it was evening already. He'd apparently been asleep longer than he himself had perceived. "Tobias is one thing, but I wasn't even hurt. We've lost time here."

"The assumption is that you lost consciousness due to a mental shock. Should I not have used fire?" Eleven looked up at him with the same expression on her face as always.

He suddenly remembered how her eyes had grown wide in surprise when he was on the verge of passing out. He sighed and shook his head. "It's fine. Don't worry about it. In fact, I can't believe you managed it in time, given the situation."

"Are you sure?" Eleven said simply, and didn't press him any further.

Quietly grateful for this, Theo left the medical office. Eleven followed a half step behind.

"...Daniel stole an Amalgam from the lab and fled," Theo said. "He succeeded in making his copy by having it feed on Nina's corpse, but then he died of an illness or something. The Amalgam he left behind continued to imitate Nina and granted Daniel's wish in a twisted form. Does that about sum it up?"

"It is different with a living human being," Eleven replied. "But feeding on a corpse, an Amalgam is limited in the restoration of the person in life. It could not behave like Nina. Perhaps Daniel saw the Nina he had brought back to life in form only, realized that his wife would not return, and fell ill in his despair."

"Hmm." Theo looked at her. "Is it that hard?"

"Yes. For those that are not Hounds," Eleven told him quietly. "With that low-quality core, the probability of it being able to maintain Nina's form is essentially that of a miracle. This is a precious example of success for the lab."

Theo remembered the day she had first come home with him. The Eleven who had analyzed the state of his apartment and tried to mimic the figure of the little sister she had never seen.

"Now that I'm thinking about it, you also actually tried to copy my sister," he said. "Even though you had no idea what she looked like."

The sound of her footsteps stopped. When he looked back, she was staring up at him.

"...I determined that it was necessary at that time." Her voice was very small. "I conjectured that this was why my mimicry ability was chosen."

It seemed impossible that she was the same Eleven who had within a few hours of joining the investigation team challenged and provoked Theo to the point where he'd felt compelled to draw his weapon. Right from the start, she'd been attuned to his desires in the belief that she was the one who could realize them: these desires that Theo had given up on putting into words and pushed to the depths of his heart with good reason. Desperately.

"...Did I deepen your wounds?"

What an annoying weapon was Theo's genuine thought. A beast that said she had no feelings, all the while awkwardly trying to be considerate. Even though she hadn't hesitated to incinerate Nina and wasn't the least bit shaken by Tobias's injuries, for some reason, she was sometimes able to stand there with a look on her face like she was entirely at a loss, like a child who had been left behind.

"You didn't." He shook his head. "You definitely didn't."

She had no intention of hurting him. Which was maybe why he felt like actually being up-front with her. Because when it came to Eleven, he hadn't been up-front enough.

By the time they left the Delverro office together, it was dusk, and people were coming and going on the street outside. He invited her to walk with him and headed for the municipal park, a green space surrounded by public facilities and shops that allowed people of all ages and genders to enjoy a respite, a soothing view spreading out before them. Many of the numerous signs and billboards visible from the park championed the peace memorial ceremony, making palpable the expectations of the people for peace.

When Theo stopped at the ice cream truck, the owner noticed his investigator's badge and doffed his hat to him lightly. "Thanks for your service."

Theo smiled and pulled out his wallet. "Eleven, pick your favorite ice cream. My treat. As an apology and a thank-you."

"We have no standard for like or dis— No, actually, lemon flavor."

"Okay. Lemon sherbet and iced coffee," he told the owner.

Ordering was one thing, but for a Hound not in the habit of eating, snacking also seemed to be a bit of a trial. Eleven took the cup of sherbet in both hands and ever so carefully stepped forward so that by the time Theo had finished paying, she still hadn't reached the bench.

As those around them smiled warmly, she reported seriously, "Theo, the ice. The ice is melting. It is becoming not sherbet."

"The way you're walking, it won't spill," he told her. "Hurry up and sit down and eat it."

Once they were seated, trouble again visited Eleven. Even if she could manage the movement of scooping with the wooden spoon, it didn't lead to any sherbet actually being scooped up. In the end, it was only after Theo demonstrated for her that Eleven succeeded in getting the now quite soft sherbet into her mouth.

"So you finally ate some…" He smiled. "How is it?"

"I have confirmed cold, sweet, and a faint sourness and bitterness. Although they are both lemon, this is different from the candy."

"Well, if you're comparing candy and ice." He shrugged. "I didn't think there was anything you weren't good at."

"The action of scooping up fine particles of ice with a plank in a particular shape is not necessary on the battlefield."

That said, however, she soon got the hang of it and dispassionately proceeded with the eating of the sherbet from the second bite on. Theo sipped his iced coffee as he watched her out of the corner of his eye. The evening breeze was cool against his skin.

"…My hometown is on the border with Cadelenza," he began. "A little nowhere place called Klyvalle. A small town in a valley. I was the first person there to be accepted to the Criminal Investigation Bureau academy. The whole town was overjoyed, but my parents were very much against it. I pushed back, though, and went anyway. I was determined to join the bureau once I graduated. For the kids living in my town, the investigators were the most real heroes. I always wanted to be one when I grew up."

Children were laughing and running around in an innocent game of hide-and-seek.

"My little sister—she was seven years younger than me. She always called me her hero."

"Was this because of something you did?" Eleven asked.

He shook his head. "Nothing big. I'd find something she lost or chase away a big dog. I didn't do anything special. But she still called me her hero. Even if I was just playing house, I never wanted to make her feel ashamed of me. So I wanted to be an investigator and work to protect people."

The wind blew harder. Before he knew it, his coffee cup was empty, and he crushed it in his hand.

"Five years ago…my sister finished junior high back home and was coming to a vocational school here in Delverro. She told me to do something to celebrate her acceptance to her new school, but I had no money back then, so I treated her to some ice cream here. And before I knew it, she was springing into action, you know? The second she got into that vocational school, she hauled all her stuff to my place. When I asked her about it later, she told me that living with me had been our parents' condition for letting her go to this school."

Eleven stared up at him. "And so that room?"

"Mm-hmm." He nodded. "But the air raids on Delverro got much more intense not too long after that, and the school locked its doors. I'd joined the bureau by then, so I was busy myself. I figured she'd be safer in Klyvalle, so I sent her home. Our parents were worried, too, and Cadelenza was an allied country. I was sure she'd be okay there."

He could still picture it clear as day. He'd seen her off on the platform at the train station, promising to come home too when he could get some time off. Heather had smiled and said, *"Leave Mom and Dad to me."* He watched the train go and then went back to working his case. Without knowing that that would be the last time.

"As soon as we closed that case, I got my boss to let me have some vacation days. Hopped into the car and left town first thing in the morning. But it's quite far away, Klyvalle. I drove and drove, and before I knew it, it was pretty late. It wasn't too much farther, but still, I pulled in at a rest stop. And then I saw this red light from the other side of the mountain, and then…everything was on fire."

"…Was it a bomb from an enemy nation?" Eleven asked.

"No." He shook his head slowly. "Cadelenza betrayed the alliance and launched a surprise attack. There's a military supply base on the other side of Klyvalle. The village was also deemed a military facility, and they bombed it all together. But the planes were quickly shot down by an enormous Amalgam the size of a mountain, breathing fire."

Eleven froze in place and then nodded. "Don't they have the obligation to evacuate noncombatants when deploying an Amalgam?"

"They do. But they couldn't let anyone get away. In order to make those bastards think that their surprise attack had succeeded. So not only was there no evacuation order, there wasn't even an alert. Cadelenza's initial foray was completely and thoroughly crushed by the Amalgam attack, and because of that, my family, my hometown, all of it was burned to ash."

Even now, Theo could not forget it. Pushing aside the people who tried to stop him, he leaped into his car and sped toward his hometown. When he hit the burned-out bridge, he crossed the river on foot and ran frantically through a heat so intense it threatened to set his lungs on fire. To find his house transformed into a pile of rubble, to be filled with despair when he saw that arm hanging lifelessly in it.

Suddenly, a cold hand touched his face. Eleven was pressing a hand damp with condensation against his cheek. The hand of a counterfeit human being with the soft skin of a person wiped away droplets of water sliding down his cheek.

"Theo," she whispered.

When he lifted his face, she peered into his eyes, as expressionless as ever, albeit with a quietness that was somehow compassionate. Calm, ash-colored eyes. Looking into them, he realized that her hand had been dry at first. It was his own cheek that was wet. He groaned silently.

"Does it hurt?" she asked. A rhetorical question.

"All this time. Ever since that day, always..." His voice in response was incredibly small.

Even after the fire was out and he could finally recover the bodies of his family, they were so blackened and burned that identification was difficult. Standing before them, he found that he couldn't accept that reality. The only clues to their identities were the chunks of metal melted onto his sister's arm and his parents' chests. Bracelet, pendant, and tiepin—gifts he'd given them himself. He certainly hadn't selected those presents for *this* purpose. Definitely not for a reunion like this.

After the village was annihilated, no one questioned the army's involvement or their responsibility. The world might have been outraged at the betrayal of an allied country, but it did not mourn the deaths of Theo's family. Left alone, he was nearly ripped apart by anger and sadness. The only thing he could do was set aside the badge that was proof of the hero.

"...After the funeral, I walked straight into a recruiting office," he said. "I thought I might feel a little better if I could make Cadelenza pay for their betrayal."

"Cadelenza's capital fell in Adastrah's retaliation, and they surrendered," Eleven noted.

"Yes. And yet...I didn't feel better at all. It was all so empty."

He'd heard the news of Cadelenza's surrender on another battlefront. While everyone around him cheered and hollered, his own heart went cold. When he thought about how weak this country was and yet it had killed his family, he vomited.

"Since then, every time I see fire, I remember. They were burned alive. I can't imagine how they suffered." He shook his head. "Every time I think about it, I can't forgive myself for being alive. But seeing as I'm still here, I want to be the person my sister boasted was a hero. But when I remember..."

Smiling in the evening sun, his sister had said to him:

"Theo, you've always been my hero. Long before you became an investigator and everyone else's hero, you were my *hero."*

* * *

Fwsh. Fabric pressed up against his cheek. Eleven had pulled out her sleeve and was using it to wipe away his tears. Paying careful attention so as not to tug too hard on his skin, she said, "You could have simply given me the order."

Reflexively, Theo looked at her. There was no heat in her calm eyes. They were gentle somehow.

"I'm certain I could have died over and over until you were satisfied."

"...Eleven, I..."

"But it's exactly because you didn't do that that you're you, isn't it, Theo?" She wiped away the fresh tears with a pale fingertip. Reflecting the evening sun, her gray eyes glittered with warmth. "You control yourself with reason. Rather than devoting yourself to revenge, you continue to be a hero your family can be proud of. I respect your intentions. Even if you cannot forgive yourself for being alive."

"...Did you think those were the words I wanted to hear?" he asked, almost in a sulk. A breeze blew past to dry his cheeks.

"No, Theo," she responded quietly. "This is me 'being closer.'"

Eleven took the crumpled coffee cup from his hands. She walked to the garbage can to throw it out, and the owner of the ice cream truck called to her with a smile. Her response was very natural; it was impossible to tell that she was a nonhuman weapon.

Her expression and her attitude were fixed. She was always quiet and never gave the impression of warmth. It wasn't that she was cold, though. Her gentle acceptance—neither rejection nor denial—was enough to get him to stand up from the bench, no matter who it was she might have been imitating. He touched the back of his hand to his eyes, but they were no longer wet.

"...Are you recovered now, Theo?" Eleven asked.

"I am," he told her. "Sorry for needlessly interrupting our investigation. I just wanted to make sure I actually sat down and talked with you. Maybe that's a bit pathetic... I mean, it's been five years."

"There are differences among people with the perception of time. For you, it's simply that it's been only five years."

"...It actually helps to have you say that." He started walking, and Eleven followed a half step behind. But then she abruptly opened her mouth.

"Although I respect your intentions," she said, "I don't understand them."

"I suppose you wouldn't," he agreed. "A weapon has no emotions as I recall?"

"But simultaneously, I am aware that from time to time, human beings who carry 'grief,' 'hatred,' and 'sorrow' caused by 'loss' are upset by the explication of that experience and will take defensive action to try hiding it."

Theo stopped reflexively. Eleven stopped a few steps in front of him and turned around. Her white-blond hair, dyed by the evening sunlight, took on a reddish hue and was set swaying in the wind.

"Having revealed your wounds, you are definitely not 'pathetic.' You are a 'hero' that your sister can be proud of." Then, as if she'd said her piece, she added, "Let's return to the investigation," and turned on her heel.

The slender lines of her back were precisely those of a young girl. He saw another figure overlaid on hers, wearing her favorite dress.

Heather. My little sister, seven years apart. The sister I couldn't protect even though she said I was a hero.

Would you still call me a hero? Am I the investigator you were proud of?

As if pushed forward by the spring breeze, Theo chased Eleven and then tousled her shiny white-blond hair. From below the mussed bangs, she stared up at him, stunned.

"Thanks," he said. "For everything."

"...It's *you're welcome*, yes?" she said, the same as always, albeit a touch awkwardly this time.

Theo felt restless somehow and patted her head roughly. "Yep, that's it."

It was a strange relationship. But he felt a little comfortable with how they were now, in a way he couldn't quite put his finger on.

When they got back to the office, the results of the handwriting analysis and the report from Narcotics Control had just arrived.

"...So Pastor Tom MacKenzie's handwriting is a match with the essays from Jim Kent's university career?" Theo said. "I guess MacKenzie approached Penley with an eye on the synthetics technology and Nina's 'children.'"

"What does the report from narcotics say?" Eleven asked.

"They were already monitoring the flow of pharmaceuticals to watch over illegal use and the like. I had them use that information net to go after the flow of drugs prescribed after synthetics operations. There's an antibiotic that over-the-counter medications can't replace, so I figured they would've had to have been stocking this, but..." Theo frowned.

Narcotics Control had narrowed the diversion point down to five places in total. All were private support groups or apartment buildings.

"...The closest is slightly under two hours from here by car," Eleven said.

"How about we hit that one, then? We have no other leads."

Theo was reluctant to head out again, but after a few hours of sleep, he wasn't in too bad of a condition. They hurried toward the residential address.

■

By the time Theo stopped the car, the world around them was quite dark. He peered at the building that was registered as the base for the private support group and furrowed his brow. "No lights on? Is it only in use during surgeries?"

"Given the time of day, it's not unusual that the lights would be turned off," Eleven noted. "It is outside of business hours."

He got out of the car and raced over to the building, gun drawn. Three of the same kind of three-story residential homes were pressed up against one another, and the premises were quite large. But there was no security guard, no guard dog, and he couldn't see any kind of security system.

"…Eleven, any sign of Amalgams?"

"There is not, but it's too quiet," she replied. "It's possible that this is a trap."

Theo steadied his breathing and put a hand on the door. It opened easily. Inside was dark and silent. And the sharp scent of blood wafted through the air.

He turned on his flashlight and readied his gun as he entered the building, but he ended up putting the weapon back into its holster after taking only a few steps. There was no sign of anyone around. No sign of anyone *living*.

"…What happened here…?" he murmured, stunned. A step ahead of him, he heard the splashing of water.

The average everyday had been abruptly cut to pieces. People who had been in the middle of cooking, play, stories, prayers—their bodies now lay on the floor with holes in their abdomens. All young girls and elderly people.

The floor was a sea of blood; there was nowhere for him to set a foot down. The peaceful after-dinner quiet had been ripped asunder, and the diners had all breathed their last with looks of surprise on their faces, unable to understand what was happening. The children had collapsed, clutching toys and picture books, or else with their hands pressing against their stomachs.

They were all in the same outfits. The room was decorated in motifs of goats and angels, with a map of the continent on one wall, together with a doctrine. This was, without a doubt, a base for Roremclad, a shared home for believers in the religious group.

The people on the long benches of the chapel had all died with their heads tilted back to the heavens. Blood trailed from the holes in their abdomens, and it was clear that some things had crawled out of them.

Theo shone his flashlight over the area and caught sight of a painting of a goddess brandishing a sword and leading the people. Long hair like woven light itself, white gown fluttering. He took a look at the nearby lectern and gasped. A single photograph covered the book that was likely their sacred text. It showed Eleven in profile in a military uniform. Scribbled across the back was the word *angel*. Judging from the handwriting, he was certain it was Jim Kent's work.

"Theo, over here," Eleven called.

He put the photo in his pocket and hurried to join her. And was baffled when they came out at the back of the building.

The trail of blood led to the waterway flowing next to the site and ended abruptly there.

CONFIDENTIAL

Chapter 5
Faithful Weapon, the Hound

AMALGAM HOUND
Criminal Investigation Bureau:
Special Investigation Unit

The faces of Theo and his team as they gathered in the bureau office were grim. Tobias swung his empty left sleeve and sighed. His gaze was turned toward the photograph of Eleven pinned to the board.

"...So we did find Roremclad's base," he said. "But not only were there no clues about Jim Kent, you found a bunch of dead bodies and a photo of Eleven?"

"This was taken secretly. Did you notice, Eleven?" Emma asked worriedly.

"No," Eleven replied without the look on her face changing. "There is too little information; I can't discern when I was photographed. I apologize."

"I am concerned about the photo, but if their target is Eleven, then we don't have a lot of wiggle room," said Theo. "Let's consider it from the perspective of the objectives of Jim Kent and Roremclad."

He indicated the five blue pins stuck into the map.

"At present, we know of five bases. All of them have been partially renovated and set up to allow for synthetics surgery. At the same time, believers were living together in these bases. But they were all dead, holes ripped open in their abdomens. All young girls and elderly people."

"Awful." Emma scowled. "I mean, moving the men and abandoning the other believers to produce Amalgams."

Tobias's face was also grim. "They made living sacrifices of all these believers, produced the Amalgams, and likely made soldiers of the men. Roremclad has plenty of firepower. Make no mistake, they've dotted their i's, crossed their t's, and now they're finally going to make their move."

"If they're continental unificationists, then their final objective will be unified control of the entire continent," Theo noted. "And if they do it in steps like they have with the Amalgam production, now that they've amassed their militia, they'll be attacking their first target."

"So is that going to be the place where they found Eleven?" Tobias asked. "The city of Delverro?"

"I feel like that's not really much of a reason." Theo frowned and pulled out a map of Adastrah. "But where else would it be? What's their criteria?"

Emma looked troubled as she peered at the map from one side. "If it's the birthplace of the Amalgams, they'll go after the lab. If they're focused on the center of the country, it'd be the capital, right?"

"Both of those places have tight military security," Tobias noted. "Both too difficult for an initial foray."

"The influence of the military is less in Delverro than in other cities," Eleven said. "It would take them time to reach the city once a request was made. Additionally, Delverro is one of the leading cities in the country in terms of shelter maintenance. There are many evacuation routes per capita. If they succeeded in an attack against Delverro, they would succeed in proving their strength and could perhaps recruit people to their cause."

"Makes sense. Pretty solid… So annoying. We can't let them use this as propaganda," Emma said, not bothering to conceal her indignation as she crossed her arms.

Tobias smiled slightly at the childish gesture, but his cheeks quickly tightened again. "Our man hiding in the bushes has revealed himself at last. They'll pick the most flamboyant stage possible."

"And with as many people as possible," Theo agreed. "Their bigger purpose is to spread the name of Roremclad."

"Oh no. Hold up. So then…" Emma looked at Theo and Tobias anxiously and then back at the office calendar.

The date of the peace memorial ceremony was circled in red.

◼

Theo stared at Eleven standing on the roof with her eyes closed. Her cloud-colored hair moved with the wind, her skin was so pale as to be translucent, and her small lips were like flower petals dropped into milk. Calm expression with no hint of emotion, androgynously slender body. Anyone who didn't know what she really was might indeed mistake her for an angel.

If all the Roremclad believers knew about her existence, then the threesome arrested for the bank robberies wouldn't have been afraid when they saw her. So had Jim Kent found Eleven somewhere and photographed her because she physically resembled the angel he'd been championing? Or had he learned about Eleven and her true identity first, and then become so fixated he took pictures? Either way, Theo's team had no leads.

They'd searched every nook and cranny of the Roremclad base, but there were no videos or written records, and when they chased down the bank account, the owner was already dead, a hole in his abdomen. They had an eyewitness report of a truck coming and going from the facilities, but they couldn't pin down where it had gone. They'd looked into every record of any kind—security camera footage, call records, the vast library of notes left behind by Daniel Penley—and hadn't gotten a single hit. The search of the sewers had also come up empty, and they hadn't been able to learn anything about the Amalgams' feeding behavior.

Eleven opened her eyes and looked back at Theo. Her gray eyes met his straight on again today. "There's nothing. I can't detect a core signal."

"…I guess it's more difficult now," he said, nodding. "The cores have no doubt gotten pretty small."

They were assuming that Roremclad's Amalgams had been given parts of Nina's core. Since Nina herself had been difficult to pursue, it was likely nigh impossible to go after her children.

"We are also unable to see their feeding behavior," Eleven noted. "It could be that the Amalgams have ceased activity and are on standby until an order is given. In which case, they are mimicking their surrounding environment, and they cannot be found by human beings. There is the option of me patrolling the sewers, but…"

"No, let's not do that." Theo shook his head. "We'd be in trouble in an emergency without you. Just keep watch for Amalgam signals. I'll look over everything again and see if there isn't some clue to Jim Kent's whereabouts."

"Understood."

They had no time. And yet they were unable to find any clues. Theo grew more impatient with each passing second.

The day of the peace memorial ceremony marched relentlessly toward them, and they still couldn't pin down Roremclad or Jim Kent.

■

Eleven waited in the hallway for Theo to leave his apartment, and the elevator stopped on their floor. Jamie popped his face out and broke into a smile when he spotted Eleven.

"Hey, Eve," he said, walking over to her. "You going to the peace memorial ceremony today?"

"No," she replied. "I'm working."

"Oh yeah? Guess you're busy, huh? So you don't, like, get dressed up or anything?"

"No. It's not necessary." Eleven was wearing the same clothes as always. In contrast, Jamie was in a jacket and tie. It was a rare look for him with his generally casual outfits. She judged the conversation concluded there, but Jamie did not go away. "Is there something else?" she asked him.

"Oh. Yeah. Well…" He scratched his head. "I was just thinking it'd be great to go to the peace memorial ceremony with you, but if you've gotta work, yeah… Guess I'll go by myself."

"There is no issue with going alone. The peace memorial ceremony is a place of prayer and repose of souls."

"R-right, I guess so... Sorry," Jamie responded with slumped shoulders and a manner befitting the word *disappointment*.

Eleven discerned that there was an issue in her handling of the situation, but she also sensed the completion of Theo's preparations and looked behind her. Leather shoes stepped on a pebble on the floor and made a sound—Jamie was heading back to the elevator.

"Okay, I'm off then," he said. "Good luck with your, uh, work, Eve."

"Yes. Thank you very much."

"...So, um, Eve? I know this is maybe a weird thing to say, but..." He scratched the back of his head and stared at his feet as he turned toward Eleven once again. "The first time I saw you...I thought you were for sure an angel, all pale and beautiful, y'know? That's why, um, I wanted to get closer to you somehow. Any way I could."

"I am not an angel," she told him.

"Ha-ha-ha! Yeah. I guess you would say that. The world's an ugly place, but if there's beautiful people like you in it, I sort of feel like I can maybe love it a little. Like, if there were *loads* of people like you." He waved a hand with a smile and got into the elevator. "Ha-ha, you know."

Eleven simply watched him go, but something about his attitude bothered her, and she was rooted to the spot.

Not meeting her eyes, muscle tension, unnatural smile, unsettled gestures. As a pattern, "nervous," "anxious," and "impatient" were applicable. However, if she focused on his eyes alone, she determined it to be something closer to "envy" or "longing." Jamie's earlier attitude was "secret confession."

He displayed interest in me from the very start. That does not constitute a secret. If secret *applies to anything, it is his final words: The world is an ugly place, but if there were more like me, he could love it...*

She examined various similar patterns from past experience but could not come to a conclusion. What about this world was he saying could be loved by increasing the number of Amalgams, which did not know love?

...Human beings easily surpass my understanding.
Eleven gripped her investigator badge and greeted Theo as he came out the front door.

With no progress made on the investigation, the day of the peace memorial ceremony had arrived.

■

The ceremony to mourn those killed in action in the continental war and to pray for peace was about to start.

Although civilian life was finally getting back to normal, there were people who'd returned, people who hadn't, and people whose whereabouts were unknown. There were far too many people with unhealed wounds. The day to pray that the souls of those sacrificed might find respite and to hope for peace going forward had come.

The city welcomed the peace memorial ceremony with a bright mood, but the air inside the Criminal Investigation Bureau was tense.

Theo tightened his necktie and listened carefully to Captain Paloma's words.

"I believe you all know this, but there are many points of concern with regard to the peace memorial ceremony. It's likely that Roremclad, led by Jim Kent, will make a move. Thus, Delverro is on high alert, and you will patrol the area you are assigned in cooperation with the municipal police. You will move in groups of two or more. You are to call in any anomalies immediately. Check the list for your assigned area. Let's go." Paloma concluded the meeting, and the investigators started moving.

The ceremony in the city of Delverro was simpler than those of other cities in the country: just speeches from the mayor and military personnel decorated in battle. It was also being held only at Central Park, so they could split into groups on alert outside and those who would be standing by at the bureau.

Emma sighed, midrange katahr in hand, a gloomy look on her face. "Are we actually going to be okay here...? I mean, the mayor didn't really understand what the deal was."

"All we can do is have faith and give it all we've got. It was pretty much everything we could do to simply get enough firepower out on the streets." Theo checked his gun before tucking it away in its holster. Special units were patrolling the ceremony venue, and snipers were in position to maintain control from above. They really couldn't prepare any more than that.

"Jim Kent could also be wearing a disguise and lying in wait within the venue. Be suspicious of everyone, man, woman, young, old—everyone. No panicking, keep in contact. That's everything. Let's go." Theo ended the conversation, and the group split into two and got into their cars.

Eleven opened her mouth. "Why wouldn't the mayor agree to change the location of the event?"

"Probably because he didn't believe a word of what we were saying," Theo told her. "But I'm not surprised he'd be resistant. Plenty of people just want to pray together, to feel that they're not alone beneath a sky where there's no worry of an air raid."

When they reached the area they'd been assigned, there were already a number of people walking down Main Street. Dressed in mourning clothes, carrying flowers, they had conflicted looks on their faces, wedged between the sense of security that they were now safe and the feeling that they had lost something precious. With lilies and other white flowers in hand, the people came. Like a funeral procession.

■

The bell struck noon at the Central Park clock tower. The peace memorial ceremony solemnly commenced.

Starting with a speech from the mayor, the ceremony proceeded apace with words of comfort for the spirits of those lost in battle and speeches from the civilian organizations that provided support to the families of the deceased.

Finally, Master Sergeant John Heseldine came to stand on the podium, showered in applause. The master sergeant was bashful, medals pinned to his chest.

"I have been on many battlefields, but I've never been so nervous as I am right now," he said, his voice full of energy over the speakers. True to his words, his hands were shaking. "As a survivor, I cannot forget the deaths of all those who were not able to return to their homes. They fought nobly, and I hope that you all will please remember that these were the heroes who brought us this victory. Please never forget the smiling faces of those you've loved."

Birds flew by high above in the cloudless sky, chirping loudly. The people sitting in the very front row of the audience noticed Heseldine's right hand was shaking quite excessively and felt that something wasn't quite right. No matter how nervous he might have been, this was not normal.

"I feel fortunate to be standing here in this place safely, and so I have made a decision as a survivor," he continued. "And that is to maintain a record of the things that happened on the battlefield and to never let the cause of this war fade from memory so as to ensure that this tragedy is never repeated. While we pray for the repose of the souls of our comrades lost in battle and the many who lost their lives, I pray that we will be the last heroes."

He threw his arms out as if to catch something dropping down from the sky. And then he called in a clear voice:

"Glory to Roremclad!"

The crowd took a moment to process this and stared stunned.

Shwrrsch. Flesh and bone opened up from inside the master sergeant's body. Sharp claws pierced Heseldine's chest, and his torso was ripped vertically into two. Fresh blood jetted out; the venue erupted in screams.

The hands of parents were slow to cover their children's eyes, and high-pitched shrieks rang out. People kicked over chairs and pushed others to try and escape.

Gawking eyes took it all in.

* * *

Body of white clay shuddering, ripping off the flesh of Master Sergeant Heseldine and faced with so many targets, the automagiton—the Amalgam—howled ferociously.

■

"Emergency! We've got an emergency here! An Amalgam has appeared at the ceremony venue! All units, mobilize to get control of the situation! I repeat—"

As they gave updates over the wireless, the sniper squad began their attack on the Amalgam. Rifle bullets shot through it but seemed to have no real effect. The goggling eyes whirled toward the exact position of the snipers, and they felt a shiver of fear.

"That—it's an Amalgam!"

"Chief! We had a direct hit on the position of the core, but it's not stopping!"

"Stay in position! The core is just small. Keep shooting and we'll—"

As the squad leader tried to encourage his team, his head was abruptly taken clean off his shoulders. In that split second when they struggled to understand what had happened, the rest of the squad all fell victim to the same fate.

Liquid splashed, and angled rifles clattered to the ground. Men in black grinned at their victory beneath their goat masks and set out in search of their next prey.

■

The chaos that overtook the peace memorial ceremony was immediately transmitted to Theo and Eleven on Main Street.

"Emergency. This is an emergency. Shots fired in Central Park. Amalgam confirmed, raid by armed insurgents. Special forces respond immediately. Teams, promptly evacuate—"

News burst forth from the wireless. Before he'd even had time to process the information that was coming in fast and furious, Theo was directing the wave of citizens to shelters.

Thanks to the facilities built during the continental war, there were fortunately many paths leading from Main Street to a shelter. Theo raced over to people who fell and picked them up before they could be trampled by other citizens, lent a hand of support to people with weak legs, and ran around guiding civilians. While he was unable to get in touch with Tobias and Emma, the information coming over the wireless grew more tangled. Perhaps everyone was trying to send messages, and it was too much for the system. His cell phone's communication functions were also disrupted.

He hurried to scoop up a child who had fallen in front of him and brought him to the mother, who had tears in her eyes. "He's all right," Theo told her. "Just get to the shelter. Listen, son, you make sure you stay with your mom, okay? Promise?"

"Please make way for someone in a wheelchair."

He'd no sooner had the thought that this voice was too cool for the situation when Eleven came running along carrying an elderly person together with their wheelchair. He let out a sigh of relief at how utterly dependable she was, and in his ear, he finally picked up the wireless from Detective Operations.

They'd managed to get 80 percent of Main Street evacuated, and Captain Paloma gave orders now for any free hands to go and provide backup in Central Park. When he told Eleven this after she had returned from the shelter, she immediately raised and lowered her eyelids.

"Understood. Tobias and Emma are still helping evacuate and say they cannot leave their posts yet."

"Got it. We'll go on ahead, then. Leave the rest to the police." Theo took Eleven and started running for Central Park.

When he saw the plaza, the main gathering place for the people, Theo was stunned into speechlessness. He couldn't believe his eyes.

Bodies covered the ground, buried in white flowers. All the corpses were so violently disfigured that it was hard to process them as having originally been human. About the only things that clearly retained their shape were torsos equipped with bulletproof vests and fragments of arts rejectors.

Theo furrowed his brow at the painful scene. He raced over to a collapsed police officer nearby who seemed to have merely tumbled to the ground. But bullets were embedded in his back, and from what Theo could tell from the way the bullets had landed, they were the type used in mass-produced machine guns that could be acquired cheaply.

Armed insurgents and Amalgams. Even if the special forces were there, he wasn't sure whether the shelter would hold up.

Theo gritted his teeth, but then he heard a sound and immediately raised his gun.

An Amalgam punched at the stage set up for the ceremony and knocked it flying. Appearing out of the accompanying cloud of dust, its body was white like a clay doll. It was smaller than the specimens he'd seen on the battlefield, but its head reached above the streetlamps. Half of this massive bulk was taken up with the mouth in the abdomen, where fangs dripped with blood. It chewed up and digested arms complete with bone caught on the edges of its mouth.

This form was specialized in feeding. The way it stood on all fours, stretching its neck out—it was all unusual.

Theo heard new screams and gunfire from in the distance. He couldn't wait for backup.

He quietly released the safety on his gun. "Eleven, do you think that thing's core can be destroyed with a handgun?"

"I will check its armor. Please fire when the core is exposed," she said simply and lightly kicked at the ground.

The Amalgam opened its mouth wide and charged, destroying the stage as it went. It gave a bloodcurdling scream and stomped over the corpses.

But Eleven did not shrink back. She transformed both of her arms into swords and slid them along blood and dead flesh, slipping past the massive Amalgam and nimbly slicing into its legs. In contrast to her own nimble landing, the Amalgam crashed into the sea of blood with a *thud*.

It quickly rose up as it devoured the dead with its abdominal mouth. Without waiting for the sluggish voraciousness to end, Eleven leaped high into the air. Her silver blades glinted in the sunlight and traced out a crescent moon. Theo could spy a sparkling fragment of red in the cross section of the Amalgam's severed neck.

Not letting this chance get away, he steadied his hand and pulled the trigger.

The core shattered like glass. The Amalgam stopped moving and melted into mud.

Eleven dropped back down to the ground mixed with blood and mud before shaking the former from her sword leg and transforming it back into a human leg. "No armor, slow movement. But the core was too small. Is it difficult for human beings to dispose of?"

"Mm." Theo holstered his gun. "If it's visible like it was now, that's one thing. But it's tough to get a good shot with the flesh on top of it."

Eleven walked back over to Theo but then abruptly lifted her face. Following her gaze, he belatedly noticed the sound of a propeller and saw a plane flying above his head. A heartbeat later, it dropped a mountain of flyers on them.

At the same time, a man's dispassionate voice began to play over the loudspeakers in every corner of the city.

"We receive the blessings of God; our time has come. God has spoken in prophecy to our Roremclad father. And He says unto us that each life we take brings us closer to paradise. Thus, we shall create a corner of paradise from Delverro, the land that welcomed our father, the land to which the angel descended. Our previous wandering was nothing more than a trial in preparation for this day. We take this land as the first keystone toward flying the same flag over the entire continent, together with the angel of strange form dispatched by God. Glory to Roremclad!"

Theo heard an explosion off in the distance as the broadcast ended. Black smoke rose up from between buildings. People yelled over the wireless, and he couldn't really pick out one voice from another. Papers fluttered down from above. He snatched one out of the air, and the word *Roremclad* jumped out at him along with the drawing from

Bob Derry's apartment. The flyer, printed on cheap paper, showed a girl in a laurel wreath brandishing a sword, standing proudly atop a mountain of skulls.

"You've got to be kidding me." Theo clicked his tongue and crushed the handbill deliberately underfoot. "Eleven, any signals?"

"There are no enemy signals in the area," she told him. "Setting aside the Amalgams, how shall I handle enemy soldiers?"

"…They're not going to listen to anything we have to say," he replied. "But killing them will only add fuel to their feeling that they're fighting a holy war. Priority is on arresting them. Render them helpless. And—"

"…This—Yell—Hill—request—someone—help—"

A voice mixed with static crackled to life over the wireless. Maybe it just happened to have been tuned to that channel—the voice quickly cut out. It was Yellow Hill Road requesting backup, regardless of jurisdiction.

If they were frantically going through every wireless channel, then the others are…

Theo struggled to make a decision. Eleven was indeed powerful, peerless. But he himself would barely be able to lay down protective fire and help with the evacuation. They were up against a true monster here. Would he be of any help? Was the speaker of this wireless message even alive still?

But the park before him had been turned into a scene straight out of a nightmare. Trampled lilies, the plaza a sea of blood and corpses. The end of the innocents who had simply come together to pray for peace.

"…Theo, is something the matter?" Eleven asked. Her gray eyes were as quiet as ever, the surface of a placid lake.

When he saw himself reflected in them, he felt somewhat calmed and took a deep breath to steady himself. If an investigator's duty was to protect the people, then he had to run toward whatever slim possibility that existed.

"Request for backup," he said. "I don't know what's going on out there, but we can't expect anyone else to come to the rescue. We'll have to do this ourselves."

"Understood. I will accompany you."

The road was buried under abandoned vehicles, so they would have to move on foot. Theo started running, still holding his gun, and Eleven followed without a word. He'd been running when she went in pursuit of the bank robbers, too. But his heart pained him even more now.

Every time he came across someone collapsed on the ground, he checked their pulse; if they were alive, he carried them to the shelter; if they weren't, he set them down on the edge of the sidewalk. Find someone on the ground, check for a pulse, carry them down the sidewalk to the shelter. Find, check, carry. Find, check, carry.

Thanks to the inexhaustible Eleven, this almost automated operation went smoothly. But it wore Theo down mentally even further.

As he confirmed one death after another, he scowled. At this rate, the voice on the wireless would be the same. He clenched his hands into fists and hurried ahead.

Running alongside him, Eleven abruptly opened her mouth. "Report. Passenger vehicle approaching from Thaley River Road. Several enemy signals from Alderta Avenue."

"If I'd known this was how it was going to go, I would've brought a machine gun!" he cried, frustrated. "Handle them!"

"Roger. I will regroup soon after handling Alderta Avenue." She had no sooner finished speaking than she was running ahead by herself. She leaped from a streetlamp to the roof of a building and disappeared.

Theo rebuked his legs as they started to tremble and kept running like the world was on fire.

■

Eleven looked out over Alderta Avenue from her position atop the building. Within range of her sensors were four Amalgams and three squads of human beings in possession of firearms. The few remaining survivors were already in the hands of the enemy.

The human beings weren't exactly fighting together with the Amalgams. It seemed that they were simply chasing the Amalgams as they fed and shooting anyone they came across. This was definitely not the coordinated action of trained soldiers. Their only objective appeared to be mass slaughter. They killed everyone, with no differentiation between civilian and police, and let the Amalgams feed.

How great would the damage be if an Amalgam noticed a shelter and learned to feed efficiently?

…*Theo does not desire that. Therefore, I must prevent it.*

Eleven stood on the edge of the roof and waited until her targets were passing directly below. The Amalgams were searching for their next prey, and they came toward her position, mowing down trees and kicking over cars.

She selected a surprise attack via free fall. She swung the blade of her leg and cut away the Amalgam's core along with its head. Before it had finished turning to dirt and collapsing into a tree, she was already on the ground and closing in on the enemy. She defended against the gunfire with crossed arms and thrust her palm toward a torso, intending to rupture the intestines. Her opponent did indeed flinch at this. But the feeling against her hand was too hard.

Synthetics?

Rather than unconsciousness via a striking blow, Eleven chose to sever all four limbs with her blades. She felt the shudder as the synthetic joints and connecting nerves were cut loose. The human being cried out in anguish and dropped to the ground, while the severed limbs flailed on their own on the pavement.

Human beings in the process of synthetics replacement and Amalgams. Eleven began calculating Theo's odds dealing with them independently, but before she could run much of a simulation, bullets came flying at her. She crushed these in one hand and used the momentum she'd absorbed from the machine gun to punch her opponent hard in the side of the head. Perhaps this part was still that of a human; his feet tangled beneath him, and he dropped to the ground. He struggled to get back up. She detected no civilian survivors in the area.

Enemy neutralized within five minutes. Rejoin Theo.

Eleven readied the machine gun she'd taken and raced off at top speed.

Theo felt himself reach his limit and stopped running at more or less the same time as the passenger vehicle turned off Thaley River Road. Out of breath, he waited and watched as it was forced to stop, blocked by the stream of abandoned vehicles.

A disheveled man jumped out of the driver's seat, while a little boy and a pregnant woman got out of the back. They had managed to get away as a family somehow.

Theo gripped his investigator's badge and ran over to them. "Criminal Investigation Bureau! You need to evacuate! This way! Hurry!"

The man looked at Theo with visible relief. He scooped up his son, took his wife's hand, and led the family toward Theo. They weren't injured, but the mother was so heavily pregnant, it looked like she could barely walk; running was out of the question.

Theo wrapped her arm around his shoulders and gritted his teeth in frustration. All the chaos was no doubt putting her under a lot of stress; her breathing was uneven, and her face was pale.

"Just hang on, ma'am. There's a doctor in the shelter. You'll be all right." He offered encouragement as a distraction, and the mother nodded several times while she intently put one foot in front of the other. He left the anxious son to his father and hurried toward the emergency entrance with the mother.

A large shadow abruptly fell over them.

What on earth is that...?

Before he could look up, whatever it was dropped down in front of him, smashing the trees that lined the road.

An Amalgam swollen to the size of a truck. It must have already fed plenty, but still unsated, it turned its empty eyes toward Theo and the small family. Massive fangs clacked open, clots of blood stretched out into threads between them, and the stench of rusty breath overwhelmed him.

Theo pushed the family behind him and readied his revolver.

Can I drop it with one shot...? An Amalgam this enlarged?

His finger on the trigger trembled. In that moment of indecision and hesitation, the Amalgam charged. Theo heard high-pitched screams from behind him and reflexively fired, but the Amalgam didn't so much as flinch.

He whirled his head around, looking for somewhere to run. He wanted to at least keep the family safe.

A fallen tree leaped up and swept the Amalgam down from one side. The creature tumbled away and slammed into the lane of cars, setting off all the car alarms.

Eleven tossed aside the tree in her hands and looked back at Theo with the same expressionless face as always. "Are you all right?"

"Y-you are really— Ah! Behind you!" he cried.

Eleven whirled around and caught a car flying toward her. Her heel dug into the pavement, but her face remained expressionless as she tossed the passenger vehicle to one side and turned her leg into a blade.

The Amalgam roared at her and pulled itself upright. It pushed its way through the cars, its focus entirely on Eleven now.

Theo was about to use this opening to lead the family to the shelter, but the mother groaned with an anguished expression, clutched her stomach, and crouched down.

The son raced over to her, his face pale. "You can't come out yet! Not yet! Stay in Mommy's belly!"

His voice was shrill, and the Amalgam's buggy eyes turned toward the family. Its gaze was mechanical. But it had definitely reacted to the child's voice.

Theo shuddered.

Another Amalgam or human beings with few weapons—which would the creature prioritize attacking, given the lessons it had learned thus far in its rampage?

The Amalgam wailed with a bone-chilling howl and started toward Theo and the family. Eleven immediately leaped up and sliced at its head. It wasn't until her blade was digging halfway through its chest that the Amalgam finally slowed down, but even Eleven could only brace herself so firmly with just one leg. The Amalgam threw her off, easily knocking her slender physique flying.

She hit the ground as though the impact hadn't even tickled, but then dropped to her knees.

Theo could hear the sizzling of burning flesh, see the white smoke drifting up. Her blade leg was melting.

A single drop of the fluid dripping from the Amalgam's wound dissolved the asphalt where it fell.

"They made one hell of a monster...!" Theo spat and then gasped.

Eyes still turned toward Eleven, the Amalgam was lifting a car. The little boy was shouting something. The Amalgam roared and threw the vehicle. Eleven never took her gaze off the beast, but with her leg in the middle of regenerating, she couldn't stand up yet.

Theo's mind went blank.

Would Eleven be beyond recovery if she was crushed by a car? No.

But a memory came to vivid life in the back of his mind. The charred remains of his family. Comrades flying through the air. The young soldier blown to smithereens. So many victims. White flowers and hunks of flesh. Police officers dying before his eyes. A mountain of corpses.

Could he watch it again? Could he watch another life be scattered before his eyes?

Before he knew it, he was running and throwing himself at Eleven. He scooped up her small body, and as he half fell forward, a tremendous wind blew overhead. He heard the roar of the glass shattering in the storefronts, and antitheft alarms began to screech and squeal.

When he sat up, Eleven's eyes were wide in surprise, her pale lips trembling. But before he could say anything, she pushed him down and stood firmly on the pavement with her regenerated leg.

The next car that came flying toward them, she knocked away with a single punch and then started running. She snatched up a broken road sign, leaped onto the head of the Amalgam as if about to take flight, and brought the road sign down with all her might.

Klankrrrshht! The sign was embedded in the Amalgam's head. The viscous liquid that oozed out of the Amalgam at once began melting the sign, but Eleven nevertheless forced it further into her opponent.

The flesh split apart with an ugly crackling sound. A fragment of the faintest red peeked out from the cross section, catching the light.

"Eleven! Don't move!" Theo shouted, yanking his gun into position.

The look on Eleven's face did not change, but her hair fanned out around her, and she kept pushing the road sign into the Amalgam's head. She stabbed the leg that she'd only just regenerated into the road and forcibly pinned the creature to the spot.

Gunfire. Recoil against his shoulder.

It was only when Theo saw the Amalgam turn to mud that he understood he'd shot out the core. He heaved a sigh of relief and returned his gun to its holster.

Eleven tossed the road sign away and pulled her leg out of the road before quietly walking over to him. "Are you injured?"

"No. I'm fine, thanks to you… Right. We have to get them out of here." Theo looked back at the family. The mother seemed to be in pain, but the son was gaping at Eleven. Theo struggled with how to explain what had just happened, but before he could say anything, the boy spoke.

"Are you a tiny Amalgam, lady? I've seen 'em on TV. They get better in, like, two seconds when they're hurt."

"Yes, sir. I am an Amalgam," Eleven replied without hesitation. The father's eyes flew open, but the son raced over to her. She dropped to her knees to bring her eyes level with his.

"Okay, so! Okay!" the boy cried excitedly. "That monster there—are you gonna get all of 'em?"

Theo watched the exchange carefully. The boy had his hands tightly clenched, and tears welled up in his eyes.

Eleven blinked slowly and then met the boy's gaze. "Of course, sir," she said. "I promise you will become an elder brother without issue."

The boy's face brightened. "Promise!" He ran back to his mother.

Even as he marveled at how unexpected Eleven's response was, Theo called out to the family, "Let's evacuate now while we can. Son, you're doing a great job protecting your parents. Keep it up."

Theo once again lent his shoulder to the mother to help her stand up, while Eleven ran ahead to the shelter. They had taken only a few steps when a group of paramedics came running over with a stretcher, and the family was safely whisked away to the shelter. All that was left on Yellow Hill Road were car alarms and emergency sirens.

Perhaps searching for enemy signals, Eleven had her eyes turned toward a different road.

Theo walked over to her. "Eleven, back there, you—"

"You were foolish," she said, her voice many times harder than normal.

He reflexively stopped in his tracks, and she slowly turned around. The usual calm gray of her eyes now glittered incandescently.

"Why did you cover me?" she demanded. "I am a Hound. It is possible for me to recover quickly from damage sustained in situations such as a collision with a car. There is no rational reason for you to shield me."

"Maybe you're right," he protested. "But your leg was melted, and—"

"I will not die. But *you* will!" she roared angrily. This was the second time she had raised her voice. Theo was stunned. She grabbed the lapels of his suit and forced him to look at her. She was staring straight at him, her gray eyes shaking so much they threatened to spill over.

"You know very well the fragility of human beings!" she yelled. "Where was the need for you to court danger like that?! If you had it in you to shield me, then you should have used that power to evacuate the family!"

"I couldn't just leave you!" he cried in response. "Even if I know you're strong, even if I know you're a Hound! Even if I know it's dangerous, I can't just abandon you!"

"Is that any justification for leaping in front of a flying car?! One mistake, and you would have died! I am your Hound, not your little sister!"

She shoved him. Not hard, but for Theo, it made a definite impact. He stared, shocked, and the expression vanished from her face. Abruptly, like a switch had been flipped.

"...Please excuse me. I apologize for my rudeness—very unlike a weapon."

"No." He shook his head slowly. "I'm the one who's—"

An explosion cut him off. Cars flew through the air, and he heard

gunfire, people screaming, and the shrieks of Amalgams. It seemed they had no more time to rest, no more time to talk.

■

Emma aimed her katahr and gently pressed the trigger. A Magirus Shell hit the Amalgam climbing the exterior wall of a residential complex and burst open, pinning down the Amalgam's ugly bulk with ice. The other one trying to pass through the courtyard was also frozen in place, and Emma panted as she reloaded with a fresh bullet.

This residential complex had always had a shelter in the basement. Thanks to that, the residents had mostly been able to evacuate, but if the Amalgams found the shelter, the occupants of every household in the complex would die. That fear alone fixed Emma's shaking sights.

She'd heard Amalgams were fairly resistant to magic, but it was still annoying when they cracked the frozen edges and tried to break free. Without the time to wonder whether lightning might be more effective, she fired her next bullet. Her brain was hot like it was on fire because of the heavy consumption of her magical powers, and the left side of her body was growing numb. She pushed all that aside and asked over her shoulder, "Tobias, how're you looking?"

"Rough," he replied tersely. "Everything but the heads are probably synthetic."

"No wonder guns and magic aren't working, then," she said.

Hiding behind a wall, Tobias fired at enemy soldiers in the hallway. The strange sound the bullets made upon landing piqued his curiosity until he realized that the human parts had also likely been worked on. A hail of bullets dug into the wall shielding him.

Emma froze another Amalgam that was trying to break free and turned around. The elderly couple slumped down there proceeded to shrink back, clutching each other's hands tightly. Although she was happy that she and Tobias had managed to secure them when they were late evacuating, there was no opening in which to get them out of there. She gritted her teeth.

"Emma, throw up a Moke for me in the hallway," Tobias said. "I'm going in."

"You mean smoke?" she asked. "Judging from the way the freezing magic hits, it'll have to be—"

"Right. I'll leave you to it, then."

By the time she looked back, he was already parkouring upward and reaching for the roof. She didn't even have the chance to cry out and stop him before he disappeared above.

She fired at an Amalgam as it started to move and then retrieved a test tube from a pouch. "Asking for the moon is proof of how much you trust me. Yeah, yeah! Fine, I get it!"

She pulled out the stopper, took a deep breath, and blew magical power into the tube. The liquid inside frothed and bubbled violently. She waited for a moment when the gunfire ceased, threw the test tube into the hallway, and fired a magical bullet at the liquid that spilled out onto the floor. The frozen liquid sent up puffs of white smoke that blanketed the hallway in the blink of an eye.

Emma intently peered out at the damage. She saw the smoke abruptly waver and looked back. She could hear not only gunfire but also cries of distress and heavy thuds. She held her breath and braced herself alongside the elderly couple.

Emma leaped up when she saw a man come tumbling toward them. Tobias stepped over him with a smile. His brand-new synthetic left hand was dyed red.

"Sorry for the wait," he said. "Shall we go?"

"...I'm more afraid of you than of them," Emma muttered, but an incredible shriek unlike that of any beast drowned out her words. There was no way a human being could produce a sound like that.

The shrieking continued. Her skin broke out in goose bumps, and she felt her insides trying to escape her body.

She was not the only one to lift her face questioningly. The Amalgams around them also stopped and looked up at the sky, and then they charged through the wall in the direction of the awful voice.

After carrying a severely injured person to the shelter, Theo hurried out onto the street. Eleven cut down her nth Amalgam before shifting her blade back into a leg and walking over to him.

"Eleven, what was that sound?" he asked, looking up at the sky.

"It was most likely the cry of the command individual," she told him. "Its voice is quite clearly different from the others, and all the Amalgams reacted by moving toward its source at once. I conjecture that it was an order to regroup."

Theo wrestled with himself for a second and then grabbed the machine gun he'd seized from Roremclad. He'd been firing nonstop, and he wasn't exactly sure how many bullets it had left. But while the request for military mobilization had been accepted, it would take time for them to arrive. For the time being at least, he and Eleven had no choice but to keep fighting back on their own.

"…If they're gathering in one place, that's actually good for us," he said. "Better than having them scattered around the city preying on people."

"It is a fight against time, so I am in agreement with that opinion. However, I am the only one who can respond to a group of Amalgams."

"That's the issue. You know of any arms dealers selling rocket launchers?"

"I do not," she replied briefly before turning her eyes to the machine gun. "Would it not be more effective for me to handle the Amalgams independently while you evacuate civilians?"

"It might well be. But I'll need a weapon for that, too. And…" He sighed and twisted a finger into the machine-gun belt. "I could never forgive myself if I let you go alone. Come on."

"…All right. Let's go." She started walking next to him but then abruptly opened her mouth again. "Although I absolutely do not understand your foolish, inefficient, and reckless behavior."

"Well, gee, sorry!" he replied.

"This is precisely why I have determined that a weapon like myself is useful and necessary for you."

Theo stared at her. "Is that a good thing?"

"If you determine that it is a 'good thing,'" she said, glancing up at him, and his eyes widened unconsciously. Perhaps because of the angle or some trick of the light, her normally expressionless face looked to him like it softened the slightest bit.

As he followed her in the direction the voice had come from, a car came out from around the corner. Ahead of it, a truck-sized Amalgam was eating a vehicle with the mouth in its stomach. It swallowed the car whole, along with the person whose arm hung limply from the driver's side window. It had apparently stopped selecting prey targets—the Amalgam was shoving into its mouth whatever happened to be in front of it, whether that be a car or a streetlamp or a Roremclad warrior who had been working with it only moments earlier. Several other Amalgams of a similar nature were scattered along the road: a true hellscape.

A manhole shot into the air, and water jetted upward. No, not water—a pale, muddy Amalgam that quickly took on a more material form. Its body swelled as it pushed into the road and buildings, forcing the people hiding inside to start running as the structures collapsed. Multiple sets of eyes swiveled to focus on the new prey, and hair-raising howl followed hair-raising howl.

"Eleven, do whatever you can to keep them busy!" Theo shouted. "I'll get the people away!"

"Roger. I will do 'whatever I can' to eliminate them."

Eleven picked up a half-destroyed car and flung it with both hands. It slammed squarely into the face of an Amalgam charging after terrified civilians, and Eleven stomped down on the monster from above. Theo fired at an individual pushing ahead while Eleven was otherwise occupied, and when it shrank back, he hurried the civilians away from the scene. Crazed with anger, the Amalgam swung its head around, and Theo turned the barrel of his gun toward it, ready to defend himself. But the Amalgam abruptly split in half, the parts falling to either side, and legs transformed into sharp blades came down lightly on the asphalt.

The Amalgams were undaunted, surging in one after the other. They reacted to anything that moved, even if it wasn't a human being—one snapped at a rolling manhole cover; another bared its fangs at a flashing police light spinning emptily. Would the people be safer if they didn't move? Either way, they'd be eaten alive if they didn't get out of here. There was nowhere left to hide.

Heads were lopped off, arms, legs; Eleven danced along on the tips of steel toes. She had no sooner shut one Amalgam up with a tossed car than she was pinning another to a wall with a streetlamp. All on her own, she was fighting off a small army of the creatures, but still, one managed to break away and come after the civilians desperately fleeing. Theo pushed them toward the shelter as he pulled the trigger, sights set on the Amalgam's head. After he'd emptied a full magazine into it, it finally turned to mud and melted away.

...If I have to shoot them that many times, all the bullets in the world won't be enough!

He helped someone up and scanned the ground for any guns that had been left behind. But then he heard a cry for help and whirled around.

A young man was running, with several Amalgams in hot pursuit.

Eleven raced over and knocked off one of their heads. Another slipped and fell on the mud its companion melted into, and Eleven kicked it aside, as she swept the legs out from under yet another. But that didn't stem the tide.

Theo hurriedly shoved the last of the civilians with him into the shelter, picked up a fallen machine gun, and started running. Eleven hit the Amalgam that was about to crawl over the fallen youth with a road sign, and in that opening, Theo yanked on the youth's arm and dragged him away from the spot. When he got a closer look at the young man, he realized they'd met the one time in the elevator at his building.

"Th-thank…you," the man panted.

"As long as you're safe," Theo replied, himself out of breath. "Where were you? Did no one tell you where to evacuate?"

"A-Alderta Avenue. Those monsters attacked everyone, and I was so scared, I couldn't move."

"...I guess you would have been," Theo said sympathetically. "Any other survivors?"

"No..." The man shook his head. "Just me. Thank God you're here. No one came to Alderta Avenue, so I thought we'd been abandoned by the police..."

Something in the youth's words gave Theo pause. Officers had absolutely gone to Alderta Avenue. He opened his mouth to point this out, and the young man thrust his hand forward to shake Theo's at basically the same time.

Before Theo could take the man's hand, it was cut off, and its owner was kicked aside.

The man flew through the air and slammed into a mailbox. The metal buckled beneath him, and he dropped onto the road. Before Theo knew it, Eleven was standing in front of him, as if to cover him.

"What exactly are you doing, sir?" she demanded quietly.

Theo shuddered as he abruptly realized what felt so odd about the situation: Not a drop of blood was falling from the man's severed arm.

Coughing, the man got to his feet and looked at Eleven through messy hair. He smiled. "How mean of you, Eve. You never once called me Jamie." His voice was hoarse.

Saying the name to himself, Theo yanked his machine gun up in front of him. This other nickname for *James* suddenly clicked with the motivation behind the successful creation of the human copy, Nina.

Theo fired every bullet in his gun; the metal body grew hot, and yet he still felt no relief.

Full of holes, the man laughed at his tattered clothes. There was no blood.

"Since when?" Theo yelled angrily, switching out the magazines. "How long have you been hiding in that form, Jim Kent?!"

The youth grinned and leaned back against a mailbox.

Jamie's skin and flesh slid away, revealing tendons and fat and blood vessels like wicked flowers sprouting branches or snakes slithering upward. The fleshy mass showed its true form. Skin clacked into place around it like puzzle pieces.

* * *

Short hair. Eyes and eyebrows that angled upward. Prominent nose and jaw, threatening visage. And a distinctive scar on his forehead. Jim Kent smiled cruelly at Theo and Eleven.

"What a pleasure. My angel, thou who are radiant as a star."

Theo aimed his gun again. And then the world shook as something slammed into him from one side.
"Theo!" Eleven cried, her voice growing distant.
Earth and sky traded places, and his body forgot what gravity was. He tumbled along, tossed out onto the road. Instead of crashing into a car or the hard concrete, he hit a black net stretched out across a wall. The mysterious softness absorbed the force of the impact, and the net set him down safely on the ground.
He quickly remembered that Eleven had used this fabric when apprehending Jacus Ghilane. The net melted away and turned into a band that wrapped around his left arm.
"Eleven…!" He whirled around and gasped.

A herd of Amalgams were fusing together to become a writhing white wall. In the center, Kent held the hands of his cracked body up to the sky.

His arms shot through Eleven's slender torso, making an offering of her shining, red core.
Her left arm was gone, and her remaining limbs hung lifelessly, motionless.

"You bastaaaard!" Theo fired his machine gun at Kent. The cheap weapon didn't have a very tight shot, but even so it managed to hit him dead-on.
Kent, however, simply turned his head to one side. He appeared entirely uninjured. The Amalgam bodies closed in following the

sweeping movement of the row of arms that sprang up, digging into the asphalt.

Theo leaped out of the way, but the wave of blades pressed in on him, churning up the asphalt and knocking even the surrounding cars flying. He, too, was knocked off his feet and sent rolling backward.

I've got to do something... Something...!

Gritting his teeth at the pain coursing through his body, he managed to pull himself up somehow. A gun wasn't enough. He needed more firepower. His eyes chased over the area around him for something, anything. Then they landed on something, and he hurried toward it.

■

"That man's running away," Kent told Eleven, and she lifted her face. With her core exposed, her operational capacity had plummeted. When she confirmed movement under her skin, Kent unfolded his flesh like resin and pulled her close.

His core and his body were both like and unlike those of an Amalgam. Which was why she hadn't been able to detect him until he reached out to Theo. Was he using something other than fortunite? Perhaps a rare substance not even the Hounds were privy to? She stared, attempting to ascertain the answer, and Kent grabbed her jaw and turned her face toward him.

"He's just garbage," he told her. "He doesn't have the first clue about what you're worth. Isn't that right, Eve?"

"...What is your objective in manipulating the Amalgams and transcending human form?" Eleven asked.

"You already know the answer to that, don't you?" Kent smiled. "Paradise. We're creating a beautiful land for a new humanity made up of rational actors like you Amalgams."

"Did you kill believers and destroy the city simply for the sake of a fiction?"

"I did. Unlike you, they were all foolish, greedy, irrational human beings," Kent affirmed with an expression to which the word *ecstatic* applied and put a hand to his chest. "They were unnecessary for my paradise, but life is life. I will have it used meaningfully. There. Take a look."

His flesh rippled, and his chest opened up. The heart sitting inside of it was half the size of a lung and thumping away. It had a crystalline red luster to it, but the blood filling it was muddied and concentrated, a sinister reddish black.

Eleven stared. "That can't actually be...the philosopher's stone..."

"It's ugly compared with the cores of your kind, but at long last, it's reached the level of usability. I've made it this far, Eve. By my own power!"

"...How can this...?" Her voice was small. Now that she knew the truth about how he was different from the Amalgams, she could see their own foolishness as well.

The philosopher's stone: the name the sorcerers gave to the almighty substance that could transform into, substitute for, and reproduce anything and everything. But human lives in the thousands were required to make it, so production of the substance had been prohibited by international law hundreds of years ago.

This man had gone so far as to break that law in his quest to approach the Amalgams. He had been fortunate enough to have been born human, and yet he'd thrown that away, sacrificing thousands of lives.

"Why would you go to such lengths...?"

"Why? It's obvious, isn't it?" Kent said with a smile, looking incredulous that Eleven would have doubts. "If you and I are going to love each other, then it has to be once we're both the same kind of being, right?"

Eleven had no words. She closed her eyes. This all went beyond her comprehension.

Dr. Tokinos and his colleagues had sought an alternative to the philosopher's stone for many years. Which was why they had given the name fortunite—the stone that determines destiny—to the rare mineral that they eventually found.

Amalgams had originally been constructed as an alternative battle force to reduce the number of compatriots sacrificed. They were to take over the dangerous front lines and keep the peace for human beings. Even if they were used for applications unintended by the military, the intentions of the doctor and his fellows remained firmly unchanged.

And now all those papers, all that research done by the doctor and his team were being trampled by muddy feet because of "love," something Eleven couldn't even comprehend. For this reason, lives she was meant to protect were tossed into the gutter.

Eleven had no emotions, but she had a mission. She had the doctor's hopes. And above all else, she had a wish to grant—Theo's.

Her core burned. It held heat. She firmly pushed Kent's hands away. "I personally understand 'love each other' as a sick joke," she told him.

"Ha-ha! I've finally got you. I'll be happy with whatever you want to say to me," he continued without seeming the least bit bothered. "Do you have any idea how I trembled with joy when I found out you were in Delverro, when I learned that the angel I'd found that day was here?! There is no being more ideal than you. *You* are my Eve."

The fleshy body that Kent controlled stroked her core. Being made to know that she was on the brink of operational cessation, the feeling of flesh other than her own touching her—Eleven deepened her understanding of what "hate" was.

She quietly extended her tissue structure into the form of a belt and sent it crawling toward her core.

Kent appeared not to notice. He touched her cheek and said, in a manner to which *in a trance* applied, "Eve. Without emotion or love, you carry out your missions rationally. Beautiful creature. Build paradise with me. You and I shall be the first of humanity in that lovely, logical paradise."

"Unfortunately, I have two points to make." Eleven stepped on his face before he could say anything further. The blade of her foot shot through his oral cavity and down through his abdominal cavity.

"One. I am a mere weapon. Love, life, death, paradise—none of these are my concern."

Her restraints now loosened with the impact of her attack, she pulled free, returned her core to her chest, and looked down at him.

"Two. You will not go to paradise. You should go to Hell for the number of lives you've stolen."

Kent gaped at her, and Eleven pushed her blade even more deeply into his body.

"I am in command. Hear me, fear me, bow down before me."

He claimed they were the same kind of beings; this should reach him, then. She broadcasted a control signal at maximum output.

"Step down, fake. I did not give you permission to touch me."

The body bounced back, and Kent collapsed with a face to which *stunned* applied. The shaking that came to her through the ground grew more and more intense. Eleven brushed the dirt off her clothes with both hands and took a step to leave the area, but the lump of flesh writhing at her feet called out.

"Wait! Why, Eve? How could you do this? Do you choose being kept and killed by humans over freedom?!"

"Sir. You have gotten the wrong idea." She kicked away a lump of flesh and turned back toward Kent. The philosopher's stone was exposed, and she stared at the man whose own foolishness and ugliness had now also been laid bare.

"The mission of the Hounds is to protect and reduce the sacrifice of human beings," she told him. "There was never a place for us in a paradise created through the killing of humans."

The vibrations were at last almost upon them. Eleven left Kent to let his eyes wonder and leaped up, leaving him behind for good.

A tanker truck skidded toward her on the other side of the wall of fused Amalgams. Theo jumped out of the driver's seat, raced toward the wall, and fired his gun. The sharp *bang* was followed by the roar of a massive explosion. Cars and Amalgam flesh bounced back. A pillar of fire singed the sky, a column of black smoke rose up, and the blast shattered all the windows in the neighboring buildings.

Pushing against the movement of the wind, Eleven landed and caught Theo with her body just as he was about to plunge headfirst into a car.

Averting the collision and protecting his head, Eleven said, "You are only capable of reckless action, it seems."

"...With a monstrosity like that, it's not as though I could choose my methods," he told her.

The surrounding vehicles ignited, and the whole area was on fire, but she nevertheless heard Theo loud and clear. She knocked back the twisted door of a car that came flying at them and endured the explosive blasts.

By the time the blowback had died down and Theo was able to stand up, Kent's Amalgams were almost all enveloped in flame. Lumps of flesh reared up to try and escape the heat, but they crumbled to dust before they could get very far.

"The fact that we learned that disposal by incineration is effective is a fruitful result," Eleven remarked.

"I suppose it is," Theo agreed. "Now all that's left is to deal with the surviv—"

Eleven shoved him away and leaped into the air when her sensors picked up a dramatically amplified signal.

A body punched the ground just a hair away from where Eleven landed, somehow retaining its shape even enveloped in flames. She hid behind the trees along the street, but the fleshy mass came straight for her, perhaps chasing her core signal. She rolled away just as the tree was broken clean in two and fell to the ground.

It is still operational. She checked Theo with a hand when he tried to approach her.

The fleshy body should have scattered as dust already, and yet a charred, black mud doll was pushing its face out from the inside. Absorbing the burning flesh, the doll manifested the face of Jim Kent, cracked like a rock with a magma core. The viscous, burning mass opened something like an oral cavity and shouted in a static-coated voice, "Eve! It's you—I need you for my paradise! Where do you think you're going?!"

Every time he howled this dissonant war cry, droplets of the lava flesh scattered. The philosopher's stone was still in the reconstructed flesh of the chest area. Was the stone the only thing protecting him from the fire?

"Eleven! Get in!" Theo roared, pulling up next to her in a car he'd found nearby. She immediately jumped into the passenger seat, and he slammed his foot down on the accelerator. "Goddammit! I can't believe this! You've got the world's worst stalker! How do we destroy that thing?!"

"We need it to burn with that intensity of flame in a state where the core cannot be protected with the flesh... Or..."

"The military's still not here... So I suppose we have no choice. The last resort," Theo muttered and yanked on the steering wheel.

Behind them, Kent absorbed the Amalgams that charged toward him to become a giant burning everything in his path. His words were already nothing more than incoherent screams. Theo could no longer make out what he was saying.

"We'll lure him away," Theo said. "Safe to assume that he's chasing you?"

"Yes," Eleven affirmed. "It seems he is pursuing not through visual identification but core signal."

"Is he? We'll head straight for the dump, then. That's our only option now to keep him burning."

Data flitted through the back of Eleven's mind. At the dump, it would indeed be possible to continue the incineration of the target until it was completely burned up. There was only one action required for that.

"...I understand. Let's do it." She glanced at the black belt of tissue still on Theo's left arm.

■

The car flew from Delverro toward the dump. Theo shuddered as he stepped out of the driver's seat. Kent had been chasing them the whole time, burning up the road they passed down. If they didn't hurry, Kent would quickly catch up with them. Theo had called the dump ahead of time, but maybe they had all evacuated; there'd been no answer. He shot the lock out of the door and kicked it down, but Eleven pulled him back before he could go inside.

"Theo, I leave these with you." She handed him her investigator badge and her gun. The items given to her by the Criminal Investigation Bureau.

"What's the point of this?" he asked.

"I will lead that fake into the furnace," she told him. "But there is a possibility of losing these when escaping."

"...Got it. But if you lead him into the furnace, will you be able to make it out before the incineration starts?" he asked, accepting her badge and gun.

Eleven slowly blinked her eyelids up and down. "A Hound cannot state things it cannot do."

"All right... I'm counting on you. We'll stay in touch over wireless." Without saying anything more, Theo started running for the control room. All he could do now was have faith in Eleven.

The door to the control room was also locked, and when he pulled out his gun to shoot it, he finally noticed that Eleven's sleeve was still tied around his own arm. He'd forgotten about it because Eleven had both of her arms. Was it all right for this to be so far from the main body?

No...she didn't take it back from me in the car. She must've decided I needed it.

Theo knew she wouldn't do anything reckless. He kicked in the door and entered the control room. When he checked the state of the incinerator through the glass at the front of the room, he saw that he would be able to control everything from the console panel.

"Eleven, I'm in the control room," he said into the wireless. "I'm opening the intake ports."

"Roger. Please do. The target has come within a lureable distance. I am heading toward the incinerator." She had no sooner finished speaking than the building shuddered heavily to one side.

Surprised at the earthshaking footsteps, Theo turned around just as a jiggling, white mountain passed by outside the window. He tightened his grip on the badge Eleven had given him and stared in anticipation at the incinerator.

Finally, Eleven slid inside through the intake port, along with a particularly large shaking of their surroundings. The momentum of her entry propelled her up the wall, and white fleshy masses poured in through the three input ports. They had lost even the shape of Kent, nothing more than bizarre monsters hot in pursuit of Eleven.

The supposedly enormous incinerator was filled with pale, muddy Amalgam bodies in the blink of an eye. Eleven stared at them from where she landed on the wall.

Theo nervously picked up the wireless. "Eleven, are they all inside?"

"Yes. All the signals have assembled. I will close the intake ports."

Theo doubted his ears. He was the one operating the controls, so what was she talking about?

But then he felt a tugging on his left arm, and in the next instant, he heard heavy shutters closing. The intake ports. Surprised, he sent his gaze racing around and was stunned to find that a hand had extended its slender fingers from a black sleeve and pressed the button to lock the intake ports.

"No—you can't! Stop!" he cried. "Eleven, get out of there right now!"

"I'm very sorry. I cannot carry out that order," she replied dispassionately.

As the Amalgams howled repulsively, countless hands reached out for Eleven, perhaps reflecting Kent's desires. She leaped at them as if throwing herself into their arms.

Platinum hair swung from side to side. Legs that were now longswords descended from above, a graceful dance that was entirely without mercy. Her opponent had no way of defending against her. The platinum blades pierced the massive core, and instantly, the blades deployed like branches and leaves that shot through the Amalgam body.

Eleven lifted her face. Intuiting what she was going to say next with those penetrating eyes, Theo jumped at her left hand. But the fabric wrapped around his head and yanked him backward, and when he lost his balance, it pulled the lever. A mechanical announcement played. A siren blared, announcing the starting phase of incineration.

When the fabric was peeled from his face as he sat flat on his backside, Theo felt a small hand pat his head before pulling away. He looked and found the black fabric fluttering to the floor. He grabbed it and leaped up urgently to the window.

Perhaps sensing the danger to their life, the Amalgams swarmed the intake ports, shuddering and wobbling. But each time they did, Eleven's blade became bone and pushed them upright before pulling them back into the incinerator. How much of the mass of that small physique did she change into those blades? Her body from the waist down was semitransparent crystal, a frost-covered tree to pin the Amalgams in place. The crystal glowed a faint fortunite red.

Theo threw himself at the window and grabbed the wireless. "What are you doing, Eleven?! You'll be burned up, too!"

"The philosopher's stone is a magical crystal that will regenerate as long as it exists. The only way to completely burn it up is to separate it from the physical body of the Amalgam and keep it in flames. Currently, I am the only one who can fix it in place in this state."

"So what?!" he cried. "You don't have to commit suicide with them!"

"It is acceptable to me. I decided from the start that I would overlook operational limits and be of use to you this time, Corporal Theo Starling."

Having grown too much in size and with nowhere left to go, the Amalgams writhed and shuddered, shrieking, making the inside of the incinerator look like the very picture of hell. After looking down on this, Eleven finally returned her gaze to Theo.

It was the same quiet gaze as when they first met at the underground fight club.

The incinerator ignited, and the temperature rose. Even if he pressed the emergency stop button now, Theo wouldn't be able to pull Eleven out. He groaned and banged his head against the window.

"What do you mean, *this* time?! What did I ever do to you...?!"

In the edge of his field of view, the incinerator's interior grew red. Fire. The brightly burning flames lit up one corner of the nightmares he had daily. The soldier who had rescued him from the wreckage, the one who had been pulverized. The quiet voice encouraged him from the ridgeline of his memory. In his nightmares, the corpse repeated, "Please retreat."

In the car, Eleven had said that perhaps the soldier had felt proud of saving him. A strange comment from her. Had he been right to feel something off in it?

What if he'd only assumed it had all been a nightmare when it had in fact actually happened?

"Are you all right?"

Memory and reality overlapped with a *clack*.

Eleven calling out to Theo over the wireless, through the glass, and the soldier who saved Theo that day. The small physique. What if her hair and face and body type had been hidden beneath weapons?

"...It can't have been *you*? Did you save me in the Alkabel campaign?" His voice was impossibly quiet, but Eleven responded with a faint smile. As if she was looking at something dazzling.

"I failed to support your withdrawal. So I decided that I would make sure to be of use to you the next time we met. The moment I heard your name at the base and ever after."

The flames grew more intense. Despite the fact that the Amalgams were writhing and shrieking discordantly, despite the fact that the edges of the clothing that Emma had bought her were catching fire, Eleven was calm. Her empty left sleeve flapped in the scorching wind. Flame and sand danced up, becoming a vortex like a wall between her and Theo. Distorted by the heat, the static over the wireless grew louder.

"That's why I will now turn to my pride and send these foolish creatures to hell."

Theo's vision blurred. *Don't say that. It's not like you.* The words caught in his throat, became a lump of heat, and bled out through the corners of his eyes.

In a break in the whirlwind of sand, Theo saw her, and his eyes opened wide in surprise.

The fire was about to envelop Eleven's platinum hair. Lynchpins like frozen tree roots burned bright and red, on the verge of turning to dust. And yet a faint smile played on her lips, her cheeks pushing upward the slightest bit, awkwardly.

As she was swallowed up by the swirling flames, she very clearly smiled.

"Theo. Have I been useful to you?"

His view was blocked by a wall of flames, and he could no longer see the inside of the incinerator. The roaring flames raced around inside the closed space. The voices of the Amalgams grew distant, and all he could hear over the wireless was static. He stood rooted to the spot. The shaking of the window grew weaker, and he remained frozen in place until the incinerator entered the cooldown phase.

■

Using a ladder from a maintenance door, Theo descended into the incinerator and began digging around in the sand. There was no sign now of the fleshy bodies that had filled the space. Everything had been burned to ash, and now they were nothing more than a quiet pile of sand.

Although it had cooled off inside the incinerator, it was still hot enough to make sweat bead on his forehead as he sniffed the air. There was surprisingly little smell. He looked down at the investigator's badge Eleven had given him and the swatch of black in his hand.

Had Eleven been planning to do this right from the start?

Just one time. The memory of their first meeting was vague in his memory. Had she remembered it through all these years? That brief moment that Theo had tucked away as a nightmare?

"Eleven, answer me!" he called. "Eleven?"

Krsh. He set his leather shoe onto the sand. Sweating and enduring the heat somehow, he walked around calling her name, and the movement sent shivers up his spine. Memories of loss came rushing back to

him. He remembered that day he ran, chest aching, scared that even his lungs might be burned, more frightened.

The thought that he might find himself alone again in the same way sent a pang through his heart and shudders through his body.

"Eleven!"

His voice echoed emptily inside the incinerator.

Amalgam bodies would burn in fire. This has been more than proven by the attacking Amalgams and by the transformed Nina. There was no way Eleven's body would have been able to withstand the flames of the incinerator.

Did Hounds not even leave bones behind? Or did he have to search out that miraculously beautiful heart in this vast expanse of sand—the crimson mineral that would decide her fate?

If I can just get her core back to the lab. Or...

Theo realized he was grasping at straws and gritted his teeth. Even though he'd been so opposed when he heard she was transferring to Detective Operations, even though he'd been so disapproving for so long.

But I still couldn't hate her...

The belated regret that he hadn't talked with her more sank into his heart. Just when he was finally starting to understand her. He lowered his eyes, pained, and his gaze fell upon the fabric he was clutching. Although there was no wind, the end of it was fluttering in a fixed direction.

It can't be. He quickly unrolled the band of fabric and let it hang above the sand. It swayed as if pulled by something. Holding his breath, he followed this movement. He could hear his heart pounding in his ears.

The fabric stopped above the sand, as if pulled to a particular, specific location.

He dropped to his knees and pushed aside the still-hot sand. Not caring whether his suit got dirty, paying no mind to the sand that flew up to his sweaty forehead, he simply—intently—dug. He dug and dug and dug. And then.

As he reached in to dig even further, a cold hand clasped his. Bloodless, pale skin and the slender bone structure particular to a small girl.

Theo gasped, grabbed the hand back, and pulled up with everything he had. He pushed sand away with his free hand and caught sight of soft platinum hair.

Eyelids lifted, and gray eyes were fixed on him.

"...Eleven...!"

He began digging out the sand around her with both hands. She stretched out her lone hand and cleared her face with a familiar lack of expression on it. When she sat up, her shining red core was exposed with her chest opened up to either side. Fortunately, her core appeared to be undamaged.

Thank God. Tears of relief sprang to Theo's eyes, but these immediately turned into tears of terror.

Eleven set a right hand—different from the one Theo had taken—on the ground followed by a left hand, sat up, and scratched at the sand with yet another hand on her back. Pulling free of the sand and exposing a naked body that was smooth like a plastic doll and absolutely devoid of any human characteristics, Eleven looked at Theo and opened her mouth. But before she could speak any words, an ocean of sand poured out. Yet another hand cleared this sand away.

"Y-y-y-y-y-you! *Youuuuuuu!*" he yelped. "What the hell are you, really?! You have *got* to be kidding me! This is goddamn absurd!"

"...Please wait a moment. I am prioritizing sand removal and restoration of my appearance," she said, somewhat businesslike, after she was done vomiting sand. Then she got to her feet, staggering slightly.

Theo nearly passed out when he saw the total of seven arms on her torso.

While he held tight to his flickering consciousness, Eleven reproduced the bare minimum in terms of skeleton and clothing, recreating the version of her from before incineration—in form at least. Her insides were apparently hollow, but she could move now.

"I apologize for the wait," she said. "Annihilation of all enemy signals and the philosopher's stone confirmed. Mission complete, Theo."

"You…" He gaped up at her. "You're a *monster*…"

"Yes. I am a weapon," she agreed. "I am grateful for the assistance. Please take my hand."

"You're seriously just too much. I can't even begin to figure you out…" Theo smiled, his mind a jumble of relief and exasperation, as he took Eleven's hand and stood up. Then he yanked her toward him and wrapped his arms around her surprisingly light body.

He could touch her. There was enough of her here for that at least. The feel of her soft, white-blond hair and slender shoulders reached his arms loud and clear.

These mundane facts warmed his heart. He sighed in relief until he emptied his lungs.

Still held up in his arms, feet dangling above the ground, Eleven spoke in a muffled voice from his chest area. "Theo, what is this action? Your intention is unclear."

"…I'm just confirming that you're alive. I didn't know what I'd do if that was the end." He closed his eyes tightly. He felt like he was truly touching her.

Eleven's physical body was, just as it appeared to be, that of a teenage girl. He couldn't completely believe that this slim figure had thrown not only people but cars and street signs and, in the end, even endured the flames of an incinerator. Thinking about it all now, he shuddered as he grabbed her shoulders and pulled her away from himself.

"Don't you *ever* pull such a foolish move again," he said. "But if you do, you'd better give me a good reason why it's okay!"

"Understood," she replied. "Since the regeneration ability of the Hound is extremely powerful, we will regenerate without issue given time as long as our core is undamaged, even if we lose our entire body and only the core is left."

"Not now!" he cried. "That was *not* the kind of plan that you can explain after the fact!"

Eleven looked like she didn't entirely understand, but she blinked and said, "My apologies. The manual does say that, excluding the case where output is remarkably low, the regenerative ability does not decline outside of disposal through a fixed procedure."

Theo automatically put a hand to his jaw. That thick Hound operation manual. Now that he thought back, he hadn't been able to take the time to really go over every single page. "Sorry. That's on me. But I still need an explanation. My heart can't take it."

"Understood. I will make certain that I explain in the future," Eleven said in her usual manner. Almost like nothing at all had happened. Even though the sensation of grabbing her hand stretching out from the sand remained vivid and fresh in Theo's own hand.

He sighed and turned on his heel. He was dripping with sweat. "Great. You can move. We're going back up top right now. It's way too hot for me in here."

"I understand."

There was a pleasant breeze when they got back up aboveground. They contacted R&D, who said they would send a team right away. Until they arrived, Theo was on standby at the front entrance to the dump.

"It's only natural that you wouldn't remember me," Eleven said from where she stood next to him. "It was an unusual situation."

"Well, normally, you wouldn't expect someone who'd been blown to bits to still be able to speak, so…"

"In fact," Eleven continued quietly, "because the existence of Hounds is top secret, I was instructed to not use my regenerative ability insofar as possible. Which is why when I protected you from the mortar attack, I did not immediately repair myself."

"Then…" Theo reflexively turned to look at her. "Me carrying you and running was actually keeping you from…"

"That is not the case." She glanced at him and said coolly, "It was because you held me and did not let go that I was able to support the parts of you that were lost so that you could run until you reached the base. Whether or not that would have happened if I had waited for my recovery... I did not calculate it, but the probability would have been low."

Theo inhaled sharply, not having even considered that possibility. Then he heard the motor of a truck drawing near. Piled high with equipment, the truck pulled up at the gate, and someone hurriedly got out of the driver's seat. The man dispatched from the research facility asked Theo a few simple questions before rushing into the dump with his team. With that, Theo and Eleven were free to go.

"...You didn't have any dog tags," he said to her. "So I felt like that was the least I could do. But that's why I survived, then... Life truly is a mystery."

"You are a commendable and rare individual," she told him. "On a battlefield where the person next to you could die at any moment, there are no human beings who stop for the dead. Much less for an injured Hound."

Theo looked down at her. She was gazing at the dump with a quiet look.

"That's why...I pondered your blue eyes, eyes that glittered like stars in my memories. So many of your comrades had been killed, your own life was in danger, yet in that place full of death, even still your eyes shone with innate goodness."

Although being complimented in this way made him break out in hives, he felt like he was being given a good-bye speech.

"Hey," he said, grimacing. "Save that for when I'm about to die in the line of duty. Our job doesn't end here."

"...Is it all right for me to continue working with you?" Eleven lifted her face.

Feeling awkward at seeing himself reflected in her gray eyes, Theo roughly tousled her white-blond hair. The soft hair without a single burnt end. "Of course. There's no partner more useful than you," he told her. "Let's go."

He started walking, and she stared up at him, her bangs still unkempt.

"Yes. Yes, coming." She slid into the car's passenger seat, and he couldn't help but laugh at how she moved so much like an eager puppy.

■

A month after the nightmare ended, many citizens and people connected with the case gathered in an event space in the city. Lined up at the front were an overwhelming number of photos. All of those among the dead.

Under tight security, people came together once more to pray and offer flowers in the hopes that the souls of those who lost their lives in the continental war and the Roremclad attack would find peace.

Many civilians had died, and many police officers and special forces members had been killed in the line of duty. Many bereaved families had seen their loved ones return safely from the war only to lose them in the attacks. Because more than a few victims had been eaten by the Amalgams and no bones remained, a number of empty coffins were also buried.

So many people were overwhelmed with grief at their loss and spent their days in mental shambles. Even so, as long as they were alive, tomorrow would come. Time alone passed cruelly. Theo knew that only too well.

"I'm sorry to keep you waiting," a voice said.

Theo stood up from the edge of the flower bed and smiled at Eleven. She carried swollen paper bags, looking sharp in the white and smoky-blue dress Emma had picked out for her. The hair accessory Rocky had gifted her "as a reward for a young lady working so hard" gave brilliant color to her platinum hair. Her billowing skirt swayed in the breeze, giving a peek of her slender legs.

If she hadn't been working, she would have seemed like nothing other than a cute, stoic girl. Many of the passersby followed her with their eyes, looking back over their shoulders.

"…That's quite a lot," Theo said. "I heard you were only going to buy a few snacks."

"In handling the requests from Emma and Tobias, the amount inevitably grew large," she told him.

Theo took one of the bags and started walking with Eleven alongside him.

Once the Roremclad attack was settled and the processing afterward taken care of, Theo finally got a bit of a long vacation. He'd accepted Tobias's suggestion of bringing some food to his house on that first day off and having a little party, and so he and Eleven had been pressed into going shopping.

Theo glanced down at her. She continued forward, unaware of his gaze.

That day, when he and Eleven had finally returned to the city, Tobias went weak in the knees in relief, and Emma embraced Eleven in tears. Because of the ongoing chaos, they hadn't been able to maintain contact, but they had worried about Theo and Eleven for all the fighting they were doing. When they returned to the Criminal Investigation Bureau, Rocky had uncharacteristically run up to welcome the four of them and sighed with relief from the bottom of his heart. "Thank God," he'd said.

Now that things had finally calmed down, Theo wanted to bask in the fact that they were both still alive. Eleven looked like she didn't really understand what that meant, but she was apparently fine with it if it made the rest of the team happy.

They headed toward the meeting spot where Emma, the first to notice them, waved enthusiastically. Unusually for her, she was wearing a dress. It was the same design as the one Eleven was wearing, but in a chic wine red. Tobias and Rocky looked up and greeted Theo and Eleven with smiles.

"That's all of us, then! And we *so* do not look like we belong together!" Emma cried. "In a way, it's kind of amazing. I did tell you to actually dress up, though, didn't I?"

"I *did* dress up," Theo insisted. "I don't know how many years it's been since I wore a suit that wasn't a work suit..."

"Son, that outfit's got a real whiff of old man to it," Rocky said. "Men *my* age are wearing things like that."

"You of all people are one to talk! You and your oversized baseball jacket, Gramps!" Theo protested.

"...Tobias. Are the clothes of Theo and Rocky not very good?"

"They're fine, Eleven. Don't even worry about it. C'mon, gang. Let's get going already."

Chatting and laughing, the group started walking toward Theo's home. Although the roads had been repaired and the cars and trees cleared away, the buildings in the area were under construction, and the noise was enough to drown out all five of their voices.

Against the backdrop of the town racing intently toward recovery, people passed by in mourning clothes and children ran around with bags from the toy store. As they walked so short a distance, so many lives moved through Theo's field of view.

"It's okay now, right, big bro?"

Surprised, he looked back and saw a young brother and sister finishing their shopping and meeting up with their parents. Theo shrugged. Right. That would have been impossible, wouldn't it? Hearing his little sister's voice—of course it wasn't her.

"Theo, the light is green," Eleven said.

"...Yeah. Sorry. I'm coming." Theo ran to cross the street.

Eleven stared directly at him. Her penetrating gray eyes reflected him without a single lie.

He was finally able to meet her gaze head-on.

To my dear readers:

I must express my deepest gratitude to you who have picked up this book. In this world filled with entertainments, there is a multitude of crime suspense dramas, of buddy stories with humans and something not human. Of all those, you were kind enough to choose this one. Thank you so much.

For me, fiction is an escape from reality. No matter what happens in the real world, I want to forget all of it at least for the time I'm immersed in fiction. And so nothing could bring me greater joy than if you were able to forget reality even if only for a second while reading this story.

Please allow me to speak a little to just you who have read this book. When I first wrote it, the imperial year was still Heisei. Comparing the work at the time with the book that you have read now, I note that the worldview, the characters, the story—everything was different. But the designation *Hound* and the character names alone were one and the same.

While a hunting dog is a force turned quietly, viciously on its prey, it is also a beloved friend. A hunter knows to pay great care to it lest the dog's teeth be turned toward unrelated people or animals. This nature matches the idea I had in mind of a devoted partner who works diligently for people at the same time as they are a powerful weapon. So I gave them the name *Hound*.

How would it be if such weapons were immortal monsters, able to freely change shape and grant your every wish? They would be a very convenient creature for you. In what fashion would you employ them?

I settled on the character of Theo from this imagining. I thought that it's not possible to use the Hound only for good unless you have a strong sense of justice, a good moral compass, and a rational mind.

And so his stiff investigator character was born, and I settled on his teammates.

The reason I chose bird names for Theo and the rest of the main characters is because I wanted them to fly around freely in the world of imagination. The way I write novels, my pen can't move unless my characters move about for me. When they get stuck and stop, my pen also stops.

But I didn't give Eleven a bird name. From the Heisei era to now, Eleven alone is unchanged, always focused on her master. Before I even wished for her to fly, Eleven started to run. If she were your partner, what name, appearance, and personality would she have?

But I digress. It's a bad habit of mine, going on for too long. You are no doubt yawning, so I will end my anecdotes here. I am truly blessed to have received the assistance of so many people to bring you this book. Thank you so much for meeting me here.

Midori Komai
May 2022

AMALGAM HOUND

Criminal Investigation Bureau: Special Investigation Unit

NEXT EPISODE

Theo and Eleven infiltrate a luxury cruise ship in order to investigate a suspicious medical company that claims to revive the dead!

AMALGAM HOUND 2

Criminal Investigation Bureau: Special Investigation Unit

On sale summer 2024!!